"Come on, Gin, what's your problem?" Tina could fret like a baby. Gin didn't answer. She had stood for long intervals of devotion before the Rembrandt, but now . . .

In a peculiar state of suspension, she admitted to herself that something seemed wrong. Something indefinable.

"Don't you see anything?" she asked softly.

"What do you mean?"

"The painting . . . Does it, you know, look all right to you?"

Tina sighed.

"I keep thinking," Gin said, though she'd only that minute actually thought it, "something about it isn't quite the same."

"The same as what?"

"As before."

"What're you suggesting?"

"Nothing. I don't know."

"Come on. What're we talking about?" Then Tina straightened and laughed. "Oh no. Don't tell me. You do lead a rich inner life." But once more she drew closer to the painting and squinted. "Okay, if it's not the Rembrandt, what is it?"

THE SANTA FE
REMBRANDT

Cecil Dawkins

IVY BOOKS • NEW YORK

Ivy Books
Published by Ballantine Books
Copyright © 1993 by Cecil Dawkins

Library of Congress Catalog Card Number: 93-90209

ISBN 0-8041-1101-4

Manufactured in the United States of America

First Edition: October 1993

1

WEDNESDAY

She woke with a sense of foreboding she couldn't at first account for. Then she remembered and sat up in her Taos bed, staring without seeing at the *santo* of St. George on his little steed in the niche above her foot locker, the mauve sheet from the thrift grasped to her throat in both fists, thinking: *Oh, God, I'm finished.*

Usually a reluctant riser, she leapt out of bed and crossed the room in three strides, pulled on her jeans, ran a comb through her lifelong trial of hair, grabbed her backpack and, biting into a cold Sara Lee croissant, launched herself into the clear September morning.

She hurried past adobe walls to the corner of Acequia Madre, then on down Garcia, sidewalks lined with big old cottonwoods, and along one diagonally cutting block of Canyon Road to the Paseo. There she had to wait for the light to change on Alameda before she could jog through the park, on the path beside what was left of the river, toward the Old Santa Fe Trail and the plaza.

In the Sangre de Cristos above the town the aspens were getting ready to turn. Soon hordes armed with cameras and knapsacks would be winding upward on the twisting road, bound for outings under bright leaves and the dense blue canopy of sky. Ginevra Prettifield, Gin to almost everybody, longed to be up there instead of jogging toward the plaza, no longer groaning that she was finished, wondering instead what she was doing with the damned job anyway. For six months now she had been assistant director of the Waldheimer Museum atop Otero Hill overlooking Santa Fe.

How had she got the job in the first place? Not by virtue of one meager degree in art history. Didn't everybody have a degree in art history? She had taken it not with an eye to entering the ranks of the gainfully employed but because even as a child she had liked to color.

Maybe Davies had hired her because she was the only applicant who spoke fluent Spanish. Being bilingual was one of the job's criteria. She was bilingual not by intent but by accident. The accident had been an arrow shot through a coonskin cap. Her great-great-grandfather Andre Beauchamp had been a mountain man, a Frenchman who came to the American West to make his fortune sometime before dime novels celebrated life with the Indians. His was the coonskin cap. The arrow belonged to her great-great-grandmother, a born tomboy though Andre Beauchamp, chasing her through the forest, laying hold of her pigtail, even without the help of dime novels had no trouble identifying her as an Indian maid. A Sioux, to be sure, though Gin kept quiet about it now that it was fashionable to be part Indian. No time at all ago, it wasn't. But now everybody claimed to be some kind of octaroon Cherokee.

When her Sioux great-great-grandmother put up her nose at *Beauchamp* and asked what kind of name was that, Andre told her it meant "pretty field." "Pretty field" she understood, and not much to his liking called him that thereafter. So while his distant cousin, who had gone to England, became Andrew Beecham, Andre Beauchamp became Andy Prettifield.

Ginevra had grown almost up in the Mora valley, till one day her widowed mother moved them both, lock, stock, barrel, and Brody, a Dane-dachshund mix, to Santa Fe. But for Andre Beauchamp's wanderlust, she might have grown up on the Champs Elysées. She liked to think of that.

Or, prompted the voice of balance for she was a Libra, on a reservation in South Dakota.

She knew she couldn't have gotten the job because of her looks. Anyone seeing her soaking wet would note that her ears were too big and her legs too long. There were a number of things about herself she didn't like. Take her hair. She tied it with a ribbon at the nape of her neck and hoped for the best. She could cut it off, but with a neck like a gander? Her hair was a catch-22 situation.

And her nose. She admired the noses on coins, but where those dumped, hers dimped. Her mouth was too long. The upper lip looked like somebody had swatted her. And when she felt anything deeply a vein crawled like a worm from her widow's peak to the inner edge of her eyebrow. The eyebrows themselves she had to brush down or they made straight for her hairline like a werewolf's.

Be positive, was her friend Tina's philosophy. Tina was always building her up. "That's an incredible smile."

"Right. But if it gets out of control it looks like somebody's cut my throat."

Sweeping around the rug-shop corner, heading up the rise toward the plaza, she put these thoughts out of her mind because they smacked of a weird sort of antivanity. She disdained vanity as a featherheaded piece of personal baggage serving the precepts of male chauvinism. She hoped to achieve detachment from worldly measures, and to that end wore no lipstick, did nothing to her hair but apply the brush, and dressed for work in nondesigner jeans. She also wore, low on her hips, a thousand-dollar concha belt, sterling and turquoise, simple and heavy. But that wasn't vanity, was it? That was an investment. It was natural, wasn't it, for her to wear her wealth upon her person like her Sioux ancestors?

Maybe Quillan Davies had hired her to serve his vanity: he could strut his expertise before an admiring neophyte. If so, the gambit worked. She liked everything about the English director, from his accent to his Charlie Chaplin walk, twirling an imaginary cane, that he sometimes fell into for her delight and edification. She'd felt an instant affinity the minute they met. She was sure he'd felt it, too.

Woolworth's was the only store left on the plaza for townspeople, the others having given away to "trading posts" for tourists. It opened at nine A.M. Unfortunately so did the museum. She was supposed to be there when Juan Romero, the museum's temperamental guard, unlocked the gate.

She turned the La Fonda corner into the plaza and hurried down the sidewalk under the portal. At Woolworth's they were just unlocking the doors. She flashed a smile at the cashier with the fistful of keys, swung in her too-long-legged stride down the aisle to the Back to School Department, and crossed her fingers.

Luck was with her. She picked up a sheaf of Pink Pearl erasers shaped like lead pencils and wrapped in cellophane and a first grader's small chrome pencil sharpener, and hurried to the checkout, where the same cashier, the fistful of keys now hanging from her belt, was opening the computerized cash box. She paid the cashier and, there on the counter, tore open the cellophane and bent one Pink Pearl eraser with her thumb. She sagged with relief and smiled.

"It's not all dried out," she said to the cashier, and the cashier obligingly smiled back. Left on their own, most pencil erasers on this high, arid desert plateau turned to stone. A day or two out of wrappers, you couldn't use them without leaving an ugly streak.

She slung her backpack over her shoulder and headed across a spoke of the plaza's star-shaped pattern of sidewalks. The white wrought-iron benches were usually settled at this time of day by the village longhair in a sweatband muttering to himself, a drunk sleeping it off, tourist couples consulting chamber of commerce maps, cyclists in rubberized shorts kneeling beside mountain bikes, preparing to attack the road to the ski valley. Where was everybody?

There they were. A crowd clustered at the northeast corner of the plaza watching men being hoisted aloft in a cherry picker. Something wrong with the traffic lights. Cables snaked across the street. Over by the Governor's Palace flanking the north side of the plaza, built by Oñate ten years before the Mayflower landed, the Indians, instead of spreading their wares on the sidewalk under the portal, were milling around, dressed for a parade in fringed buckskin and Navajo velvet.

Tina sauntered toward her across the cobbled street. Gin couldn't believe it. Usually Tina painted till the wee hours and slept all morning. They'd tried being roommates but it hadn't worked—partly because of conflicting internal clocks and partly because they were afraid of being codependent. Also, Tina was a slob and Gin the opposite. They lived in adjacent studio apartments in a run-down adobe compound off Garcia. Ginevra Prettifield had discovered Celestina Martinez, from Santa Ynez pueblo, in a high school art class and they'd been friends ever since.

"Hou," Gin called, their customary greeting. Tina frantically waved Gin back with a covert motion of her hand behind the folds of her skirt. What was going on?

"Oh, Gin," Tina said, exasperated.

Somebody yelled, "Cut! What the devil . . . !"

The cherry picker zoomed down at them like the neck of a hostile dinosaur. "Have you any idea what you've done?" shouted a man with a megaphone.

"Why didn't you tell me?" she said to Tina.

"Take ten!" the megaphone shouted, and all the dressed-up Indians sat down on the curb.

"What do you think you're *doing*?" Gin asked.

"Making a little spending money," Tina said. She'd hired herself out before as an ethnic extra. Gin disapproved. Indians had been shortchanged too long in the motion picture industry.

"Do you have a speaking part or what?"

Tina shook her head. "I'm just local color." She picked up the small gold watch hanging from a chain around her neck and squinted at it. She was blind as a bat but too vain to wear her glasses. "You're late to work."

"I know. I can't stop. I'm in a rush."

Tina fell in step and hurried up Washington beside her. "I'll have a break in about an hour. How about lunch later? Burrito Company?"

"I can't. Not today. Why don't you bring something up the hill?"

"What's your hurry?"

They rushed single file down the sidewalk past a parked semi full of movie equipment pulled up over the curb and blocking pedestrian traffic. They were always making movies in Santa Fe.

"God, where are your boots?" Gin said as they came abreast again. "You come about to my nipples." Tina usually wore high-heeled boots to make herself taller, but here she was in moccasins playing Indian. "Mutt and Jeff," Gin muttered. "We're a comedy act."

"Do you have to *fling* yourself down the street?"

"I'm in a *hurry.*"

"Okay, *okay!*"

Tina stopped in the middle of Washington with her hands on her hips. She looked like a flamenco dancer with her braids looped in rosettes over ears Gin coveted.

The assistant director plowed up the street alongside the library, mostly fenced off because they were putting up a new building though she wished they wouldn't. A hardhat whistled down at her from a girder. She knew why. She hadn't had time to tie up her hair. Down, it fell into twirls and tendrils and made her look like a tramp.

She stuck her hand in her pocket to keep from throwing him a finger, hurried through the library parking lot, turned up Marcy, then north and again across the Paseo, her mouth open to the September air under a royal blue sky, paint it that color who'd believe it?

Quarter past nine. She bent to the hill. If she could get past Don Juan with his eyes full of grieved longing, and duck past Regina Philipson at the reception desk, and slide by the door to the gift shop where Olivia . . .

Drat, here came the bus from the Sheraton full of Ted Torrence and his group. Now she'd never get to the East Room without being seen.

The tour group had almost finished in there last night, Tuesday. The museum was closed on Tuesdays, but this was a privileged group, well-heeled patrons of the arts who might with proper treatment become donors, and their private visits had been arranged by Quillan Davies. Their visit last night had been cut short by dinner reservations at the Old Adobe, which held reservations for exactly sixty seconds, if you were late you could just go hungry. Gin had met them briefly in the East Room and answered their questions. Yes, it was an unusual collection for the Southwest, particularly the old masters. Didn't the Rembrandt remind her of his *Polish Rider*? Yes, she agreed it did call to mind the famous painting at the Frick in New York City, which she told them was her favorite Rembrandt. She had not, however, told them about her visits to *The Polish Rider* on rainy Saturday afternoons while she was a student at Barnard. The Rembrandt painting in the Frick on Madison Avenue had perversely reminded her of home.

The Waldheimer, overlooking Santa Fe from the north, had been constructed by the firm headed by Lacey Ebrams, a small woman in tweeds summer and winter, even to her small tweed hat, who had come into construction by accident, having built her own house then planned houses for several of her friends, and then been begged by others to do no less for them. Her buildings were notable for their double-adobe wall construction, which supplied amazing insulation, actually a house within a house, their pink brick floors, red corrugated high-pitched roofs, and pitched ceilings of inlaid vigas. The white walls were finished in some sort of fresco Lacey Ebrams had discovered in Italy—a favorite plaster finish of sixteenth-century Italian nobility—and taught to her crew of Spanish craftsmen from Truchas and Chimayo. The walls had a subtle translucence, a glow emanating mysteriously from within. Gin thought the elegance of the Waldheimer deserved the art it was built to house.

What luck. Ted Torrence's group detoured into the gift shop. As she moved past she could see hands turning the poster carousel. Olivia was nowhere in sight, probably behind the locked case at the other end of the room. Trust Nobody was Olivia's motto. Everyone was a potential kleptomaniac, even the idle rich. Everybody wants something for nothing, it's a game, it's a lark. You couldn't be too careful, according to Olivia.

More luck. Mrs. Philipson was not at the reception desk. This time of morning she'd be watering the plants, starting in the Northwest Gallery (early painters of Taos and Santa Fe), and working her way through the Georgia O'Keeffe Room, then Frida Kahlo, surrealist painter and mate of Diego Rivera, thence through the offices and on to the East Room, where the four old masters shared the space with twentieth-century Europeans.

She made it unnoticed to her office and, with a breath of relief, slid her backpack off onto the desk. Rummaging, she brought up a Pink Pearl and the first grader's pencil sharpener. If that didn't work . . .

Not time yet to worry, she told herself. She counted it one

of her strengths, this ability to tell herself when it was and when it was not time to worry. Fitting eraser into sharpener, she turned it in her hand until the eraser was honed to a fine point. She put the pencil-shaped eraser behind her ear, where anyone noticing might suppose she had need of it. As indeed she had. For the night before—chatting, explaining, acting every inch the assistant director—she had flung out an arm to indicate something or other, and the point of her pencil had come into brief but disastrous contact with the Santa Fe Rembrandt.

No one had noticed. The group was gathering up belongings—large notebooks in fitted leather cases, big carryall purses for cameras and gear, sketch pads, portfolios.

The vein had made its way down her forehead as she stood there alone beside the picture, staring at the pencil mark on the masterpiece while their voices echoed down the vaulted corridor and thinned in the evening air of the courtyard outside.

She'd bent over the painting, surveying the damage—a pencil mark an inch long. She bent closer, switching ends of the pencil. But the pencil mark was so close to the frame she couldn't get at it. And the rounded-off eraser, hard as old chewing gum, was worse than useless. It would only have further defaced this strange, uncharacteristic masterpiece which proved to her that Rembrandt, in the fifth decade of the seventeenth century, had been caught, for some reason compelled, by a landscape made famous by the Frick Collection's *Polish Rider.*

Now, the morning after, she was making her way down the corridor, trying to look normal, when a voice quick with annoyance stopped her. "Miss Prettifield!"

Startled, she turned toward the Northeast Gallery, where the museum showed the work of contemporary artists.

"Ah, Benito, there you are!" How stilted. Better to keep her mouth shut and make do with a questioning smile. She thought Benito Montoya was the finest painter at work in Northern New Mexico, though his bold semiexpressionist swatches disturbed visitors looking for pictures of adobe walls and wrought-iron gates into lushly flowering courtyards.

She stepped into the gallery where Benito, helped by Juan,

was hanging his show. Huge canvases were stacked like truants, face to the wall. Only one had been hung. It confronted her across the room—abstract, though she thought she made out in the bold, broad strokes a barely discernible figure big as a sky you could only imagine. But she knew better than to mention it and win Benito's savage scorn.

"What are you going to do about that window?" Benito scowled, a stocky young man with horn-rimmed glasses and a shadowy beard. "The light will destroy all the paintings on this wall till after noon."

The problem was always there, though other painters had been too grateful for a show to complain. The morning light was one reason the Northeast Gallery was relegated to rotating shows.

"We'll bring up a folding screen from the basement," she said brightly. "We can set it up and use it in the morning and fold it when the sun has passed."

His sigh was heavy with dissatisfaction. "We can try it. But when it's folded it has to be taken out of the gallery."

Where did the little prick expect her to put it? She loved his paintings but she was less fond of Benito. But she couldn't worry about that now. She had to worry about the pencil mark on the Rembrandt. Any minute the tour group would leave the gift shop and make for the East Room.

"Juan," she said, "as soon as the show is hung, we'll go to the basement and bring up the folding screen."

Juan looked at her reproachfully out of dark Latin eyes in a long, narrow face. Juan chose always to be in love with somebody. At the moment he chose to be in love with her. He looked at her accusingly, as if she'd condemned him to this heavy obsession he carried like a globe on his Atlas shoulders. But she wasn't drawn to men who liked uniforms and guns at the belt.

Voices from the gift shop sounded close. The tour group drifted toward the hall. She hurried down the corridor, relieved to have it to herself. The Santa Fe Rembrandt hung in the place of honor opposite the door. She could see it down the length of the corridor. Once she'd made it, she closed the arched double doors and approached the painting on tiptoe, like stalking an edgy prey.

2

The canyon was broad and deep. Its walls reached into the sky. It was late afternoon, the shadows already halfway to the top of the eastern wall. Sunset would come early, as it always does in canyons. The broad-topped butte in the background looked a lot like the Pedernales behind Georgia O'Keeffe's house at Abiquiu.

Gin stood there waiting for the Rider to appear. She was half in love with the Rider. Who was he? Where was he going? Why had Rembrandt identified him as the *Polish* rider? (Some said he hadn't, that the name had been bestowed later, probably because of the clothes—flamboyant jacket, hat possibly fur, red trousers.) Perhaps because the Poles were great horsemen and the young man appeared so at ease upon his mount. It was a strange mount for so romantic a figure—a nag with such heavy shanks and knobby knees it might have been Rosinante.

But it could have been a hot-blooded charger the way the Rider sat, one hand on his hip, clutching what catalogs identified as a war hammer. What on earth was a war hammer? He also had a quiver of arrows, a dagger, and a sword.

The Polish Rider was a strange, romantic painting, unlike Rembrandt. He had done few landscapes and only one other equestrian painting in his long career, and that a commissioned portrait. Was *The Polish Rider* a portrait? She suspected it was.

The young man was lovely, his face both strong and gentle as he stared not ahead at the path but boldly aside, at you, the viewer, standing just off the canvas along his way. And the look on the Rider's face asked in return: Who are *you?* Were you waiting for me?

10

Those exiled years in New York City, the Frick had been a refuge. She'd spent long hours before the painting, perhaps because the lonely rider in the vast desert landscape reminded her of herself.

But if it was a portrait, then a portrait of whom? Nobody knew. She'd never for a minute believed he was a Christian knight off to do battle with the infidels as some art historians hazarded, though such things still apparently happened in 1655, the date attributed to the painting. In the 1650s Rembrandt had created many of his finest works: *Aristotle Contemplating the Bust of Homer, Anatomy Lesson of Dr. Joan Deyman, Jacob Blessing the Sons of Joseph, Bathsheba.*

During this epochal period, he also painted *The Polish Rider* and what looked like the same landscape sans rider, known simply as *Barren Landscape*, which was the Santa Fe Rembrandt.

He had painted a number of moving portraits of Titus, his son by Hendrickje Stoffels, called by some "Rembrandt's concubine," the woman he lived with after the death of his beloved wife Saskia. But if the paintings were correctly dated, Titus would have been a boy of about fifteen when the picture was painted, and the Rider was a youth at least in his twenties. Such musings occupied her on the dingy New York afternoons she'd spent under his compelling gaze.

But she might stand all day before the Santa Fe Rembrandt, the Rider would not appear. Where had Rembrandt van Rijn, the Netherlander, come upon such a parched landscape? He had lived all his life in lowlands amid dikes and marshes near the sea. What in the desert landscape had so captured his imagination that he'd painted it at least twice?

The painting at the Frick had everything in common with the painting at the Waldheimer except for the foreground. In the Santa Fe Rembrandt, the foreground was simply sand-colored clay, while at the Frick the lonely rider was the painting's central feature.

The painting at the Frick was about four feet by five, but the Santa Fe Rembrandt was much smaller, a very small painting for the Master, who liked large canvases. To the Englishman Davies she had pointed out what looked like the curve of a horse's neck in ocher paler than the surrounding rocks. Had Rembrandt almost added horse and Rider here? But Davies had laughed and called her a romantic. That was true. She knew it. Perhaps that was why, of all Rembrandt's work, *The Polish Rider* most drew her. It was a romantic painting from a classical Master.

Quillan Davies surmised that the Santa Fe Rembrandt was only a very successful preliminary study for the much larger painting. But she argued that Rembrandt would not have gone to such trouble over a preliminary sketch. The small gem of a painting—though developed in the structural style of the 1640s—had a monumental effect, the brush strokes broad, bold, the colors warm, intense.

At which Quillan Davies disarmed her with a toddle or two in his Chaplin walk, twirling the imaginary cane, and dismissed the whole thing with, "Let's go down the hill for lunch. We can get our names on the blackboard before the crowd." For the exchange director had abandoned the pudding of the British Isles for the chili of New Mexico, and down the hill at Josie's you chalked your name on a blackboard on the porch to reserve your place, then sat on a bench in the sun, waiting for the summons.

The visiting director had bought two season tickets to the opera, claiming he'd no idea who he'd ask, then taken her to all three of the summer's offerings—*Carmen* and *Rigoletto* and *The Barber of Seville*. They'd sat side by side those Santa Fe nights, sky quilted by stars, and she'd felt grown-up and sophisticated.

Moving to shield the painting with her body should anyone open the East Room's arched door, she bent with the Pink Pearl poised for the coup, its rubber tip honed to a fine point. Last night the pencil touched the painting along the bare yellow strand at the bottom.

She bent closer, scanning the painting from one side of the frame to the other and back again. She straightened and squinted. She bent from the waist. But no matter, the painting was clean, the mark was gone. There wasn't a sign of it.

3

In a hiatus so short she soon forgot it had ever existed, she felt a flood of relief—the Rembrandt was intact, it had never been marred, she hadn't damaged it after all.

But where was the pencil mark? Not that she was really thinking. It was more as if thoughts unbidden collided in her brain.

Behind her, tall Ted Torrence opened the door and his group entered the East Room, Ted lecturing in his actor's voice. She turned and, smiling vaguely with what decorum she could muster, hurried past quizzical looks out the door and down the hall to her cubby of an office, where she stood looking out the one big window over the flat rooftops of Santa Fe. Below her, the slope tumbled down, full of gray-green chemiso with golden tops and patches here and there of wild purple asters. She could hear but not see the traffic on the Paseo under the hill.

After a while, she took her keys out of her backpack on the sofa and moved to the door marked DIRECTOR in gold block graphics. She fitted the key to the lock and turned the knob. Nothing happened. Turning the key, she had locked the door. Another failure. She had left it unlocked overnight.

The drapes were pulled across the large window that, like hers, overlooked the town. In the darkened room she was met with the smell she associated with Quillan Davies—a compound of some subtle after-shave and the Turkish tobacco he smoked in the handsome meerschaum. He had departed yesterday morning for the annual Regional Museum Conference in Dallas, leaving her in charge. From there he would go on to visit the museums in New York City and D.C. In a serendipitous meeting at a cocktail party in New

York City, Quillan Davies and George Cameron, the permanent director, had arranged the exchange between themselves. George Cameron was an incorrigible Anglophile and Davies was fascinated by the American Southwest.

She let her fingertips trail over the desk in the middle of the room facing the door. Usually, entering, she found the Englishman, his back to her, swiveled around to the floor-to-ceiling window and the view of the town as he talked on the phone. In the darkened room she felt rather than saw the tobacco crumbs scattered over the polished walnut surface. She absently scooped them up in her fingers and sniffed them as she crossed the deep pile carpet and drew open the drapes.

He's twice your age, whispered the voice of reason as she watched a flock of grosbeaks clamor in the piñon trees.

But the Libran voice of balance amended, *Not quite.*

Quillan Davies—amused, melancholy air, graying sandy hair, face round as a cherub's, in baggy tweeds reeking of tobacco—was hardly a Prince Charming.

She was sitting again over coffee in the kitchen of their sweet, spacey landlady Magda Sanchez who, arms full of bangles, laughed at her with gypsy eyes. "When I married my first husband, I was nineteen years old. He was thirty years my senior, the village stud. Everyone gave the marriage a week, but it lasted till he died, and it was the best of all my marriages."

She felt lucky to have been hired over better-qualified candidates. Davies assured her it had been because her résumé stated that in summer school at Boulder, Colorado, she'd taken a course called Museum Practices, which he thought might come in handy as he knew nothing whatever about museum practices in the USA. Whereupon she'd confessed that all she'd done in Museum Practices had been to stuff a weasel. The weasel had ended up looking like a hot dog with a head and a tail.

A possible solution to the mystery of the vanished pencil mark came to her as she toyed with the drapery cord. She spun to the desk, picked up the phone and dialed, absently scooping the tobacco crumbs into a neat little pile and again sniffing her fingers. She circled, playing with the cord, while the phone went on ringing.

Then a click at the other end and, "Yeah?"

"Croy? Is that you?"

"Naw, Scahlet honey, this not me, this foxy ol' Rhett."

Croy Beuly also lived in the East Side compound. Although he played the light and frolicsome wit, she suspected he was, deep down, as dark and broody as Hamlet. He worked in the gift shop at the old Territorial Governor's Palace on the plaza. He never took a job with a future because he was a writer, wasn't he? and a real job might interfere with his "vocation." He called it a vocation because he was a lapsed Catholic from New Orleans. So he made his living waiting tables, or mâitre d'-ing, or, just now, at the gift shop.

"Run around the corner, will you, Croy, and see if you can find Tina. She's with that movie crew. Tell her to get herself up here."

"Anything the matter, luv?"

She could see him with his tumbled hair, dishwater blond, thin face smiling across the glass-top counter. "No, nothing. Nothing's the matter. Everything's fine. I just want to talk to her is all."

"Sure. Okay. Right away. Want to hold?"

"No. Tell her I'll be in the East Room." She put down the phone, looked at the Pink Pearl eraser, and jammed it into a mug on the desk already full of ballpoints and advertising throwaways. Then she pulled the drapes and hurried back to the East Room.

Ted Torrence had moved on to the small Dürer drawing, probably a preliminary sketch, of a hare, a fox, a strange creature perhaps of the imagination, and an owl in a hollow tree.

"Critics once laughed at Dürer's drawing of a rhinoceros," he drawled in his carefully modulated voice, "because, they said, rhinos didn't look like that. As it turned out, the critics were right—about the *African* rhinoceros." This was Ted's pièce de résistance about Dürer, so he took his time. "But he had drawn from someone's description of an *Indian* rhino, which did look like that precisely, right down to the armor plate." His dark hair swept back in wings and a crown of it peaked out over his forehead. Put a mike in his hand, he'd look like a fifties' crooner.

The group surrounding him chuckled. Gin had heard it all before. She smiled vaguely in their direction and moved toward the Rembrandt.

Mrs. Trowber returned her smile. She was a cheery soul, always ready to call it a morning and head for lunch. And she liked a joke. Ever since the group's arrival at the beginning of the week, her low laughter had rumbled down the hall like a bowling ball.

There was something froglike about Toby Trowber, with her bulging eyes and her head as flat at the back as if she'd been nursed on a cradle board. Her legs were thin and the rest of her plump, and her voice was a kind of croak. Like many a gentleman losing his hair, she let hers gain in length as it otherwise lost till it fell in strands to her shoulders.

Victor Weldon stood a little aside from the group, looking at the Rembrandt, apparently not listening to Ted Torrence. A broad, strongly built man, cheeks pitted from ancient acne wars, his hair in permanent disarray, victim of his raking fingers, he was a man who, with the blandest of looks in his faded blue eyes, gave the impression of suffering.

He studied the Rembrandt, frowning a little. She moved anxiously behind him and asked inanely, "Is anything wrong?"

He shrugged. "There's a little glare."

Eric Albin spoke up. "*There* you are!" he said to her. "We were hoping you'd join us for lunch."

She worked up a smile for Eric. In his mid-forties, he dressed in denims and sneakers, wore his hair to the top of his collar, and flirted with the women in the group, who seemed to regard him as charmingly boyish. But his real attention, if she read him right, was reserved for their leader, Ted Torrence, who lived in Upper Canyon Road with a gallery director named Herman Rawsche.

Groups like this tramped through the museum about once a month. Full-page ads in glossy magazines offered fall in Santa Fe. A six-day guided tour highlighting the arts and crafts of the Southwest. Led by Linda Burnabum, Archaeologist (or Ted Torrence, Santa Fe Painter; or Markham Bloye, Renowned Local Potter). Tour groups were cordially invited to a special brunch at Santa Clara pueblo as guests of the family of a famous Indian craftsman. Join the fun.

The ads always promised behind-the-scenes tours of the Maxwell Museum of Anthropology at the University of New Mexico in Albuquerque, and the Pueblo Indian Cultural Center, The Wheelwright and Waldheimer museums in Santa Fe, the Museum of Indian Arts and Culture, and the Museum of International Folk Art, as well as visits to the Spanish-American weavers and woodcarvers in Truchas and Chimayo, with an authentic New Mexican lunch at the famous Rancho de Chimayo, originally the heart of a hacienda chartered by the king of Spain.

The visit to the East Room was usually an afterthought, the tours losing momentum after the Southwest galleries—Georgia O'Keeffe, and the early painters of Taos and Santa Fe—and Frida Kahlo, who'd thought of herself as an amateur, the crippled appendage of the robust great man to whom she had devoted herself, while the great man devoted himself to his art, his politics, and his other women.

Not the whole truth, Gin's Libra self corrected: Frida Kahlo'd had her own affairs, one with Leon Trotsky, and—it was rumored—several with women.

But it was the East Room that displayed those paintings the museum had primarily been built to house—the Dürer drawing, the small Rembrandt, the Van Dyck portrait of an English nobleman, the Turner landscape with castle, and the works of Picasso, the exquisite Matisse, the still lifes by Derain and Juan Gris and Marie Laurencin and Braque, and the small, perfect Cézanne. Not one of them a painting you'd expect to find in a small museum in the American Southwest.

The group around Ted Torrence was different from groups that usually passed through. There was a cohesiveness about it foreign to a tour group randomly convened—students with notebooks and ballpoints taking academic credit for broadening experiences, art teachers on sabbatical, widows from the East Coast who had always meant to see the West while their husbands were alive and now made the pilgrimage alone.

Mrs. Trowber whispered something to her and stifled a guffaw in deference to the lecture across the room.

"Did your group know each other before the tour?" Gin asked softly.

"I didn't know any of them," Mrs. Trowber whispered. "Still don't, if you want the truth. They stick to themselves. You see, they're a pod."

"A what?"

"A pod! A pod!" Mrs. Trowber laughed, then lowered her voice. "What! You never heard of a pod before either? I mean, besides a hull full of peas or a family of whales?"

"What does it mean?"

"Well, as I understand it"—Mrs. Trowber raised her penciled-on eyebrows in a significant look—"they all met years ago in Southern California, when they were grad students or young instructors at UCLA. Decided they wanted to stay together. We all have dreams like that, don't we—when we're young and in school, with twenty-seven best friends we can't live without, jabbering away till three in the morning over a jug of red wine about religion and philosophy and maybe buying a tract of land and everybody building his own house but sharing the washer and dryer and riding lawn mower and swimming pool? That sort of thing."

Gin thought it sounded familiar. "They must all have independent incomes."

"It would seem so," said Mrs. Trowber, "though I've heard whiffs of difficulties in the financial department. But I gather they're into some scheme to set it right . . . Stock market ventures would be my guess."

What was keeping Tina? Gin glanced at her watch. Over by the Dürer, Alice Maynard—short, dark hair in bangs, pink paisley print flaring girlishly from square shoulder straps—turned and gave her a slow, head-ducked smile, shyly coquettish, like a little girl at a party.

Alice stood beside Eric Albin, who said he was a jewelry designer. (My dear, it's work you can do anywhere. I just draw my designs as the inspiration strikes, and when I feel moved to it make my casts and send them on to Uncle Roderick's foundry in Arizona. Then they go to Uncle Roderick's chain.) She'd visualized a chain necklace full of little gold charms, but of course he meant a chain of jewelry stores.

Eric wore a thin flat band of gold around his neck, exposed

by the three open top buttons of his collarless terry shirt, and a matching band around his wrist—both, she assumed, designed by the model himself. Eric and Alice seemed particularly close, in that sexless bond often formed by timid women and feminine men.

"Everyone in the pod," Mrs. Trowber said, "seems to do the kind of work you can do anywhere. That one, for instance." She pointed covertly, with the forefinger of the hand holding the top of her cardigan together, to the tall woman with thick glasses that, as she glanced their way, reflected the morning sun from the windows and obscured her eyes. "She's the crime writer. Sheila Wadsworth. Maybe you've heard of her."

"Crime writer?" Gin stared back at the glaring spectacles that seemed to be watching, reading their lips. The gangly woman struck you as awkward, unsure, inept. Then her jawline suggested otherwise.

"Makes a fortune out of what's called the 'new journalism' writing up ghastly things—serial murders or the scatter shots of madmen in towers or the bodies of little boys unearthed in suburban gardens . . ."

Mrs. Trowber's voice trailed off as a man and woman moved toward them—the man tall, with a clean profile and a squarish patch of gray on the side of a head of otherwise dark brown hair, the woman small and lopsided, with the hint of a hump, graying hair in a bob, wearing wrinkled cotton slacks.

Mrs. Trowber greeted them and turned to make introductions, but at that moment Tina Martinez swept down the corridor, now in her boots. Her heels announced her arrival long before she entered the room.

"This better be good, Gin."

Gin drew her toward the Rembrandt. "You found the pencil mark last night, didn't you."

"What do you mean? What pencil mark?" Tina said, with familiar impatience.

"You worked here in the basement last night. I gave you my keys." Tina served the museum, as well as several of the galleries in town, as conservator. Gin had recommended her for the job, as replacement for a man who'd been coming up from Albuquerque a couple of times a month. She would probably keep it as long as she cleaned up after herself and left the museum basement in tolerable shape.

"You don't have to tell me what I did last night."

"You were working on the Frederic Remington."

"*I* know what I was working on."

"Come on, Tina. You came upstairs and took a look at the paintings—I've seen you do it."

Tina glanced at the tour group and lowered her voice. "I haven't a clue what you're talking about."

"But you must have seen it," Gin said, "because it's not there anymore."

"*What's* not *where* anymore?"

Slow down, try again.

Gin explained—haltingly, hesitantly—how, the night before, she had inadvertently flung out an arm that, unfortunately, had a pencil at the end of it.

Tina turned to the painting and stood looking at it with one arm crossed over her breast and clutching the other one hanging at her side, a habitual pose. "Where?" She leaned forward, hands on hips. "I don't see a thing," she muttered, "but there is a glare."

There seemed to be glares everywhere. On the other hand, whenever something seemed wrong with a painting, any painting, it was usually attributed to glare.

Gin moved to shield the painting from whatever reflection it might have been picking up, and Tina moved farther back, then closer, then bent in her nearsighted way with her nose inches from the canvas.

Finally she straightened. "You must have imagined it."

"I didn't imagine it. It was at least an inch long."

"Well, if you find it, let me know and I'll make it vanish again."

A voice behind them murmured, "He painted so few landscapes."

They turned. It was the man with the square gray patch in his hair.

Raoul Query said, "And this one's so unusual. It might be Spain, or"—he smiled—"the American Southwest."

But he wasn't looking at the painting, he was looking at

the two young women—one tall, one small—and judging them to be Hispanic, or Spanish as they said out here, and/ or Indian. The museum tour, till then tedious, had suddenly become interesting. "Are you sisters?" he asked.

"Yes," said Tina, who was into games.

"I see," he said, smiling, realizing there was some joke. "I would very much like to paint you."

But it wasn't a real suggestion, only a compliment.

"Which one of us?" Tina asked. "Or is it two for the price of one?"

Gin dissociated herself from Tina's teasing. "Are you one of the peas?" she asked.

The smile broadened. "I'm a member of the original pod."

"Oh. Does that mean others have joined since the founding fathers—and mothers—so to speak?"

"Yes. Some have married and brought in wives and husbands. Some have divorced and one or the other gone his or her separate way."

"I see," she said. "You mean when there's a divorce one of the parties leaves so they won't be bumping into each other in the communal laundry?"

"Not always," he said. "Sometimes both parties stay, and eventually bring in another husband—or wife, as the case may be. I am, in fact, one such."

"Oh," said Gin, embarrassed. "I'm sorry. I didn't mean . . ."

"Don't be. My wife and I remained the best of friends."

"How civilized," said Tina, looking from one of them to the other.

Raoul Query's gaze shifted downward. He smiled at Tina. "I think it's a shame when people who once loved each other become enemies. My wife, as a matter of fact, remarried. Splendid fellow."

"Are they on the tour? I mean, your wife and . . ." Gin asked, feeling immediately the impropriety of the question, born as it was of curiosity and her habit of sorting.

"Her husband is," he said, his face suddenly drawn, as if the skin had momentarily shrunk and tightened. He nodded toward the broad man with the suffering eyes, presumably the splendid fellow. Gin was finding Raoul Query handsome and charming, and that put her on guard. She distrusted handsome, charming men. Of medium height, he somehow gave the impression of being taller. His hair, with that strange squarish patch of gray above his right ear, grew thick and straight, like fur, though a little wavy at the front.

She'd noticed him at once, on the pod's first visit to the Waldheimer, and tried thereafter not to look at him. He had a subdued, patient air, and when one or another of this collection of art lovers made a particularly unfortunate gaffe, his eyes sought hers with a tolerant smile, a bid for connection, which she had pretended not to notice.

The new husband seemed older, and he was not good-looking, or particularly charming, which she found to his credit. He was talking to the one they called the commander—fortyish, in some kind of summer uniform with epaulets on the shoulders of his white short-sleeved shirt. Tall, towheaded, his neat, white, short-clipped beard like a bandage holding up his jaw, the commander looked habitually self-conscious and shy.

"Do you always dress in identical jackets?" Tina asked. Both husbands wore navy blue blazers. "Is it some kind of uniform? I mean, to identify you as mates of your mutual wife?"

But Raoul Query only smiled. In spite of herself, Gin found something likable about him, perhaps the pleasant, detached, ironic tone in everything he said.

He moved between them to look at the painting, hoisting his hands to his hips, flaring the skirts of his jacket as he bent. "Remarkable, isn't it," he said, swinging back around. "Till yesterday I didn't know it existed. Look at the impasto, the depth of color." But he hadn't really looked at either, he was looking at Gin.

"Are you some kind of expert?" Tina enjoyed luring visiting experts into making fools of themselves.

He smiled. He was onto her. "I'm a painter of sorts myself," he said, "though I don't claim to be much good."

False modesty, Gin thought.

"I was just a commercial artist with ambitions beyond my talent, and I needed something I could do anywhere."

So he could live with the pod.

"But I show in a gallery here. I can write off the tour as a business trip." He smiled.

"Which gallery?" Tina asked. You could classify a painter by the gallery.

"The Phoether."

Tina called it the Phinn and Phoether. It was full of sportsmen's prints and paintings of anglers in waders in the middle of mountain streams—all guaranteed to appeal to the husbands of tourist couples. If the husband liked a painting, a sale was sure to follow.

Raoul Query said, as if reading Gin's mind, "Paintings for dentists looking for something for their office walls." He glanced at the Rembrandt and immediately back at her. "Perfect," he murmured.

Her face went hot.

"You think so?" Tina said with a wicked smile.

"Oh, no question. Look at those rocks." But he wasn't looking at the rocks. "A rock is the damnedest thing in the world to paint."

She felt Tina's eyes, with their own lively smile, moving from one of them to the other. Tina often accused her of being unapproachable, and Gin accused Tina of coming too much under the influence of whomever she was in love with at the moment. "If I threw caution to the winds . . ." Tina would be leaning with her fingertips on the dresser top, examining herself closeup in the mirror.

"You'd wear lipstick and green eye shadow."

"No. I'd wear kohl. Do you know what kohl is?" She pronounced it with a round fruity *oh*. "Powder of antimony"—she said it like an incantation—"worn by women of the East."

Now Ted Torrence's group was in front of the Turner—a painting of landscape-cum-castle under roiling clouds on a headland over a bleak, cold sea.

"It's an early Turner," Ted was saying in his patronizing way. It's *only* an early Turner.

Ted always did it like that—paused briefly, studied the Turner, then took that patronizing tone about the greatest nineteenth-century landscapist of them all. Gin bristled when she heard it, which wasn't too often—she tried to avoid Ted's lectures. Oh, please, she thought. Get on with it. She needed the gallery to herself.

Now Ted became the serious critic. "Some of his seascapes rivaled—even surpassed—those of the Dutch Masters." But as the pod cocked heads and frowned weightily at the painting, Ted smiled, flipped a dismissive hand at the Turner. "Not, I think, this one, however."

The pod obligingly chuckled.

"Did you know," he went on, "that after Turner died the curator who received his paintings at—I believe it was the Tate—" (he knew very well it was the Tate)—"destroyed all of his later work? The pictures were impressionist, you see, and the curator simply thought the old man had lost his marbles and wouldn't have wanted his reputation spoiled by such daubs."

The pod obligingly groaned. Gin groaned silently with them. She could have wept each time she thought of those lost Turners.

"The man was an eccentric—secretive, unsociable, never married. Though I understand a widow bore him two children in his middle years."

Small touches, tossed out like that, created a time warp—and made Ted an intimate of Turner's circle.

"When he died he left his fortune toward the support of 'decayed' artists—his term. But distant relatives, not the widow and children, contested and got the money."

The pod obligingly *tsk*ed.

When they moved toward the Rembrandt, Gin and Tina and Raoul Query stepped aside.

"I've got to get back to the plaza," Tina whispered.

Gin smiled at the group and wadded Tina's skirt firmly in her fist. Tina looked down in amazement.

"And this," Ted Torrence solemnly intoned, "is the gem of the collection." The pod cocked its communal head devoutly. After a moment of respectful silence, he went on. "Rembrandt's early paintings, when he was still in Leyden, his hometown, were painted on oak panels bought readymade. He prepared them with a thin layer of chalk, then covered that with an oil-based imprimatura that gave the whole a brownish tone.''

Get *on* with it. Gin hugged herself with her arms crossed to keep from dancing with urgency.

"But after he moved to Amsterdam, he painted mostly on canvas. This painting is on canvas. A fairly late work.'' He paused to give this fact significance that Gin couldn't see it had, and they all raised knowing eyebrows. She kept her eyes on Ted, avoiding Raoul Query's, which were on her.

"He applied a double layer of ground—reddish earth pigments—then usually a gray or grayish brown mixed with lead white. That way he built the background and set the color tone of the painting.''

The pod scribbled in notebooks, all but Victor Weldon. He was eyeing Raoul Query with a look both intense and enigmatic. Then he looked at Gin with direct, unsmiling eye contact that lasted until, flustered, she looked away.

"Or—'' Ted paused, as if recalling some casual drop-in at the painter's studio ''—sometimes he made his ground of a single dark layer of silica sand tinted with brown ocher and lead white, probably the technique used here.''

Someone murmured something about *The Polish Rider*, and Ted said, "Um, yes, one sees a similarity of subject,'' as if this were too obvious for comment, and Raoul Query gave her that small complicitous smile, while behind him Victor Weldon moved closer. Tina, caught trying none too discreetly to free her skirt, boldly returned his look. He gave them a melancholy smile and glanced at Raoul Query.

"Charming the ladies, Raoul?'' Raoul Query flushed and turned his attention to the painting. "Or admiring this particular Rembrandt?'' Tina's eyes flashed from one to the other. Impatient, Gin turned away to the pod and Ted Torrence.

"Afterward, of course, as you all know . . .'' Ted bestowed on the group a colleague's smile. The man belonged on stage. ''. . . he sketched in the forms, worked up features, glazed over dark areas, adding details of costume, shadows, nuances . . .'' All rattled off while the pod scribbled furiously. Alice Maynard stopped mid-tilt and glanced around, hopeless of keeping up. Victor Weldon, hands clasped together in front of him, moved up beside Alice, bent his head, and murmured reassuringly.

". . . bringing the whole into his particular kind of unity with little tricks of his own"—Ted smiled, indulging the Master his small, painterly foibles, and the group smiled too—"like applying the back of the brush to lend texture, much as modern painters use a palette knife. For, as we all know, thick brush strokes reflect light and add dimension."

Heads nodded, notebooks again came under the pen, but finally, just when Gin thought it might never happen, Ted Torrence edged them toward the door. Faces smiled. Someone called "Good-bye." Raoul Query said, "We'll see you tonight," and she remembered the Montoya opening. It had completely slipped her mind. It was scheduled to begin at eight with a reception for the trustees to which Ted had wangled the pod an invitation. At nine, the public would come in.

Raoul Query gave her a parting smile and moved off with the rest. Did Alice Maynard step away from the handsome, charming Islander and grasp Eric's arm more firmly? Alice and Eric hurried on ahead, leaving Raoul Query behind.

Finally she and Tina had the room to themselves.

Tina said, "Let go of me, Gin."

"No, look, wait a minute."

"I've *got* to get back to the plaza."

"The pencil struck about here." Gin pointed.

"You mistook a hairline 'crack," Tina said. "All old paintings have them. What are you worried about?"

Good question. What did it matter what had happened to the pencil mark? There was the painting, frame and all, intact, like before. "It looks okay to you?"

"Come on, Gin, what's your problem?" Tina could fret like a baby.

Gin didn't answer. She had stood for long intervals of devotion before the Rembrandt, but now . . .

In a peculiar state of suspension, she admitted to herself that something seemed wrong. Something indefinable.

"Don't you see anything?" she asked softly.

"What do you mean?"

"The painting . . . Does it, you know, look all right to you?"

Tina sighed.

"I keep thinking," Gin said, though she'd only that minute actually thought it, "something about it isn't quite the same."

"The same as what?"

"As before."

"Before what?"

"You think I'm crazy."

"You're not being absolutely unequivocally lucid."

"How late were you here last night?"

"Till about ten. I left right after Juan and Benito finished unloading the paintings for the opening."

Right. Benito's cousin used the pickup during the day and Benito couldn't borrow it till after work. They would have unloaded at the back of the building, at the basement entry, and brought the paintings up in the elevator.

"Reuben drove me up the hill," Tina said. "They asked him to give them a hand, and he did, grudgingly. He's miffed, you know."

How well she knew. On the East Side compound, Reuben was their difficult member—a painter without a gallery, who had never yet had a show of his own in Santa Fe. Due more to his temperament than to his work, Gin thought.

"They finished at about eight," Tina said. "I worked on the Remington a little later. I had to clean it and revarnish the frame."

Later, when Tina got home, Gin had not mentioned the pencil mark because she thought she could fix it herself and no one the wiser.

"There was a regular mob in the museum last night," she muttered. "Does it really look the same to you?"

They both bent over the painting.

"What're you suggesting?"

"Nothing. I don't know."

"Come on. What're we talking about?" Then Tina straightened and laughed. "Oh, no. Don't tell me. You do lead a rich inner life." But once more she drew closer to the painting and squinted. "Okay, if it's not the Rembrandt, what is it?"

Gin shook her head. "I haven't the faintest."

"You mean maybe last night somebody whipped up this elaborate copy and substituted it? Who? Those idiots in Ted's group? Or maybe Juan? Or Benito? Or Reuben?" Tina laughed to soften her tone, which had been almost angry. "You're just giving yourself frissons."

It did sound ridiculous. "I guess I'm being weird. This isn't some kind of joke, is it, Tina?"

"You're asking if *I* took the Rembrandt?"

Gin eyed the painting out of the corner of her eye like it was something she was afraid of and might have to placate.

"Or maybe you've never really looked at it before," Tina said, "and always overrated it just because it is, after all, a Rembrandt."

Gin shook her head. "You think I'm filling your mind with foolish doubts."

"You're not filling *my* mind with anything." That angry tone again. Gin bit her lip. Tina was a trusting soul who wanted a world in which she could get on with her painting without distractions. "If that's not the Rembrandt, it's a damn good copy," Tina said.

It was. A good painting. Brilliant, as a matter of fact, not the work of a hack. A painter that good wouldn't have to deal in forgeries. None of it made any sense.

She stood in silence, looking at the landscape so like the painting at the Frick that the Rider might simply have ridden off the canvas and out of sight, and the stillness of the painting came back at her with something like a dare, asking weren't these yellows a touch too yellow, and the pinks of the rocks too pink? And the rocks themselves . . . Hadn't Rembrandt's rocks been defined more by the impasto, so that they were almost the idea, the essence, of rock rather than rocks themselves, whatever life vouchsafed to rocks breathed into them by the Master? While *these* rocks, though they were indeed rocks, lacked the weight of those other rocks. *These* rocks were airy, light, touched into being by a different muse entirely.

These rocks. *Those* rocks. She tried to shake herself, but the shake was more of a shudder.

"Where could it have come from?" Tina asked in little more than a whisper.

Gin couldn't answer.

"Anyway, what's in a name?" Tina's laugh was sharp, unnatural. "Take the cave paintings in Lascaux . . ."

They'd seen them one summer on a college tour to Europe. Gin had never been so moved by paintings in her life.

"Nobody knows who painted *them*," Tina said. "Nobody bothered to sign his name. If he had a name. He might have been known by a particularly egregious grunt."

"Why do you say *he*?"

But Tina ignored her. "*They* can never be sold, or hung in museums. They're just there, for all time, in the living rock."

The paint still wet to the touch, the guide had said as they looked up at the giant figures on the cave wall.

"So what are you saying? I'm supposed to ignore my feelings?"

"Come on, Gin, you've developed a hyperactive imagination."

Still they stood looking at the painting. After a while, Tina jiggled Gin's arm. "So what are you going to do?"

Gin turned and looked at her. "You think I should do something?"

Tina met her eyes with a look almost of defiance. "I don't think anything."

Gin said, "You're a great big help."

4

"So what'll you do?" Tina said when they were in Gin's office with the Mr. Coffee plugged in. "I mean, with Herbie out of town?" That wasn't Davies's name. His name was Quillan. But they agreed that the interim director looked like Herbert Marshall from "Movie Classics," which they watched regularly on Magda's tube. That same sad, bemused air, as if he looked out at the world from a higher plane.

"I don't know."

"If that's not the Rembrandt, then where is it? It's such a small painting. It couldn't just walk out of here."

"Not without help," Gin said. Then she sighed and said in what she hoped was a take-charge voice, "Okay, we know it was there when I left last night."

Tina raised her eyebrows questioningly.

"Because of the pencil mark."

"Oh, right, the pencil mark." Was there a note of doubt in Tina's voice?

"If the painting's missing," Gin said, and a shudder spiraled from her shoulders up her throat, "that corresponds with the pod's visit."

"But they had already left when you inspected the pencil mark."

"I don't mean just last night. I mean their whole visit, this week."

"It also corresponds with preparations for hanging Benny Montoya's show."

"I know, I know." Gin circled in front of the window, feeling cold for such a sunny morning.

"Or Benito and Reuben and Juan coming and going down the freight elevator last night, carrying paintings. Or me,

THE SANTA FE REMBRANDT 31

working in the basement till late. And then there's Olivia.
Are you writing off Olivia?''

But that wasn't what the assistant director was doing. She
was kicking herself. In spite of her inexperience, Quillan
Davies had entrusted the museum to her care and look what
happened. ''So now what? What do I do?''

Tina took off one boot and rubbed her arch. ''I don't
know,'' she said. ''I suppose we ought to question people.
That's what they do on television.''

''Question who?'' Gin asked. ''Juan and Mrs. Philipson
and Olivia?'' She stifled a laugh.

But she called Juan away from helping Benito hang his
show. Right, he'd helped Benito unload his paintings last
night and locked up the museum at about eight o'clock—
except for the basement because Tina was still there. He
glanced down at Tina on the couch.

When Gin asked him to go lock the East Room, one eyebrow shot up in a look she suspected he practiced before his
bathroom mirror.

''The floors have to be waxed,'' she lied.

The look on his face said Oh, yeah? He knew janitorial
service had cleaned and waxed late Tuesday afternoon, yesterday, as they always did.

Next, Mrs. Philipson. Cameron, the permanent director,
called Mrs. Philipson the czarina of the Waldheimer. The
galleries and corridors were Mrs. Philipson's empire, taken
by coup and capitulation soon after she arrived. Mrs. Philipson had a running battle with Olivia. The gift shop was the
only principality left unconquered.

Mrs. Philipson's name was, appropriately, Regina. Now
a widow, she lived in a town house off the Old Taos Highway,
but in her married life she had presided over a large residence
not far from the governor's mansion. For Regina Philipson,
taking care of the museum was a piece of cake.

Mrs. Philipson also had an ongoing argument with the
permanent director—about the plants in the museum. ''Wonderful light,'' she said, aggrieved. She had a green thumb
whose natural creativity was being thwarted. But Cameron
wanted leaf plants only, no horticultural hues to compete
with the paintings. Mrs. Philipson would turn the Waldhei-

mer into a greenhouse, George Cameron said, if not strictly controlled. This dynamo, volunteer worker, and museum receptionist—Mrs. Philipson preferred "hostess"—came in the surprising package of a soft-spoken, upright, blue-haired lady of seventy.

She left the museum last night later than usual, she said, because of the tour group. Of course the Waldheimer was closed on Mondays and Tuesdays, but she always came in for a while on Tuesdays to hector the janitorial service, to see that they dusted the tops of the frames and vacuumed the drapes in the offices and waxed in the corners.

"And Ted Torrence's group was *where* when you left, Regina?"

Oh, said Mrs. Philipson, they were nowhere near ready to leave. They were still in the Georgia O'Keeffe Room. Except, of course, for Mr. Query. Charming man. Mr. Query had stayed behind at the desk and they'd chatted a bit about the building. He admired the building. They talked about the floor plan and how well it worked. She'd given him the visitors' map of the galleries and he'd wandered about alone. "He's not much for groups and it's something of a trial for him," Mrs. Philipson said. "He appreciates the pictures and likes being left alone with them."

"I see," Gin said with a flitting glance at Tina. "Did you see where he wandered?"

Now Mrs. Philipson knew what this was all about. It was that foolish Olivia, always suspecting people. "Well," she said, "he didn't go near the gift shop or I'd certainly have noticed."

Gin saw what Mrs. Philipson had in mind. And just as well.

"He went," said Mrs. Philipson, drawing herself up, "in the opposite direction entirely."

"Toward the East Room?"

"Well, in that direction, though I think . . ." She dropped her voice. "I believe he went to the men's room."

Gin and Tina exchanged glances. The rest rooms were around the corner from the main entrance to the East Room but right across the hall from the side entry.

"He may have wanted to think . . . and take notes . . . Off to himself, you know," Mrs. Philipson said.

"He had a notebook or a briefcase with him, then," Gin prompted. Ordinarily visitors to the museum were asked to leave such things at the reception desk, but this was a privileged group, the tour being more on the order of a seminar.

"Yes, he always carries it," Mrs. Philipson said, with an approving smile.

"Do you remember anyone else leaving the group?" Mrs. Philipson rarely missed anything. "I mean, I know you were busy . . ." Gin always deferred to Mrs. Philipson, suspecting that if she and the director were suddenly to disappear, the Waldheimer would run smoothly on under Regina Philipson's small freckled hand.

Mrs. Philipson's brows met in a V over her nose. "Well, the strange-looking lady . . ."

"Mrs. Trowber?"

"Yes, that's it. She came into the hall and stood looking at the little painting facing the entry, the one you see down the corridor."

"The Rembrandt."

"She may have been sketching it, or perhaps reading about it from *Gallery Notes*." *Gallery Notes* was the pamphlet Mrs. Philipson handed out to visitors.

Gin said softly, "Then Mrs. Trowber had a portfolio with her?"

"Oh, yes," said Mrs. Philipson, immediately picking up the gist, for someone with a portfolio could easily smuggle out of the museum a small memento from the gift shop, and Mrs. Trowber's portfolio got Raoul Query—such a charming man—off the hook. "I remember it very well," she said, "as it is on the verge of falling apart."

Behind Mrs. Philipson, Tina shifted on the sofa and gave Gin a look.

"Anything else you can think of . . . Regina? It might be very helpful."

"Well, I recall being unusually tired. I was glad I'd driven to the museum. Sometimes I walk—for the exercise, you know. And as I got in my car"—an enormous Lincoln that dwarfed Mrs. Philipson—"I saw Richard just coming for

Olivia.'' Richard was Olivia's husband. ''Nobody,'' Regina Philipson said firmly, ''was anywhere near the gift shop.''

Olivia Marquez, even teetering on compensatory heels, was no more than five feet tall. But her bosom was of impressive proportions. She wore her black hair in the Betty Boop-style of the twenties, shingled at the back and curving in little scimitars toward cheeks that lapsed into dimples when she smiled, which was almost all the time. Her husband Richard adored her. Not much taller than Olivia, he was a sales representative for a pharmaceutical company. He dropped her off at the museum each morning and retrieved her again each night. The hair on his head apparently grew straight out from his scalp and he had to weight it down with oils and conditioners. But usually some of it broke free at his crown, making him look electrified. Whenever he gazed at Olivia his features fell into a foolish grin.

When Mrs. Philipson had gone, Olivia's heels clicked across the corridor from the gift shop, where she sold cards and posters and art books, and a few local Spanish and Indian crafts that had nothing at all to do with the museum. She counted everything over each night before locking up, nervous about all that responsibility.

This was her first job. She and Richard had discussed it for days, Olivia confessing, in her small voice that ran on so rapidly it left her breathless, her longing to be out in the world and, contrarily, the fears and insecurities that kept her at home. For first she had been her father's darling, and then straightaway became Richard's. But Richard had held her hand and told her that she could do anything, absolutely anything she put her mind to. So after a time he had taken her around and with great trepidation she had put in applications and here she was.

But Gin knew Olivia no better now than on the day she'd been hired. For outside of Richard, Olivia needed neither kin, nor friend, nor close acquaintance. Yes, she had stayed a little after five-thirty the night before. She'd only come in in the afternoon, to accommodate Ted's tour. And, yes, several of the group had come into the shop and looked at posters. One gentleman had bought a box.

''A box!'' said Tina on the sofa behind her, and Olivia

jumped and looked around. She was always a bundle of nerves.

Yes, she told them, you know, one of those chests they'd purchased from a Spanish wood carver. The new director, wanting to carry some local crafts, had brought in these little Yei rugs . . . and chests from this carver in Chimayo.

What size chest had the gentleman bought?

One of the large ones, the very largest—he could ship souvenirs home in it, he said—so large that he'd left it in the gift shop and gone on with the others. He had come back later and put some things in it so he wouldn't have to carry them around with him during the lecture, and he'd been upset to find that she'd locked it in the gift shop when she left for the night.

"Is it still there?" they chorused.

"Oh, no," Olivia said. He'd come back for it this morning. She hadn't meant to do it, lock it in, she'd just forgotten. But he'd only left one of those . . . rain things, you know, and maybe a hat to match, in the box, that was all. But it hadn't rained—it never rained in Santa Fe this time of year, no sign it ever would—so she couldn't imagine why . . . He was here first thing this morning to retrieve it.

Which man was this?

The one in the . . . white shirt, you know, with short sleeves and these . . . She brushed at the top of her shoulder with red-tipped fingers.

"Epaulets!" Gin said.

"That's right."

"The one they call the commander."

Olivia nodded. "And he came back this morning to pick it up. He said he wanted to get it while he had the car. They've rented a station wagon to take them around, and he had it this morning."

This morning had Olivia seen what was inside the box?

Yes, she had. For he was with that lady—Olivia's forehead crinkled as she tried to remember the name on the credit card—and this lady had bought a poster. They'd opened the chest right there in front of her, to put the poster inside.

Which lady? Could she remember?

"Mrs. Enright, I believe it was. Yes, it was Mrs. Enright." Olivia's face relaxed and fell into its habitual smile, so relieved was she to have passed this examination.

With Olivia back in the gift shop, they looked at each other.

"Now what?" Tina said.

Gin said, "You could call Tito."

Lieutenant Gonzales, of the Santa Fe police, was an old schoolmate who had once lusted after Tina. But when Tina phoned the station, Lieutenant Gonzales was said to be out on a case.

Tito Gonzales got the message on his radio at the drive-in window at Burger King and called them back. "You gotta be kidding," he scoffed when Tina told him something seemed to be wrong with one of the paintings up at the Waldheimer. He couldn't come to the museum right now. He was on another assignment.

They went back to the East Room, closed the door against museum visitors beginning to arrive, and looked at the painting again. "Do you have a good photograph of the Rembrandt?" Tina asked.

"Sure." The museum sold prints of these particular paintings and a few others. Everyone wanted a Georgia O'Keeffe. They'd had a lithographer make color transparencies.

"We might as well have a look."

Gin went back to the director's office and found the transparency in the files. As an afterthought she got the ultraviolet light from her desk drawer. She took them back to Tina, who held the color transparency up to the painting on the wall, backing off to dip her knees and eye it. She handed the transparency to Gin.

"Could be lens distortion," Gin said after a moment.

But Tina shook her head. "If it were lens distortion, it would be the same in all directions from the center. Here, look. See this line?" Tina pointed to the lower right-hand corner. "It's longer in the painting than in the photograph, and that dark area . . ." Again she pointed. "Isn't the shape slightly elongated?" She sighed, lowering the film. "But you can really only compare two transparencies, not a transparency and a painting."

"Are you sure?"

"Of course I'm sure. I mean, if this is a transparency of the Rembrandt and we had another one of this . . ." Tina's voice trailed off with the enormity of what she was saying.

"I brought the black light," Gin said, handing it over.

Tina shrugged. "It'll show differences in media and texture, but I doubt there'll be any. Turn the lights out."

When the gallery was dark, Tina turned on the ultraviolet lamp. Gin gasped and laughed. Tina's costume-department blouse was suddenly fluorescent.

"It's picking up the starch," Tina said. "If you had false teeth, it would pick them up too."

They looked at the painting. The surface glowed. "Look at that," Tina said. "It's picking up the surface varnish. The whole painting is varnished."

"Is that significant?"

"Retouching with varnish would have been done over the centuries, each layer showing up in a different fluorescent shade. But this looks like only a single layer, and very uniform. That's peculiar. Even if it *were* the original varnish, it was unusual at that time for a whole painting to be varnished. At least, the practice was just then coming in. And varnish coatings oxidize and degrade with time. This doesn't strike me as centuries old."

They went back to Gin's office and tried the lieutenant again. He was still out, but the office reached him on his car radio as he pulled to the curb in Park Plaza, where Mrs. Gutierrez's poodle had barked all night and left her nervous about intruders. A lieutenant of the Santa Fe police wouldn't ordinarily have gone on an errand principally of reassurance. Such calls were left for patrolmen when they had the time. But Mrs. Gutierrez was his mother's bridge partner, and his mother had prevailed upon him, and it was on his way to Arroyo Hondo where he was going to interview a couple whose house had been broken into the night before. The thief had only been interested in food. He had gorged on everything in the icebox, reducing a baked turkey to a pile of bones and leaving a mess on the kitchen table. Apparently he'd come on foot and left on foot.

There'd been an escape at the state penitentiary several weeks before, and one of the escapees was still at large (pre-

sumed to be in Mexico), and as Arroyo Hondo lay along the
most popular escape route, it was just possible that he'd escaped detection by the search helicopters and hidden out in
an arroyo all this time and might be the turkey thief. After
one prison break, three men thought to be in California had
hidden out for weeks in a storage locker off Siler Road. A
relative of one of them had outfitted it with water and food
and sleeping bags. So it was possible. Probably not, but the
lieutenant was meeting the dusting crew at the house in hopes
of finding greasy fingerprints.

His radio came on just as he parked outside Mrs. Gutierrez's house, and his office gave him a number to call. He
didn't recognize it or he would have put it off. But he dialed
Mrs. Gutierrez's telephone and, when Tina answered, said
impatiently, "Look, Celestina, I'll be busy most of the afternoon but I'll get there as soon as I can. When's the place
close?"

"It's open all day today and there's an opening tonight."

"I better not promise anything," he said. "How 'bout I
look in at the opening?"

The lieutenant liked openings. They were a frequent phe-
nomenon in Santa Fe. He liked the drinks and nuts and dips
and tiny little sandwiches. He could get away from home
awhile, from the wife and babies. Not that he wasn't crazy
about the wife and babies.

Gin's afternoon was chaotic. She consulted the caterers,
located the folding screen and got it to the gallery, calmed
Benito who, once he'd hung his paintings, was ready to switch
everything around, convinced Olivia that the gift shop need
not be open for the guests, cajoled Mrs. Philipson into ordering flowers after she'd said she'd never mention the word
flowers in the museum again.

Finally, on her way home to eat and change, she detoured
by the health food shop and purchased an herbal tincture
recommended for the relief of acute anxiety.

5

"Grab the door, will you!"

It was Croy, with a Dutch oven in one hand and a pot of steaming rice in the other. They were eating at Tina's. It was Croy's night to cook, but he said his place was too disgusting and they believed him. Tina's was not much better.

"What are we having?" Tina asked, but they all knew. On Croy's night they had what he called hamburger mess, a dish consisting of hamburger meat browned in the Dutch oven, and everything loose in his refrigerator thrown in—tomatoes, potatoes, peppers, limp celery, onions. Over rice it was tasty, though it was their habit to groan. On Tina's night they had tamale pie, and on Reuben and Dolly's spaghetti, and on Gin's New Mexico chili, which, unlike Texas chili, was made without beans.

Croy set his burden on the stove and wrung his hand. "Come on, love. You've got to eat," he said to Gin, and tossed her own wisdom back at her. "It's not time yet to worry."

But Gin thought it was.

Tina said, "This is what happens when you turn upwardly mobile. Jobs, money, stress . . ."

"You're all coming to the reception, aren't you? I need support."

"We'll be there with bells on, though otherwise I may be indecent," Croy said. "I don't have another thing to wear."

Gin was in no mood for their bantering. She'd never felt so alone in her life. She watched them pile up their plates. Tonight their appetites repelled.

"Wear your Mexican wedding shirt," Tina said.

"The white or the peach?"

39

Croy suffered from an unrelenting writer's block. He had showed her several stories so sensitive and delicate she wasn't sure what was going on. The central feature in his living space was the ancient typewriter that had belonged to some little-known dead writer he admired. He had acquired it through an aunt, who had been the dead man's mistress, which put the author almost in the family. But as far as Gin could see, the typewriter, a constant reminder sitting there in the middle of his apartment, only focused his frustration.

She turned her back on them. Outside the window, nothing had changed—the lace vine bloomed heavy on the coyote fence and the cosmos in their furry ruffs still lifted bright faces to the sun, heedless of the season change ahead.

They were like a pod themselves, she thought. They each had an apartment in the crumbling adobe compound, one of the few on the East Side that hadn't been renovated and the rents raised out of sight. Magda, their landlady, couldn't afford to. And if she could, her tenants couldn't have afforded to stay.

Magda had been left the compound by her last—and final, she swore—husband, Larry Sanchez. It had been in his family longer than anyone could remember. Every time a child of the family grew up and married they'd added another share-a-wall starter house till they were strung out almost to the Acequia. Those original pairs had long since flown the coop to Albuquerque or L.A., where now they were grandparents.

The little adobe row houses had charm. They shared a portal along the front, covered with lace vine like an arbor. Each house was little more than a room with a kitchen and bath attached, but they were old Santa Fe—flat roofs with parapets, jutting *canales*, exposed *vigas*. Tina's place had, across a half wall from the kitchen, a small dining area she'd converted to a sleeping niche, leaving the rest of the space for living and painting. Croy's was the most decorated—an army cot painted black with dyed red canvas, and two matching butterfly chairs, one blue, one yellow.

Reuben's had a large walk-in closet with a small, high window. He'd carpeted the floor with foam rubber and turned it into a boudoir. He lived there with his au courant, who worked as a waitress at a downtown restaurant where she made more money in tips than any of them made in salaries. ("This one," Croy had confided when Reuben brought her home, "is actually *named* Dolly.") Reuben and Dolly were at the door.

"I never said any such thing," Dolly was muttering. "I never did and I know it. You know it, too."

"You did. You said it more than once, and I don't for a minute believe—"

"Hello everybody," said Dolly.

"Grab plates," Croy said.

But Reuben—black curly hair and black curly beard linked by black curly sideburns—glared in the screen door at them with eyes so pale they burned into you like dry ice, then turned on his heels and headed home.

"What's the matter with him?" Croy asked.

"What's always the matter with him," Dolly muttered, all pink and tan from the summer, soft as cashmere, dishing up her plate. "If anybody knows, I wish they'd tell me."

Gin, at the window, felt Tina and Croy look at her. If Dolly didn't know what was wrong with Reuben tonight, she was the only one. He always pouted when there was an opening. The museum had never given *him* a show.

"Who is it this time?" he had asked her earlier in the week. "Oh, naturally. Benny Montoya. Let us by all means be ethnic!" Reuben might have hailed from another star with those strange, slanting eyes that could be as vacant as mirrors.

"Oh, come on Reuben." She had tried to reason with him. "Benito Montoya's a damn fine painter."

"His colors are garish and his ideas puerile. Everything he does is East Coast derivative." Reuben's place was crammed these days with plaster sculptures of people missing their parts— holes in their stomachs, holes in their heads . . .

"Reuben's a pain in the ass sometimes, Dolly," Croy said, letting himself down beside her on a pillow on the floor.

Dolly nodded, sighing. Pretty Dolly, with her pink cheeks and tangled hair, ate with her plate balanced on her knees. The knees, disclosed by her shorts, were as pretty as the rest of her. Croy reached over and patted one of them. Croy was protective toward Reuben's women. "But he can be so sweet," she added shyly.

Puke. Gin turned back to the purple cosmos. Women regarded Croy as one of the girls, but they fell in love with Reuben. Hard to see why. He barely noticed they were there. No matter what the scene, the look in his eyes was a little removed. His moods were unpredictable. At times he was maniacally gay, so full of energy you couldn't keep up with him. At others he fell into glum despair. He worked furiously at his sculpture, fell in love with every piece, then suddenly rejected everything he'd ever done and broke up his figures and tossed them out back, where they lay in a gruesome heap.

Gin had explained to him more than once that she didn't have the whole say as to who would get a show at the Waldheimer, which was the truth but not the whole truth. She and the director met with a panel of consultants who, she was surprised to learn, listened to her recommendations. One day she would gird her loins and recommend Reuben. When she'd been there longer. When she felt together enough to deal with him. When he got off the sculpture kick and back to his painting. Reuben was a marvelous painter continually dissatisfied with his work. He was also a marvelous potter and could have made a living at it if only he potted pots instead of the strange extraterrestrials he called his "creatures."

Tina's phone rang. Tina, who viewed the telephone as an instrument of torture, groaned with her mouth full and looked at Gin, who had tried all afternoon to reach Davies in Dallas and left Tina's number as well as her own at his hotel. Setting her plate down, Tina crossed the room to answer it.

"Celestina?" The voice on the other end of the line had a Latin accent. "Iss that you?"

"Pablo?" she said. One hand went to her hip. "Come on, Pablo. How many times do we have to go through this?" She looked at Gin and rolled her eyes heavenward.

"Now don't hang up, Tina, please. I am at the air terminal in El Paso in the state of Texas, and I 'ave 'ad a very bad time reaching you. I 'ave tried for days."

To escape all the eyes upon her, Tina swung around and

faced the wall. She lowered her voice. "I have told you and told you . . . Look, it's over, done, *kaputt, se acabó, fini.*"

"Now, Tina, don't hang up. Everything has changed. Nothing at all remains the same. It is, as you say, one whole new picture. My wife has left me."

"Good for her. It's about time. I'm not surprised."

"Please, don't be harsh. You wound me so," muttered the soft voice in her ear. "Look here, only let me talk to you."

Tina expelled a long breath that puckered her lips. "What are you doing in El Paso?"

"I am on my way to the museum conference in Dallas."

"I thought it was just regional museums in the U. S. of A."

"That is true, my dear, but, you see, they 'ave honored me with an invitation to speak a few words."

It was his nicest trait, this touch of humility she knew to be genuine.

"Tina, I am standing at the desk of Southwest Airlines. I 'ave not to be in Dallas until two days. I 'ave come on along early, on the, how you say—off-chance—you will let me see you. Save my poor wasted life, Celestina. What must I do—go on to Dallas, Texas, or take the next flight that will put me down in Albuquerque in less than one hour's time?"

"Absolutely not, Pablo. Don't even think of it." She closed her eyes for an imagined privacy, feeling three other pairs upon her. "Look, I can't talk. I have to go. Please, Pablo, don't keep this up." She put down the phone, and, without looking at anybody, crossed the room and picked up her plate. "Men!"

Croy chuckled. "You sang a different tune last summer." Last summer Tina had taught art in San Miguel de Allende and there met Pablo Esperanza-Ramos and fallen in love.

The phone rang again. Croy and Dolly busied themselves with their food. Gin put a little hamburger mess on a saucer and picked at it standing up. The phone rang seven times before it stopped, and a minute later started up again.

When it stopped Gin looked at her watch. It was almost seven. The reception started at eight. The trustees would be there, and Lloyd Noldes, president of Yucca Federal and chairman of the Waldheimer's board of trustees. Would she tell Lloyd Noldes her suspicions, show him the questionable painting? Croy asked, perhaps to change the subject uppermost in their minds—the unfortunate affair in Mexico last summer that had left Tina sad and angry and bereaved.

To fill the silence when the phone stopped ringing, Gin went along. ''Well, Noldes knows all there is to know about financial matters . . . insurance . . .'' The paintings, of course, were not insured against theft. The cost would have been prohibitive. But they *were* insured against damage. She shuddered to think . . . Once a dolt of a thief had cut a Vermeer out of its frame, rolled it up, and *sat* on it in a taxi.

''But,'' Croy said, ''he dudn' know Jack Shit about painting.''

They had to explain to Dolly about the Rembrandt.

''Well, I hope somebody took the old thing. Maybe one day they'll pay attention to young artists coming along.'' All of Reuben's women took on his grievances. Dolly looked very sweet when she pouted. It turned Gin's stomach but it didn't seem to bother Croy's. He patted her knee again and she smiled at him with large, sad eyes.

Croy said to Gin, still picking at her food, ''What would you say to him? You think he'll take some missing pencil mark seriously? What you need,'' he said, ''is an expert.''

Gin looked at Tina and let her dish settle on the counter with a clatter, and Tina jumped up, rushed across the room, picked up the phone, and tapped the Off bar repeatedly.

''Operator, oh, please, hurry, get me the number of—of the Southwest Airlines desk at the El Paso airport! Oh, please it's urgent.''

''One moment, plee-uz,'' the operator said. ''Was that the . . . ?''

''Southwest Airlines desk!'' And she implored of the ceiling, ''Oh, don't let it be too late!''

Gin said, ''God, what luck! What a coincidence!''

''According to Jung, there's no such thing as coincidence,'' said Dolly.

''Oh, *why* did I hang up on him? *Why* didn't I think?!''

''Calmly, Tina, calmly,'' said Croy, now at her elbow, plate in hand, still eating.

''Hello. Hello, operator?''

"One moment, plee-uz. I have the number. Do you want me to dial it?"

"Oh, yes, please!" And now it was ringing.

"Flying Southwest Airlines is like having your own company plane," a sprightly recorded voice announced while Tina silently mouthed the words familiar from TV commercials. "At the moment, all lines are busy. The first available—"

Then a live human voice asked her to hold. Tina danced in a circle of impatience as the Muzak came on.

"Southwest Airlines. Sorry to keep you waiting."

"Just a moment," the operator interrupted, and announced officiously to Tina, "I have Southwest Airlines on the line for you."

"Okay, *okay*!"

The miffed operator hung up.

"Southwest Airlines?" Tina said into the phone. "I spoke to a man at your counter not ten minutes ago? Pablo Esperanza-Ramos? He's . . . rather tall and looks a little like Cary Grant." Croy groaned and she gave him a look. "It's *desperately* urgent that I speak with him," she added in a small, helpless, appealing voice.

"One moment, please."

"What're they saying?" Gin asked. Tina flapped a hand at her to shut up.

"I am sorry, m'am, but there is no gentleman by that name at our counter."

"Oh, *please*, help me."

"One moment, please."

"Why was I so *stupid*! Why didn't I *think*?"

The voice at the other end of the line sounded muffled, as if the phone were inadequately covered by a hand as the speaker consulted someone else. Tina thought she heard, "But we're not allowed to give out that information."

"Right," a baritone voice said in the distance. "But this guy just bought a ticket for Albuquerque and he's out at the gate right now, ready to board. We could page him and—"

"Never mind!" Tina said triumphantly. "It's all right! Don't bother! Thank you, thank you! Thank you very much." She hung up and whirled around. "He ignored everything I said. He's on his way to Albuquerque. An hour on the plane. Another hour to Santa Fe on the shuttle, and then—''

"How can we get him straight to the museum?" Gin asked.

"Croy'll wait for him at the Inn at Loretto"—which was where the shuttle disgorged its passengers—"and bring him right up."

"Thanks a lot," Croy said.

Gin clasped her hands and held them to her mouth. Now there'd be two experts at the opening—Lieutenant Gonzales of the Santa Fe police, and Pablo Esperanza-Ramos, director of the Museo Nacional in Mexico City.

6

"What's that noise?" Mrs. Trowber, entering, asked the room at large. She got a Scotch and water from the bar and helped herself to a canapé from the tray passed by a waiter in a red wedding shirt and a black bow tie. The noise was the mariachi band at the opposite end of the gallery.

Benito Montoya's paintings—big, bold, and bright— occupied the walls with the kind of presence peculiar, Gin thought, to The Real Thing, not as if they had only been hung that morning, more as if the gallery had been built to house them.

Benito himself sulked in a corner, glass in one hand, the other a fist bulging his pocket, eyeing the guests with equal contempt whether they gazed raptly at his pictures or turned their backs on them to chat with one another.

Gin looked around for someone she might introduce to him. Across the room a woman manufactured a mirthless laugh. It raveled her nerves. These affairs left her wasted. And without a director—any director—in the offing, this one was particularly harrowing.

The Widow Trowber came toward her.

"Mrs. Trowber!" God, it sounded like Mrs. Trowber was a close relative she had mistakenly assumed demised.

"Call me Toby, child. Everybody does." Mrs. Trowber's dress was splashed with big showy flowers. Her open-toed sandals were too slight to confine her chubby feet. "That's a wonderful conch belt."

"Yes, lovely," Alice Maynard murmured.

Gin craned down at the belt on her hips. "Oh, thank you."

Victor Weldon, hands clasped together in front of him as if he didn't know what to do with them, said, "A conch is a shell. The belt is a *concha*. It looks like old Navajo pawn," he said to Gin.

"Wherever did you get it?" Alice Maynard asked.

"In Gallup," Gin said, avoiding looking at Juan eyeing her from the bar, all dressed up in white shirt and red cummerbund and black leather boots with elevator heels. After their trip to the basement that afternoon, where they'd gone to look for the folding screen, she couldn't bear the sight of Juan.

Mrs. Philipson, hair freshly done, in full-length lavender lace over purple silk, smiled charmingly and chatted with the chairman of the board while keeping a sharp eye on the catering service.

The chairman of the board was a well-set-up fifty—hair the color of taffy brushed back from his temples, cleft chin, blue eyes that went with his nature, cold and reserved. Gin dreaded speaking to him about her suspicions, and she might have to before the night was over. She fingered the herbal tincture in her skirt pocket and willed the thought out of her head with a meditative mind control technique she had learned in a weekend workshop. Santa Fe offered many kinds of weekend workshops—psychodrama, rebirthing, inscape, escape, primal screaming.

The mariachi band struck up "La Paloma."

"I keep wanting a concha belt," Mrs. Trowber said above the mounting din, "but I'd look like a horse in a studded saddle." Her laughter rolled down the room.

Alice Maynard thought, Noisy old bag. The language of Alice's mind was not as prim as the language of Alice's lips.

Where had Eric got off to? She felt self-conscious at cocktail parties. They were too like the birthday parties of her youth, when she'd stood shy and ignored in any handy alcove, watching the rowdies at play. Count on Eric to desert her just when she needed him.

She glanced hopefully at Will Nevil, the commander. Not a member of their pod, they'd known him only a month. He'd come looking for poor Ellen Weldon. He'd met her some-where—on a cruise or something, he'd said—and hadn't known of her death. He'd been quite devastated. And he'd spent all his time with them on Maui while his "good old ship," the frigate *York*, was in drydock in Pearl Harbor.

It was just such as that, his "good old *York*," that made her envy men. Men had adventures. Women were poor things by comparison. Not all of them, of course. Look at Sheila, traipsing all over the globe researching her terrifying books. But it made Sheila a weirdo, sort of. Now if a man did that it would be . . . Why *was* it so different? Sometimes it made her mad, the clamps put on women. Everyone did it. She did it herself. It wasn't fair.

Still, she didn't like Sheila. Might as well admit it. Sheila made her feel weak, silly. Well, that's what men wanted in a woman, wasn't it? Oh, it made her dizzy to think of it. She'd think instead of—of Victor Weldon there, standing off to him-self. Victor was the strong, silent type, not a chatterer like Eric. She liked that in a man.

As if her thought had reached out and lassoed him, Victor moved up beside her, smiled his thin smile, and asked, "Where are the others?" For the milling guests were mostly board members, not members of the pod. Mrs. Trowber hardly counted, having joined the tour, supposed to be ex-clusively their own, in San Francisco. Some slip-up of the tour company never supposed to happen.

But here they came, breathing a little hard, for they had elected to walk up the hill after their dinner at a gourmet place just off the plaza.

Victor Weldon watched Raoul Query enter, navy blue blazer folded over his arm, Hanna Enright beside him. Hanna had spent the afternoon nursing a migraine in her room at the Sheraton. A bright woman, not very attractive with that little hump on her back pulling one shoulder lower than the other. And such a dowdy dresser. He thought of Ellen and his heart dropped in his chest like a stone.

Alice Maynard laid a hand on his arm and gave it a pat. "Nobody gets away with anything, Victor. What goes around comes around." He supposed she was talking about karma. The woman was always talking about karma. He didn't know what to say, so he smiled.

Alice was relieved by that smile, like sun through mist. She'd been afraid she'd invaded his privacy. The crime writer joined them, holding a glass of what Alice knew to be nothing stronger than Perrier. When Sheila turned her eyes upon you magnified by those thick lenses, you felt like you'd come under a microscope.

"Sheila, dear," Alice purred.

Sheila smiled, and her face was transformed. She was after all a sweet thing. Alice always wondered where those horrendous books came from. "Exhaustive research," Sheila said. They read like firsthand accounts of the most shocking crimes of the day, the ones that held headlines for weeks on end.

"But why do such . . . events . . . so fascinate you?" Alice had once delicately inquired.

"They don't so much fascinate *me*," Sheila had replied, "as they fascinate the general reader, who shells out the cash and keeps me in the style to which we've become accustomed." She meant the pod, all of them living amid such beauty in such exotic places. Certainly it couldn't be done on a budget. Alice wished right now she was back on Maui in her little house of two octagonal rooms, one offset on top of the other like a layer cake that had slipped in the oven, making space for the sweet little balcony from which she could see the blue Pacific.

"The public's love of crime is second only to its love of war," Sheila maintained. "If you don't believe me, just watch a night of television. Look at the ratings. The star of the century is Adolf Hitler. Everyone loves a villain. Read *Paradise Lost*. Satan's fascinating but God's a crashing bore."

The commander was washed up next to Gin by the crowd. His drink, bumped by somebody's arm, splashed on her skirt.

"Oh, I say," he said.

She wore her smile like a visor. This was the sort of affair she ought to enjoy. That she didn't made her feel guilty and inadequate. "It's all right," she said. "It's nothing." She brushed at her skirt with her napkin.

He looked vaguely around the room with his face elevated and his mouth a little open. His hair and beard were the color of a baby duck. "Jolly good show." One of his side teeth was framed neatly in silver.

"I say," he said, "do you care for this type of music?" There was something naive or innocent about him, more suited to the featureless sea than the clutter of land and people.

"It's probably an acquired taste," she said.

"I suppose if you catch the bit of humor in it," he said. "Otherwise it would be bloody awful."

She'd never thought of humor in mariachi, but now that he mentioned it . . .

Olivia put in a brief appearance with her husband Richard. They smiled at everybody, sipped mineral water, nibbled at sandwiches, and soon edged toward the exit, holding hands.

Tina entered with Tito Gonzales in tow. In red and white and black, with a touch of green thrown in, she looked, Gin thought, like an exotic tropical bird.

Lieutenant Gonzales felt keenly out of place. Though dressed for the occasion in gray pinstripes, he was more at home in sweats. All this to-do about Art left him cold. The hell they think life was about anyway, with people homeless and starving. In his line of work, he sometimes felt more at one with the thieves he chased than with the rich up off Hyde Park and Bishop's Lodge Road who'd had their TVs and stereos ripped off. The lieutenant had grown up in a barrio, and he still, in his deepest heart, felt like a misfit anywhere else, the way Benny Montoya looked like *he* felt, standing off in the corner like he needed to scratch his crotch.

Benito'd come up in the world since their old days on the basketball court. More power to him. It was a rip-off, Tito could see that just by looking at what hung on the walls.

Made you want to laugh. Benny was shrewd. They'd never have looked at an honest picture of a mountain or a canyon or a man on a horse, but they'd pay through the nose for these splatters about like his own three-year-old daughter's, the bigger the better. What kind of houses did these people live in, to have room for pictures that size? Old Benito knew what he was doing. He painted what sold.

The lieutenant went over to speak to the artist, and Gin was startled by what she overheard of the conversation. Fences? They were talking about *fences*? Weren't fences people who bought stolen goods?

Tito Gonzales saw her listening. "We used to play sports together. Basketball, and we were on the fencing team. This *chulo* won statewide fencing tournaments," he said.

Tina came over with a glass of white wine in her hand. "So, where do we start?" she asked.

The lieutenant shrugged. They thought one of their pictures had been stolen and another one put in its place. How would you know the difference? "I'll start with a drink," he said, turning to the bar.

The reception was growing noisy. Guests kept arriving in Santa Fe style—silver and turquoise, designer jeans, Paris fashions. The parking lot filled with Mercedes and Range Rovers, BMWs and four-by-fours, king cab pickups and muddy jeeps. There was Onisimo Villarael, president of Corpex Corp. Guadalupe Valdez, widow of a circuit judge. Mrs. Dickie Mambes, late of New York City, in Navajo velvet weighted with silver. Andrew Beckerridge in running velour. Jean Medows in a heavy silver squash blossom over silk, and fawn-colored riding pants. Secretary of the board, Jean Medows dressed to suit herself, with a nod to the occasion. She had thick, short sandy hair and freckles, eyes that met you head-on. She and her much older husband raised Arabian horses out at their ranch in Galisteo.

Gin turned to Toby Trowber, for Juan was eyeing her from the bar. "I understand you're not a—not a member of the pod." She had to raise her voice. The mariachis were moving closer.

"Oh, heavens no. And don't think I don't feel it. They're

very cliquish." Mrs. Trowber swilled her Scotch, set the glass on the white bar cloth, took a cigarette from a leather pouch in her purse and jammed it into a stubby holder, grumbling, "You hardly taste them anymore . . . filters in the fags, filters in the holders. I ask myself what's the point?" She laughed. "Well, we all have to die of something."

Gin thumbed the herbal tincture in her pocket. She said, to be saying something, "I understand Mr. Query and Mr. Weldon have been married to the same woman. Do they get along? I mean, the two husbands?" How odd. Not only did they have the same taste in women, they again wore the identical blazers.

"The wife is dead," Toby Trowber said. "I imagine that improves their relationship."

"What a pity."

Mrs. Trowber looked at her.

"I mean that she's dead."

"Yes, well . . . I gather she was a beauty and they both in their time adored her. I see how it could be a bother to a woman, being beautiful. It's a trouble I never had." And she bowled her laugh to the other end of the room. "Well, I never missed it. Bobby and I—Bobby was my husband—we ate what we liked and wore what we liked and never tried to be fashionable. It wouldn't have worked anyway. Bobby was a roly-poly cuddly thing, furry as a teddy. He had to shave himself a neckline." And her laughter rolled along the bar where guests clustered three deep, noisily greeting one another, reaching for drinks, keeping the bartender hopping.

The mariachis veered toward the entry and sawed into serious action. Gin watched Raoul Query engage Benito Montoya in conversation. Benito was smiling. The two of them turned and stood together in front of a painting, Raoul Query talking and Benito nodding, then Benito talking and Raoul Query nodding. She'd never seen Benito so pleasantly animated.

Mrs. Dickie Mambes eyed the two painters across the room. A small, dark woman with seductive eyes, she evidently liked what she saw in Raoul Query. And no wonder. Dickie Mambes was a dried-up, stringy thing, but very rich.

Toby Trowber puffed on her cigarette holder. "I gather the

first couple—the woman's name was Ellen—Ellen and Raoul Query fell in love while still quite young. They never had children. Nor did poor Bobby and I," she added sadly, and then rolled out her laugh, "but it wasn't from lack of trying."

Gin smiled.

"Then somewhere along the way," Toby went on, "they fell on the outs, or Raoul left the group for a while. He's a painter, you know, and he'd been invited to teach at a school in New York. While he was gone, Weldon entered the scene. An importer, I gather, with his office in Honolulu."

"I thought they all lived together on one of the outer islands."

"That's right, they do, on Maui. Once Weldon and Ellen Query got together and later married, he commuted between the islands in his company helicopter—weekends, you know—and Ellen spent time with him on Oahu. Even after they married he kept his place there."

So, Gin thought, she had wrongly convicted Raoul Query of philandering and all the time it had been his wife. But something must have driven her to it.

"If you're wondering how I know all this," Toby Trowber said, "the crime writer and I have shared rooms on this jaunt. I gather Ellen Query was sort of, oh, fascinating, though I've never quite understood what that means outside of the movies. People are people, don't you think?"

Gin laid a hand on Mrs. Trowber's arm. "Excuse me, Toby." Board members were mingling with the pod. It must be almost eight-thirty. There'd be a mob when the public came in at nine. Smiling nervously she joined Tina and the lieutenant at the bar.

"Thanks for coming, Tito."

"Yeah, well . . ." He snatched a handful of sandwiches off a passing tray. Their sandwiches were pretty good, even if they did cut them up in little bitty bite-size pieces.

"You want a look at the painting?" Tina asked.

The lieutenant sighed and put down his glass. Might as well get that over with. Then he could have another drink.

But a smiling Lloyd Noldes blocked their path. Gin always suspected Noldes's friendliness masked distrust. Quillan

Davies had passed over Lloyd Noldes's wife's nephew to make Gin the assistant director. "Why didn't you hire the nephew?" she'd one day ventured to ask. It seemed to her the nephew was better qualified.

"He minced," Davies said, and minced in a circle by way of illustration, making her laugh.

"Miss Prettifield!" Lloyd Noldes said in greeting. He was so perfectly put together—dark suit, crimson tie, shirt cuffs showing a quarter inch below the sleeve—it made her feel like her slip was showing.

"Coo caroo caroo," the mariachis sang to their own accompaniment.

"Quillan got off?"

She nodded. The chairman often addressed her rhetorically. He already knew Tina. Gin introduced the lieutenant only as Tito Gonzales, and Noldes studied him as if trying to place him. Then several board members engaged the chairman in conversation and they were free to go to the East Room.

7

The Waldheimer was a small museum. But well endowed, supported by its board, blessed with the directorship of George Cameron, who dressed like a cowboy but collected like a prince, some called the Waldheimer the best in the West. Not true, Gin granted. It hadn't the breadth of the San Francisco museums, or the scope of the new Getty. But judged piece by piece, it could hold its own.

At the touch of a switch, darkness sprang into light. The gallery looked as it always looked. Across the room the painting looked much as it always had. She'd dragged the lieutenant all the way up the hill for nothing. She crossed the gallery and bent over the picture, looking for the pencil mark. Surely it was there. Maybe it had struck higher.

But she'd known she would have to sharpen the eraser to get at it, so close to the frame.

Maybe there had been a sonic boom and the painting had slipped down in its frame, hiding the squiggle. She reached out and lifted the frame on its wires. The painting was tight inside the gilt.

"Okay, tell me again," said the lieutenant, surprised to find he liked the landscape. It looked a little like the land out where his grandmother lived. "Who painted it?" he asked.

Full of doubt, Gin hesitated, but Tina said firmly, "Rembrandt," and when the lieutenant looked disbelieving added, "He was a Dutchman."

"*I* know who he was," Tito said. "When'd he come to New Mexico?"

"He didn't."

"Huh," the lieutenant grunted. "It looks like Chimayo, maybe a little like Nambe."

"Doesn't it," said Tina.

"So, what's the problem?"

Gin told him about the disappearing pencil mark.

"You coulda been mistaken," the lieutenant said. "You thought you saw a mark but it was really a hair or something."

"It was a pencil mark," she said. "Heavier at the end where the point struck. With a zig in it."

"A zig, huh?" The lieutenant chuckled. "Sure it wasn't a zag?"

Gin smiled grimly.

"That the right frame?" the lieutenant asked.

"Yes."

"You sure?"

"I'm positive. As you see, it's very old."

"*Looks* like the same picture, though?" said the lieutenant.

"Looks like," said Gin, then added in a voice both thin and faint, "but the . . . *feeling's* not the same."

"Feeling, huh," said the lieutenant. "So we got what looks like the same picture, we got the frame, but we haven't got the *feeling*?'' He laughed. ''So maybe somebody stole the feeling.''

Tina gave him a look, and the lieutenant drew himself up and cleared his throat. ''Lemme get this straight. This pencil mark and this . . . *feeling*, they were both here when you closed the place last night, and they were both gone when you come in this morning.''

Gin explained about the pod being there the night before with their leader, Ted Torrence, though the museum was closed, and how it had happened—the business with the pencil—and she had left soon after, she and Mrs. Philipson and Olivia, and Juan had stayed till about eight.

''Juan. He the guard?''

''Yes. Juan Romero.''

''He here now?''

''He's at the reception. He has to come to the openings because we leave the galleries open, and then he has to close up everything.''

''Ask Juan to come in here,'' said the lieutenant, and Tina went to fetch him.

''Everything on this floor?'' he asked.

''There's also a basement.''

''What's down there?''

''Well, there's a sort of shop, full of tools—for hanging shows and things—and a large table and easel where Tina does her work when she comes in, and—''

''What work? What's she do around here?''

''She's the conservator. She works for several of the galleries in town. A conservator cleans the paintings, does small repairs, things like that.''

''She do anything like that here last night?''

''Yes.''

One eyebrow shot up. ''Tina got a key to the place?''

''No. Only Juan and I. And the director.''

''So how'd she get in?''

''I gave her my key.''

''You do that often?''

''Not often. Sometimes.''

''Who else was here?''

"Well, Juan stayed late to help Benito unload his paintings for the show."

"Cheez," said the lieutenant, "place was crawling last night. This director—he here tonight?"

"He left town yesterday morning to attend a conference in Dallas."

"When'll he be back?"

"After the conference he's making a quick trip East, to New York and Washington."

"What for?"

"To look at pictures."

"Huh," said the lieutenant. It was a long way to go just to look at pictures when Santa Fe was full of them.

"So what else you got in the basement?"

"Nothing much." There was George Cameron's set of snow tires off in a corner, and a big side-by-side refrigerator Juan had asked to store there for his sister till she found another house. At Cameron's insistence, it had a chain around it with a padlock to keep some venturesome youngster from climbing inside and suffocating. And the bins full of paintings people gave to the museum, or died and left the museum, and the museum didn't know what to do with. One in a hundred was worth anything. If a painting had value, the family sold it. The museum just waited a decent time after the bequest, then put the paintings at auction. They mostly brought headaches, these gift paintings, and trouble with the tax people. There'd been fewer such bequests since the so-called tax reform.

Tina came back with Juan, who looked reproachfully at Gin with those mournful eyes.

"Routine security check," the lieutenant told the guard, who knew very well there was no such thing. He gave the lieutenant a look that said, Please.

The lieutenant cleared his throat. "You gotta lotta valuable stuff up here and the department runs these periodic checks. Your system ties in with the station."

"We haven't checked the alarm system since I've been here," Gin said.

Juan ran his tongue over his teeth and his upper lip bulged.

If he had to come to these openings, why couldn't they let him enjoy himself?

The lieutenant said, "This heavy equipment yard out the Old Vegas Highway? It had an alarm system went *beep* at the guardhouse when anything set it off. They hadn't checked theirs in years, either. So one day somebody decided to check it—and when it went *beep* the guards scratched their heads and asked ever'body what was that funny noise." The lieutenant laughed.

Juan took the story personally. "We got the latest 'quipment in Santa Fe," he said. "I turn it on every night and off first thing in the morning. If it ever went off you'd hear it all over town, up on the hill like this."

The lieutenant frowned. He disliked men who exaggerated. He regarded it as a female trait. "How long you worked here, Juan?"

Affronted, Juan looked away without answering, and Gin said, "Five years. Isn't that about right? Ever since the museum opened."

Juan nodded.

"Well, let's make the rounds," the lieutenant said. "Since you got a party on, we'll start in the basement. Lead the way, Romero."

Gin turned out the light and locked the East Room. The elevator, freight-size to handle the paintings, opened off the hall diagonally opposite the rest rooms labeled CABALLEROS and DAMAS. Gin hoped to get that changed while Cameron was away. Mrs. Philipson had confided that he thought it very Santa Fe. "For a man of impeccable taste in art," she'd said, "George Cameron can have lapses.

"His wife died several years ago," she added, with a look that implied his wife had held such enthusiasms in check.

The elevator descended and the door slid open. Gin reached around the corner and flipped the light switch. Even flooded with the dead white of fluorescence, the basement was full of dark corners. She had never liked the place. Now she liked it even less. That afternoon when she and Juan had come down for the folding screen, he had allowed the screen to slip aside, trapping her against Tina's worktable and barring her escape.

"I ass myself," he'd murmured, "how a beautifool woman can reseest love."

To escape him she swooped, ostensibly to pick up dirty paint rags and a scrap of paper from the floor. She was always picking up after Tina. She had picked up after Tina halfway across Europe. Otherwise they'd have left a trail of underwear, socks, postcards, passports . . .

She dropped the paint rags in the trash—acrylics—and realized that Tina, who worked in acrylics, was using the basement as a part-time studio again. Tina could lose her job if she wasn't careful.

The lieutenant examined the alarm system without setting it off. He tried all the windows—the museum was built on a slope and the basement was above ground at the back—and the big garage door that slid open automatically overhead so paintings could be loaded and unloaded near the oversize elevator that now took them back upstairs.

"Everything all right down there," Tito Gonzales said as the doors slid open to the laughter, voices, and mariachi band down the corridor. Already the crowd overflowed into the hall. Soon the public would flood in looking for free drinks. "You got the keys to the offices?"

Gin nodded and let them in. The lieutenant tried the locks on the windows and looked around while she eyed the empty pipe holder on the desk, half expecting the meerschaum to materialize. "Everything seem to be in place?" he asked. "Anything missing?"

When the lieutenant led them off to circle the other galleries, Raoul Query, sitting on top of the reception desk in the corridor to escape the crowd, watched them go. Something about the girl, some toughness combined with reticence, intrigued him and made him sad. She so carefully avoided his eyes, as if she held something against him.

But he had felt sad ever since visiting his gallery earlier in the day to deliver a few small paintings he had brought with him from Hawaii. His work was doing very well, they said. They could sell everything he could provide. It should have cheered him. They'd expected it to. He'd tried to look pleased.

Of course the pictures would sell. That's why he painted them—pictures as small in reach as they were in size, of carpenter tools on a bench, or fishing rods on a wall, or a gun case against wood paneling—paintings that sold to corporation presidents, men who played their hands close to the vest, giving nothing away. Nothing like these huge, bold canvases by this young Montoya, a sort of primitive, who took enormous chances and hated the opening, though he may have fought to get it, who wanted his pictures seen but loathed the people who looked and nodded and said how nice.

Why didn't the girl return? Where had they gone? If he hadn't thought she'd be here, he'd be lying on his bed at the Sheraton, the lights of Santa Fe spread out below him like fallen stars, in the dark, unhappy about the business of Ellen. He hoped it didn't show. How guilty should he feel, anyway? He ought to be able to forget it. He had all his limbs, and his health as far as he knew, and he wasn't old, and he had enough money, and a small talent that made him a living, and friends. Or they used to be friends. Now sometimes he thought they hated him.

Why?

Because of the business with Ellen.

Perhaps they had liked him only as part of that perfect couple.

No doubt they had been handsome, and young, and some thought gifted. They'd drawn people without knowing why. Life as a continual party had gotten tedious, but it was worse being alone together.

Ellen had a strange lack of talent for intimacy. She couldn't gossip, or talk very personally about herself, or him, or anybody else. Talk with Ellen had to be serious, about Subjects. She had liked to study—Russian literature, French history, Chinese art.

She had come to him ravenously at first, and then, once they'd made love, withdrawn for days and treated him like a stranger. Finally the days had stretched to weeks, months, years. He had shut down his own feelings, tried to do things her way, till one day he discovered he was impotent.

There followed almost a year when he found it difficult to

finish a sentence, or match up his clothes, or remember to shave or take a bath. The pod had whispered around him, wondered if he'd become a secret drinker, asking why, when he had everything. Then the surprising offer had come to teach—at a small college renowned for its program in the arts. He'd grabbed for the brass ring.

Driving him to the airport, she had said, "Promise me you'll come back. I know you won't, but say it anyway. Say you'll be back in six months or I can't stand it." And looking straight ahead at the rain-blurred windshield, where the wipers beat like a metronome, he had said it: "I'll be back in six months."

Once away from Ellen, he had an affair and found he'd recovered. When Ellen asked, he hadn't denied it. He'd thought she wouldn't mind. He'd thought she would be glad to be rid of the needs and entreaties he liked to forget.

But the marriage would have killed him if he'd stayed. That had been the choice—Ellen and death, or loneliness and life. And had he after all chosen life?

He sat there on top of the reception desk in the hall, pondering.

Though she was already married to another man, he'd flown home when he found out she was ill. Then, months later, she'd told him, "I'm so happy."

Happy? To be dying?

"There's no trace of it left. Tumor's all gone. I've quit all their poisons and chemicals."

"Your lovely hair . . ."

"Short but healthy." She laughed with delight. Those perfect teeth . . . "It's growing back. Thanks to my kahuna. The man's a saint and a healer. Rory, I'm getting well."

She'd certainly looked it. Cured by herbs and diet and visualizations? It had happened to other people.

He saw her again, there on the beach at twilight, a vision he would like to forget.

Sitting there in the corridor, taking time out from the noisy opening, heels dangling against the front of the reception desk, he idly watched a bearded youth come in the door. Jeans, ragged sweatshirt, eyes pale as glass.

Raoul Query glanced around for the guard as the fellow

marched past into the gallery and crossed in three strides to stand before a painting on the far wall. People moved away or stopped talking and turned uneasily, drinks in hand, while he rocked back on the run-down heels of his dirty Nikes and looked. He circled the room. Benito Montoya unfolded his arms and watched. The intruder moved past him, acknowledging the painter with a jerk of his head. He spent time at each painting, standing up close, moving back for lengthy scrutiny. Raoul Query watched the dark curly head move up and down, the short curly beard dip and rise.

When he'd finished with the pictures, the gate-crasher went to the bar, said something to the bartender, tossed down a drink, and turned away. The well-dressed company parted to let him through.

Passing Raoul Query there on the reception desk, he muttered, "Self-expression. They hope it'll produce a masterpiece but all it produces is gas." Then he belched.

Raoul Query smiled.

"Reuben!"

The assistant director ran down the corridor from the other end of the building. Raoul Query smiled at her, though apparently she didn't see.

"I'm glad you came," she said to the young man. He looked at her, made a right-angle turn, and, wordless, went out the door.

Gin watched him go, hardly hearing the lieutenant. "The place is secure," he said. "You hadn' got breaking and entry. The frame's the same, picture's the same. Nothing missing but a hair or a piece of lint."

Then, aware of the guests all looking at him standing in the door where the bearded young man had just disappeared, the lieutenant drew an expansive breath and gave the room a smile. "So I'mona relax, have some fun, join the party." He headed for the bar.

Gin felt stupid. The mariachis sawed away. Across the room, Lloyd Noldes laughed. At least she wouldn't have to speak to the chairman of the board tonight.

8

"Ah, Señor Query! I would not expect to see such a doubter as you in this city of Holy Faith."

"Pablo, you rascal!" Raoul Query pushed himself off the reception desk and put out his hand. "What business brings you here?" Across the hall the opening was getting noisier by the minute.

"No business, my friend. I have come to Santa Fe on a matter of the heart."

Raoul Query laughed, warmly grasping Pablo Esperanza's hand. "I don't doubt it. I thought you were in Mexico City."

"I am, I am. Still at the *Museo*. They rarely allow me to leave. They want me always in their sight. But for now I 'ave escaped."

"I'll bet you're on your way to Dallas."

"Yes, to give a little informal talk. Nothing very erudite, only a few comments—off the sleeve, as you say—on contemporary Latin art."

"Why am I a doubter, and which lady brings you to Santa Fe?" Raoul Query looked around the room and back at his friend. Seeing the direction of Pablo's gaze, his smile faded.

Pablo Esperanza said, "I call you a doubter because you 'ave always so doubted yourself, and—"

"I take it you're enamored of the assistant director."

"Assistant director is she! I'd no idea. She never said. I only know her as a painter."

"I didn't know she was a painter. Is she a good painter?"

Pablo Esperanza-Ramos's laugh was politic. He was very careful who he pronounced a good painter. "Perhaps. Someday. But she is herself a work of art. Just look."

Unhappily Raoul Query looked.

63

"I met her in San Miguel de Allende, at the art school there when she was teaching, and but for the regrettable fact that at the time I was still legally attached to my wife—"

"You're finally divorced?"

"I am, at last. And for that I give thanks to the Virgin." He blew a kiss to the vaulted ceiling. "A disastrous match, as I knew from the start. We were not—how do you say?—compatible."

Raoul Query smiled. "But you wanted her, and that was the only way you could get her."

"Ah, you are perceptive, my friend. But I was very young and hot-blooded. Thank heavens the match was barren. And now, for the first time in my life, I am in love."

Though fond of Pablo Esperanza, Raoul Query took that with a grain of salt. Saddened, he looked across the room at Gin. "And . . . the lady reciprocates?"

"In San Miguel I had reason to believe she might, until she discovered—"

"The existence of Señora Esperanza-Ramos?"

"Exactly. You 'ave said it."

"You hadn't told her?"

"My dear Raoul, I hardly thought of myself as a married man. We had been separated for years."

"I see."

"Of course I intended to tell her, but there was so little time for histories. Regrettably she found out from another source than myself. And poof! All over, gone, vanished, our little flirtation, our so piquant *tête à têtes*. And what a shame! Such chemistry. So much in common—laughter, art . . ."

"She's very beautiful."

"Yes. She is Indian. Santa Ynez Pueblo. *Norte Americano* Indian."

Raoul Query nodded. "I didn't know that. Very distinctive face."

"Yes, and figure, too. That so much charm should come in such a very small package, eh?"

Raoul Query was for a moment confused. Then his spirits lifted. The chatter from the opening seemed suddenly pleasant. For Gin Prettifield was every bit as tall as Pablo

Esperanza-Ramos. "Are you talking about the young woman there across the room?" he asked.

Pablo Esperanza looked in that direction. "*Sí*. Indeed I am. Is Mees Martinez not lovely?"

With a rush of enthusiasm, Raoul Query said, "Very. And I wish you luck, Pablo."

Croy Beuley hurried through the entry, having finally found a place to park the rig, short for rigor mortis, so named after his thirty-year-old Chevy station wagon once sat moribund for months, its tires deflated and its battery expired. It was the compound's chief mode of transportation. They all—Gin and Tina and Reuben, and even at times Magda—chipped in to pay for its upkeep and repairs.

"I had to park way down the hill," he panted. He smoothed a hand over his tousled hair. He had pulled off a disreputable sweatshirt in the rig so he could appear in his Mexican wedding shirt.

"Señor Beuley, Señor Query," Pablo introduced.

"No kiddin'!" Croy said, putting out his hand. "Raoul Query? I really like your stuff. Far out. Fantastic treatment of light."

"Thank you," Query said, studying the young man with the narrow, sensitive face.

"Ah, yes," said Pablo Esperanza. "Raoul is a very fine painter."

The very fine painter examined his friend in vain for signs of irony. "Thank you, Pablo."

"Not at all. I speak only the truth." But it was clear that Pablo Esperanza's attention was elsewhere. Tina Martinez walked toward them.

"Go," she said to Croy, patting him on the back toward the bar. "Eat, drink!" And with a smile for Raoul Query she took Pablo by the hand and led him across to Gin, standing alone watching them come.

She had expected Pablo Esperanza-Ramos, a giant in the art world, to be a tall man. Hadn't Tina said . . . ? But everybody was tall to Tina. He was about her own height, which, she reminded herself, was not negligible. He smiled as he came toward her—black Aztec eyes, lean face, good bones, a real smile.

Lloyd Noldes bore down on them. "Señor Esperanza-Ramos, welcome! Were we expecting you?" He frowned questioningly at Gin. Pablo Esperanza was, after all, the director of the Museo Nacional and also on the board of the Palacio de Bellas Artes as well as consultant at the modern museum in Chapultepec. If the assistant director had been expecting him, the chairman of the board might at least have been notified. "What brings you to Santa Fe?" the chairman asked. "Not our little show!"

Benito Montoya glared at the chairman's back.

The expert said, "I have come to see an old friend, and by happy chance my visit coincides with your opening, which I must 'ave a look at."

"Wonderful. But . . . here, let me . . ." And before Esperanza-Ramos had been introduced to Gin, Lloyd Noldes bore him away toward the trustees, whom his name would impress.

"Well, Tina, old girl, I'm off," said the lieutenant, flushed and pleased with himself. Alice Maynard, bereft of Eric, had made much of Tito Gonzales to keep him beside her, she felt so vulnerable alone. And the lieutenant had so enjoyed himself that he'd forgotten to feel guilty about the little wife at home with the babies.

Tina caught his arm. "No, Tito, wait. You can't go yet."

"But I must," he said. "I am already late."

"Look, there's an expert here who can tell us what we have to know."

"Aw, come on . . ." The lieutenant tried to free his arm. That last margarita had done him in. He was feeling sleepy.

Pablo Esperanza, pleading the pictures, broke free from the board members and circled the gallery in Tina's direction. Benito Montoya, depressed at the speed with which the expert took in the paintings, fell into a funk and turned to the bar.

"Come quickly," Tina said, taking the hand Pablo Esperanza was only too willing to give. "Don't go away!" she said to Tito.

But as she led the expert toward the East Room, the lieutenant said to himself, Oh, no. No more. Not tonight. Take an aspirin and call me in the morning. He laughed at his little joke and waved after them.

"Hi," Croy Beuley said to the artist. Stuffing his mouth with a cracker heaped with caviar, he turned to the picture nearest them while Benito watched glumly. Croy knew how to look at pictures, he had lots of artist friends. You squint, you cock your head, you move up close to get at the brush strokes, and back again for the sweep. Finally, lifting a glass of champagne from the tray of a passing waiter, he nodded. "Yes." Benito moved cautiously closer. Croy sipped champagne and said, "Fantastic treatment of light."

In the East Room, Gin flipped switches and, one after another, banks of lights came on.

"Madre mia," breathed Pablo Esperanza, "what a gem of a place!" He turned in a circle, dark eyes to the ceiling in appreciation of the glowing white of the plaster applied by the artisans of Truchas and Chimayo. He passed slowly before the Matisse, the Cézanne, the Picasso, the Juan Gris, the Braque. He paused before the Derain and looked and nodded. He stopped in front of the Marie Laurencin. Finally he turned to the old masters.

"I knew these were here," he said, "but this moment I realize I never quite believed it." He turned to Gin. "You must tell me how you acquired them. The whole world must have been bidding."

She was struck by the change in him. In place of the Latin playboy and smitten lover stood the art historian, authority stamped clearly upon his person. "No," she said, "they were given to us."

He sucked in a breath. "Ahhh!" He nodded. "Now I recall. But how lucky for Sahn-ta Fe. You must tell me how this came about."

"That's a long story," Gin said. She knew only the broadest outline herself.

"Jesús Cristo." He was frowning at the Rembrandt. "I 'ave seen it before. Boston, I think . . . You must 'ave given it on loan."

She nodded. Two years ago, before her time.

Gin told him, lightly, making a joke of it at her own expense, about the vanished pencil mark metamorphosed into a crack in the paint or a piece of lint. Listening, he bent to the painting. "So we're awfully glad you came," she finished.

He glanced at Tina. "I am glad, too, Ginnee," he said. "So," he turned back to the painting, "you 'ave fears about your Rembrandt? Well, many museums 'ave lost their Rembrandts."

He spoke so matter-of-factly. She clutched the herbal tincture in her pocket. How would it mix with Scotch? "We have only the one Rembrandt," she said. "If anything happened to it, it would be a disaster."

"But, Ginnee, losing a Rembrandt is always a disaster."

He made it sound like a common occurrence.

"But other museums wouldn't feel it so much," she said. "The Metropolitan in New York has so many."

"They have nineteen, I believe. No, that's the National Gallery in London. The Metropolitan has more."

He studied the painting up close, then moved farther back, then squinted at it inches from his face. "I am, of course, no technical expert, but I 'ave done work on Rembrandt. I'll wager, dear girl, you didn't know that," he said to Tina. "My doctoral dissertation"—he smiled—"alas, so long ago, was on his preparatory techniques. They were, as you know, elaborate. Admit it, Celestina, you thought of me as a Latin chauvinist, did you not, interested only in political muralists like Diego Rivera, eh?"

Tina murmured, "I know you're political."

"And while I am here, I understand you 'ave a whole roomful of his wife Frida's work. I must see that."

He casually took the painting from the wall and held it at angles to the light, moving it this way and that.

"I 'ave seen many Rembrandts in public collections," he said, frowning at the painting. "And a number in private ones."

"I'm glad you're here to put our minds at rest," Gin prompted.

He nodded and chuckled, not taking his dark eyes from the painting in his hands. "I know," he said. "When a rumor flies that a painting is spurious, whether true or false the museum suffers. Donors get very—what is your word?—*tight* with their pesos if they think the museum can have its eyes pulled over with the wool.''

Gin said, "I'm new to all this. But one thing I've learned: *Donor* is a sacred word."

"You are new to this? But wasn't it you, my dear, who suspected . . . ?''

"Yes. Yes, I did. I mean, it looks the same, but I had a hunch . . .'' That sounded lame. And then there's the missing pencil mark, she reminded herself.

"I see," he said. He held the painting at an angle almost flat to his eye and scanned the relief of the surface as he talked. She peered over his shoulder, trying to see what he was looking at.

"It's great luck to have an authentic Rembrandt at all," he said. "In his own time his contemporaries not only copied his style but used his signature as well. Oh, it was all very innocent, Ginnee, not at that time considered dishonest at all. It could mean *by a student of Rembrandt*, or *in the style of Rembrandt*, or *from the studio of Rembrandt*, or even *'corrected' by Rembrandt* . . .''

He turned the painting over, scrutinizing its back, running a finger around the edge of the frame where it touched the canvas. "In 1913," he went on, "a catalogue of Rembrandts listed no fewer than nine hundred and eighty-eight paintings. But in 1935 there were only six hundred and thirty, a reduction of three hundred and fifty-eight Rembrandts.''

"Good Lord, what happened to them?"

"And in 1960 there were only five hundred and fifty as I recall—a loss of eighty more.'' He chuckled. "And in 1968 only four hundred and twenty paintings were recognized as legitimate. All the others proved to be forgeries, or painted by students or colleagues or the like. So many Rembrandts 'ave been discredited by scientific and other means that everyone is wary. At one time it got so bad some even denied Rembrandt ever existed. They said all his paintings were forgeries.''

"I didn't know . . .''

"Many of those forgeries were very fine paintings," he said with a smile.

A look of amused tenderness hovered about Tina's lips.

"Look here," he said, holding the back of the painting for their inspection. "Note the weave of the canvas."

Tina reached out a tentative finger and touched the canvas.

"And the stretcher," he said. "I cannot be sure, but if I am not mistaken, this wood is yew."

Gin nodded, trying to follow.

He turned to her. "Congratulations, my dear."

In a fog of confusion, Gin said, "I'm not sure I . . ."

He smiled gently. "I congratulate that eye of yours, so new and yet so sure."

"You mean . . . ?"

"This canvas is, at the earliest, nineteenth century, after the invention of the mechanical loom. It is clearly not loomed by hand. And unless I'm mistaken yew was not a popular utilitarian wood in seventeenth-century Netherlands. Also, a painting from the seventeenth century would have markings of some kind, and custom stamps on the back."

"Are you saying . . . ?"

"Yes, my dear. You are quite right. This painting is a fake."

9

A scream broke through the steady drone of the reception and the drone fell silent.

"What is it? What's that?" cried Mrs. Trowber.

"Calm, everybody. Just stay calm." The chairman of the board cleared his throat and headed for the corridor. It had been a woman's scream. But what woman? Where was she?

But Toby Trowber beat him to it, being closer to the door of the gallery.

Oh, good Lord, there seemed to be a body. Oh dear, oh no, there were *two* bodies. But as she stood in the doorway of the Gallery of Western Art peering at one of them, behind her the other one moved, rose up, and resolved itself into Lt. Tito Gonzales, who had not quite made it out the entry into the Santa Fe night. That last margarita. He couldn't risk a DWI. He had taken advantage of the bench in the O'Keeffe gallery for a sobering snooze. The scream had penetrated the Jose Cuervo.

He sat up frowning, blinking at the lights, ran a hand through his hair to smooth it down and instead stood it on end. "What's going on? What's that?" he muttered.

Gin, in the East Room, heard the scream not as a separate event but as some weird aftershock of the blow dealt her by the Mexican expert.

Bowing apologetically, claiming the number of drinks aboard the flight, Pablo Esperanza had just excused himself and left them to visit the CABALLEROS.

When he'd confirmed her suspicions, her heart had dropped to her stomach and begun to pound. Now she felt very light, particularly her head, as if she might rise weightless to the ceiling.

And that's when she heard the scream, like an instant replay, seconds after it rang through the building, an external manifestation of her inner state. She crossed the room ahead of Tina, flung open the door, and saw Tito Gonzales standing in the entry to the Gallery of Western Art, hiking his belt, putting out a hand. His voice echoed down the corridor, "Now hold on, wait, don't move, don't touch him . . ."

Lloyd Noldes brushed past the lieutenant and Toby Trowber and disappeared into the Gallery of Western Art. The lieutenant came to life and followed. Guests flowed into the corridor and stopped, barred by the broad frame of Toby Trowber in the Western gallery door.

Gin hurried down the hall and Croy broke free of the crowd to join her. Tina followed from the East Room without closing the door behind her.

At the entry to the Gallery of Western Art, the assistant director stopped. Across the room, under the big Moran landscape, Raoul Query lay on the floor. Under his cheek a dark pool slowly spread. The chairman and the lieutenant bent over him, peering down, along with a member of the

pod—Hanna something, Gin couldn't remember. It must
have been she who'd screamed. On one knee over the man
on the floor knelt Pablo Esperanza-Ramos.

"What's happened here?" said Lieutenant Gonzales
gruffly.

"Oh, please," the woman said, "somebody do something."

The lieutenant, head clearing by the minute, reached down
and took Pablo by the collar and lifted him to his feet.
"What're you doing? What happened? What's going on?"

"Don't touch him," the chairman said to nobody in particular, kneeling in Pablo's place beside Raoul Query and
putting his handkerchief to the head wound, which quickly
stained it crimson.

Gin thrust the chairman and the lieutenant out of the way
and knelt beside the man on the floor. She couldn't find a
pulse. "Oh, God. Croy!" she shouted, though he was already beside her. She started CPR. First the chest thing—
one-two-three-four-five—pounding with one hand over the
other. Then swapping places with Croy without missing a
beat, putting her lips to Raoul Query's, breathing into his
lungs. Then Croy: one-two-three-four-five, while, cheek low
to the man's face, Gin tried to feel his breath. Mouth-to-
mouth again, keep it up, breathe in, watch his chest rise,
then Croy: one-two-three . . . Once you started, you had to
keep it up till the ambulance arrived. It was the law. They
learned that when they took the class, all of them, even Reuben, when Magda had her heart thing—they said from grief
for Larry Sanchez. Doctors put her on Quinadex, but after a
violent allergic reaction she went to the Japanese acupunc-
turist who, with a year of treatments, fixed her up.

. . . three-four-five, breathe into his mouth. God, she
thought she was hyperventilating. Why didn't somebody do
something?

"Here." The chairman tried to pull her away and take
over. She wouldn't let him. She bent her head, put her lips
to those of the fallen man (soft lips, turning blue), and gave
him the kiss of life, closing her eyes as she breathed into
him, otherwise it was much too intimate. Already she had

his face memorized to the tiny flat mole at the edge of his lip.

A thin line of blood trailed on her skirt. If he still bled, didn't that mean . . . ? One-two-three-four . . . His chest rose and fell with her breath. Behind and above her Pablo and the lieutenant engaged in a heated argument that started in Spanish and ended in English.

"I ast you a simple question!"

"To hell with you, señor!"

Toby Trowber stated the obvious. "It's Raoul Query."

. . . three-four-five . . .

"Somebody call the police."

Tito grunted, "The police are here."

Tina knelt beside Gin and whispered, "Is he dead?" But Gin couldn't stop what she was doing. She began to feel dizzy.

"Nobody leaves this building!" the lieutenant shouted. And in a lower voice to someone she couldn't see, "See that nobody leaves the building."

"Let me through. I'm a doctor. I'm a doctor. Let me through." Dried-up Dickie Mambes, the retired psychiatrist, knelt beside her. Where had he been? In the CABALLEROS probably, in no position to help. She watched his bony fingers move on Raoul Query's throat. One-two-three-four-five . . .

The chairman, hovering over her, muttered, "I couldn't find a pulse."

Gin felt like she might pass out. One-two-three-four-five. Croy's face was dark with concentration as, one palm over the other, he pounded Raoul Query's chest. Breathe in . . .

"That's right, young lady. Keep it up." Dickie Mambes, pompous idiot. Laughter bubbled up in her . . . one-two-three-four. She imagined herself fainting and all of them standing over the bodies piling up on the floor.

"Let's everybody stand where you were when the incident occurred." (That's the ticket. Get some order in the scene.) "Let's see who can account for who here." The lieutenant looked around and collared Jean Medows. (Freckle-faced broad in the riding pants looked like she could handle rush-hour traffic single-handed.) He sat her at the bar with pad and pencil the old bird in lavender brought from someplace. "Okay, get everybody's names and addresses." Pulling rabbits out of hats till some cars got up the hill.

Okay now, called the ambulance. Called the station. Herded everybody back in there with the bar—God, he could stand a drink—where Benito stood off in the corner, pissed his show was over. You don't know how lucky you are, Benito. Wanna swap places with me? The lieutenant's show was just starting. Christ, he hated Murder Ones. Sucker looked dead to him. He wished he was home in front of the television, tricycle on its buns in the corner, red plastic choo-choo on the rug, wife on the phone talking back to her mom, junior, the sweet little bastard, yelling to be hauled off the pottie.

What did the assault have to do with a stolen painting? Did he even believe in the stolen painting? He guessed he'd better. Somebody talking about the theft and this dude overheard? Or he was in cahoots and they got to arguing? Could be anything. Could be a different matter entirely. Put that out of your mind, boy. First thing they teach you at cop college is: put it down to coincidence, you're a cop-out.

Cop out. That was good.

"Can I be of any help, old chap?" asked a man in what looked like a summer uniform, voice surprisingly bass for such a tall, skinny fellow. "Who're you?"

"William Nevil, Commander, Her Majesty's Navy, on temporary leave."

The lieutenant grunted, cleared his throat, and asked Hanna Enright, "Know what happened here? Know anything about this?"

The lady looked ready to faint. Somebody thought to hand her a drink.

"I really don't know." The lieutenant watched the little broad with the slight hump bring the glass with both hands to her mouth like a squirrel with a nut, make a face, and hold it out. Somebody took it away. What, it was Scotch and she was a gin drinker? "I . . . the reception was noisy . . . my head . . . a migraine all afternoon. So I came into the corridor and wandered in here and . . . There he was, just as

you see him . . . with this gentleman kneeling beside him.''
She nodded toward Pablo. "I suppose I screamed."

"You did." Lloyd Noldes said it like an accusation.

"Such a shock." She sank awkwardly, her dress riding up
over her knees, to kneel beside the assistant director and the
young man administering CPR. She reached tentatively toward the man on the floor, then drew back her hand.

"He must have slipped," she said, "and hit his head on
the edge of the bench."

Gin thought: lawsuit against the museum. One-two-three-
four . . . Davies away . . . Cameron in England. Could the
museum sue the janitorial service? The company that supplied the wax? She bit off a hysterical laugh. It was nonsense,
of course. How could he have slipped? She breathed into
Raoul Query and watched his chest rise. Then Croy pounded.
One-two-three-four-five . . .

"This fellow already here when you come in?" the lieutenant, pointing to Pablo, asked Hanna Enright.

"He couldn't have been. He was just with us," Tina said,
putting the afghan from Gin's office over the man on the
floor.

Tito said to Pablo, "Stay put. Don't go away. I'm gunna
wanna talk to you," and Pablo murmured his denials.

The lieutenant went out into the hall. Car lights nosed
around the parking lot, looking for parking spaces. The clock
on the wall above the reception desk said nine o'clock. The
public was trying to come in. "Stay at the door," he said to
Juan. "Keep them out. Explain there's been an accident."

He went back to the room with the bar. "Okay, if we don't
want to be here all night let's try and cooperate." Where
were his people? The ambulance? Why didn't they get themselves up here?

He took Hanna Enright by the arm and led her into the
hall. "Okay, give it to me again."

She shook her head. "But that's all. I left the opening and
wandered down here away from the noise . . . and there he
was."

"With this Pablo guy bending over him."

"I believe he was kneeling . . . on one knee."

Tito waved his hand in front of his face like slapping at a fly. "Okay, awright, *kneeling*. See anybody else?"

"No, I—"

"Think about it. What else did you see?"

"I didn't *see* anything. I thought I heard the entry closing."

"How'd you know it was the entry?"

"The door has one of those slowing devices. It sort of *whooshes*."

He took her by the elbow and ushered her to the entry door. Juan stood outside with his feet planted wide apart and his hands clasped behind him. People crowded around him, asking questions, somebody's forehead white against the glass.

The lieutenant knocked. Juan unlocked the door.

"Get back! Stand back everybody! There's been a little accident," the lieutenant shouted. The ambulance siren approached from Fort Marcy. Christ, they were taking their time. Had to finish their gin game.

He let go the door and listened to the *whoosh* as it closed. He stuck his head out again. "Okay," he said, "you can lock it." Juan produced keys and bent to the light.

"Okay," the lieutenant said to Hanna Enright, letting go of her arm. She rubbed it where the short sleeve ended, and the lieutenant herded her into the gallery where shortly before he'd been having such a good time.

The ambulance turned off Hyde Park Road and crept down the drive into the parking lot.

He raised his voice. "I'mona wanna statement from everybody here." He was back into his official role, reassured by all this meek obedience that he had everything under control.

Another siren approached and died in the parking lot outside. "Wait a minute, hold on." The lieutenant headed for the hall. A moment later he returned with two uniformed officers. "Okay," he said to the room at large. "This is Sergeant Peck. He'll ask the questions and this lady here, she'll take down your answers. I'll wanna know where you were, who with, what you saw, heard—the works."

Then with the help of the sergeant—a large, blond young

man as thick in the neck and shoulders as a wrestler—Jean Medows dealt with the roomful of guests as competently as she dealt with a stable of horses.

They had all been engaged in conversations when Hanna Enright screamed.

Except for the doctor, who was in the CABALLEROS.

And except for Eric. Nobody had been talking with Eric when the scream rang out. "But," Eric sputtered, "the man is my best friend. I was at the bar . . ." When the bartender shrugged, Eric shrugged, too, and finished lamely, "I was right here, getting a handful of nuts . . . and a sandwich."

And except for Benito Montoya. No one had been talking to Benito when it happened.

And Toby Trowber. She had been alone, there by the door, taking it all in.

Taking what all in?

Why, the party, of course, and the—the music.

The mariachi players vouched for one another.

"Where's Victor?" somebody asked.

Someone else asked, "Where's Alice?"

"Who's missing?" asked Sergeant Peck, and raised his voice. "Is somebody missing?"

"Oh, they left ages ago," said Eric.

How long ago was ages?

"Ten minutes maybe."

"Some ages," somebody muttered.

Somebody else asked, "Where'd they go?"

The crime writer said, "They may have gone into town to sit on the plaza."

Toby Trowber dug an elbow into Benito's ribs and winked. Meaning what? Benito wondered. The bartender said, "Have another drink, folks," and a board member said, "A little music there," clapping his hands toward the mariachi band, which shortly began playing.

In the Gallery of Western Art paramedics lifted the victim to a stretcher.

"Keep people out of this room," Tito said to one of the uniformed officers just arriving, and to Sergeant Peck's partner, "Briggs, you ride in the ambulance."

"I'll go along too," Dickie Mambes said, and the chairman said, "Good idea, Richard."

But the lieutenant said firmly, "Nobody else leaves the building."

10

He stood in the hall watching the stretcher move out to the waiting ambulance, its lights flashing in the courtyard, hoping it turned out to be assault and he didn't have a murder on his hands. He went back to the scene of the crime and searched the floor—easy, it was so spotless and bare—and found only a leaf that had come inside on somebody's shoe. Tina's friend was still there, standing in front of a little statue on a pedestal.

"What's the matter?" he asked, moving up beside her to see what she was looking at.

Gin, fingers to lips still imprinted with Raoul Query's, was looking at the Apache woman, but the Apache woman stared straight ahead, unmindful of her or the lieutenant, or even of the Gallery of Western Art, bent on concerns of her own, one foot set firmly in front of the other on the trail.

"What's that thing?" Tito asked, pointing.

Gin said, "A burden basket." Strapped to the Indian woman's back, it extended above her head.

"What the hell is that?"

"An Apache backpack. They changed camp often. They traveled light."

"What's in it?" Tito asked, eyeing the little bronze statue.

"Whatever she needed," Gin said, "a change of clothes, food for the trip, cooking utensils . . ."

"Huh," the lieutenant said.

"She had one hand up to steady the basket. Like this." Gin put up a tentative arm as if to balance a burden.

"Where is it?"

"The arm is missing."

And the hand along with it. And the missing hand had snatched away part of the burden basket.

"Well I'll be . . ." the lieutenant said. "She stuck to the stand?"

The walnut pedestal was four feet tall. "No. She's just standing there on a felt base."

Okay, the lieutenant told himself, somebody picked her up and bashed the victim over the head and broke off her arm. So where was the arm?

"It's a bronze by Frederic Remington," Gin said, "from about 1902."

"Pretty old, eh. She worth much?"

"She's a first casting. That makes her valuable."

"We talking about, how valuable?"

"Before the damage, about four hundred thousand."

The lieutenant grunted skeptically. "A casting, huh. Must be a lot of them around."

"Not like this one. Ours was a first, and there's only one of those." The artist's original conception. Remington made changes in the early castings of his bronzes. He would cast the original, then set it aside. If he didn't think it was quite right he made changes in the cast. And the early castings, done by the artist himself, were more refined than the later ones, which might have been done by anybody.

The lieutenant circled the pedestal, frowning.

Gin said, "On the second casting of this Apache woman he moved her foot out a bit, to give her a better foundation."

The lieutenant grunted.

"And in the third he lowered the burden basket, to make the whole thing sturdier. And in the fourth—and all subsequent castings—she's looking down at the trail." Gin liked to think this reflected Remington's sorrow that the Indian's West was dying. "But he should have trusted his first impulse," she said. The Waldheimer woman's stance was perfectly natural, and very sturdy, and the burden basket looked like a burden. And that purposeful gaze, bent on distances, was compelling, less editorializing and just as moving as the downcast look at the trail, for the tribe was on the move, as it always was in those days of persecution and genocide.

"Okay, don't touch it," Tito said. "Don't touch anything." There might be fingerprints on the broken statue.

"It would be worth everything to us to get that arm back."

Yeah, the lieutenant thought, to us, too. Next thing, have the museum searched, and the courtyard and parking lot. Cheez, all these cars coming in.

"But whoever took the arm could just throw it away," Gin said. "It's not very large." Tossed out in the chemiso, it would be hard to find.

"Maybe," the lieutenant said. "And maybe he just got flustered and slipped it in his pocket."

He. She saw the assailant, a shadowy figure dissolving into the night. She shivered.

She followed Tito Gonzales back to the opening where he headed straight for Pablo and Tina, talking together at the bar.

"Okay," he said to Pablo. "So how'd you just happen to be kneeling over the victim?"

Pablo shrugged. "I left these young ladies to . . . I was looking for the men's room."

The lieutenant glanced toward the East Room at the end of the hall, where the sign outside the door indicated the direction of the rest rooms in handsome graphics.

"You went in the wrong direction," he said.

"So it would seem."

The Mexican had something to do with it. Art expert, he'd know the value of the stuff on the walls, how to unload it. "And you just happened to look in and—"

"That is correct." Pablo ignored the sarcasm in the lieutenant's voice. "I looked in and saw my good friend—"

"You knew the victim before?"

"I have known him for some years."

"You say you just come up from south of the border."

"*Sí*, that is correct. I did not know he was in Santa Fe."

"Just luck, eh?" the lieutenant said in a voice heavy with irony.

Pablo Esperanza looked uncomprehending.

"Oh, come on, Tito," Tina said to the lieutenant. "Two hours ago, Pablo didn't even know he'd be in Santa Fe himself."

The lieutenant said to her, "So you're the . . . whatcha-callit, Miss Fixit, eh?"

"What do you mean?"

"*She* said," he glanced at Gin, "you were up here last night, in the basement."

"Yes. I am the conservator."

"And now they think a valuable picture's missing and we got an assault on our hands."

"You have known me too long, Tito, to pretend to think I'm a thief and murderer."

The Mexican expert put an arm around Tina and the lieutenant noticed she didn't pull away. She was still a cute little thing. In high school he'd followed her around like a dog. Well, he had a perfectly good wife, nice trim figure, good cook. . . . The lieutenant sighed. "Do me a favor," he said to Gin. "Call my wife and tell her don't wait up."

Gin went back to her office and telephoned, then stood in the dark at her big window, looking out over the peaceful lights of Santa Fe. The view had become the mark of her rise in the world—from part-time at the library, and before that clerk in an expensive cookware shop. Why did these things have to happen when she was in charge? Till then she'd thought only about the Rembrandt, and later poor Query and the broken bronze. Now she thought about herself, soon, perhaps, to join the ranks of the unemployed.

She returned to the opening.

Sergeant Peck still interviewed guests one by one and watched Jean Medows take down their statements on a yellow legal pad. Tina and Pablo talked together at the bar. Croy leaned against the wall with his hands in his pockets. The mariachi band huddled silent in a corner. Benito Montoya scowled as if this ruined opening was no more than he'd expected.

Outside, colored lights turned in slow arcs and lit up the courtyard and parking lot. More sirens approached and died. Gin crossed the room to where Lloyd Noldes talked, arms crossed, to the Englishman they called the commander. She waited beside them, summoning courage. *You need a little drop of courage,* her mother used to say when Gin was small and the world too big, handing her an Oreo cookie.

Finally the commander moved off. As the fingerprint crew made their way into the Gallery of Western Art, she felt the vein worm its way down her forehead. She moved up beside Lloyd Noldes and murmured, "I have to talk to you."

11

While the assistant director told the chairman—quietly, hesitantly, to lead him into it gently and upset him as little as possible—of the missing pencil mark and Pablo Esperanza's confirmation of her suspicions, while Lieutenant Gonzales's reinforcements spread out through the museum, dusting the statues, the frames, even the light switches in the Gallery of Western Art, and while certain members of the pod from Maui went to St. Vincent Hospital to see about Raoul Query, certain others met in the bar at the Sheraton.

But Toby Trowber went straight up to the room she shared with the crime writer to recover from the hot flash she'd had at the museum and renew the powder beading in the creases of her neck. As she combed her hair, her eye fell upon a notebook open on the dresser and she read, "One swift, sure blow to the lower occipital where the spinal column enters the cavity of the skull . . ." She shuddered and went back down to the bar. She needed a drink.

On the glassed-in terrace overlooking the lights of Santa Fe, the pod had their heads together. She longed to hear what they were saying, but when they didn't invite her to join them, perhaps didn't see her there in the door, she took her brandy to a small inside table by a bit of wall between open French doors.

Judging from who was out there and who was not, it had been Hanna Enright and the commander who had gone off to the hospital, though the commander was no more a member than she was herself. In the meantime, Victor Weldon and Alice Maynard had rematerialized.

Mrs. Trowber sighed, lonely there at the little table all by herself. At times like this she did miss Bobby.

"If you ask me, he had it coming." It was Eric Albin's voice.

Alice Maynard's voice trembled on the verge of tears. "I'm sure it isn't serious."

Victor Weldon murmured, "Drink your drink, Alice."

Sheila Wadsworth said, "You wouldn't say that if you'd been there. It was a nasty wound. He lost a lot of blood."

They all fell silent. Sheila was the expert. Her books were full of blood and gore and lengthy discussions of The Weapon.

"Bloody awful," said Eric Albin.

Sheila said, "Raoul was struck by a weapon the assailant either took away with him or hid somewhere in the museum."

Victor Weldon cleared his throat as if to speak, but Alice Maynard broke in nervously and ran on about the opening until Sheila interrupted. "Where did you two go? One minute you were there and the next . . ."

"Oh," Alice said, "we tired of the crowd and escaped down the hill to the plaza. We sat on a bench and enjoyed the night air—little boys gliding by on skateboards, lovers on the grass, people promenading round the square much like a piazza in Italy, right down to the ice-cream cones." She laughed a little hysterically.

The group on the terrace fell into what the crime writer might have called a pregnant silence. Mrs. Trowber rummaged in her purse for a match and, not finding one, went to the bar to get some from the bartender. As she turned back, the pod on the terrace was pulling up chairs to accommodate Hanna Enright and the commander.

"Chap hasn't regained consciousness," the commander said. "Nothing we could do so they sent us home."

Nobody said anything. Mrs. Trowber found the silence

baffling. You'd expect them to be full of outrage and sur-
mises. Then somebody said something she didn't catch because two couples came in, laughing and talking, and drew
chairs up to a table near the bar.

Then Mrs. Trowber heard Hanna Enright say, "Raoul's not
been his usual self. He hasn't been able to sleep since . . ."
She broke off.

"You can say it," Victor Weldon said softly. But nobody
said anything.

"Poor Ellen," said the deep voice of the skinny commander.

"I wouldn't be able to sleep either, if I were him," Alice
Maynard said.

"You don't know what you're talking about," said Hanna
Enright.

"No," said Alice Maynard, with a lilt of sarcasm. "*He's*
the only one who knows."

Who was *he*? Mrs. Trowber wondered. Raoul Query?

"What's the use talking about it," Sheila Wadsworth said,
"if we're not going to do anything? And now I suppose we
never will."

"Why do you say that?"

"We've waffled too long, and we have no evidence."

Laughter from the table by the bar blotted out the rest.
Mrs. Trowber drank her brandy too fast. She coughed, pulling a handkerchief from her purse. The commander got up
from the terrace table and passed her on his way to the bar.

Eric asked, "What was in the fax?"

Victor Weldon said, "They'll take possession on the dock.
They wanted to pay cash."

"Great!" Eric said.

Victor Weldon gave a scornful laugh. Mrs. Trowber had
the impression that Victor Weldon despised Eric Albin. "Not
at all great. Any bank where you deposited such a sum would
have to report it to the government. It would look like drug
money. We'd all be investigated."

"Then how *do* we take it?" Eric asked, and Sheila Wadsworth said to the table at large, "One day I'll get a book out
of this."

"An irrevocable letter of credit," Victor Weldon said, "released on the dock in exchange for the merchandise."

"What will our share be?" asked Alice Maynard in a girlish voice.

"About a third," Weldon said.

"A third of what?" Eric wanted to know.

"This time, one million. Over five years, they'll pay something like sixty. We'll get a third of that."

Hanna Enright said, "But it seems so wicked. It makes me feel awful."

"You'll feel better when you see the money," Eric Albin said.

"Only because we *must* have it," Hanna Enright said. "But does the end ever really justify the means?"

As the commander turned from the bar with a drink in his hand, Mrs. Trowber crushed out her cigarette, took up her purse, and toddled out to the lobby. Her head felt large and full of pressure. What on earth had she stumbled into?

Croy and Gin and Tina and Pablo Esperanza waited with their own nightcaps in the Victorian parlor bar at La Posada. Earlier, Tito Gonzales had taken Pablo to the station for questioning. The others had followed in the rig and waited in the dead fluorescent light on uncomfortable chrome and plastic chairs. Then, threatening dire but vague consequences if Pablo left town, the lieutenant released him and headed for the hospital on the off-chance that Raoul Query might regain consciousness and be able to talk. And if he didn't regain consciousness . . . Several murders of late were still unsolved, and he was already under pressure from above.

Tina had wrung from the lieutenant a promise to call them at La Posada with news of Query's condition.

Gin slid off her chair and stretched out on the floor—stress gave her a pain in the neck—and the bartender stepped over her with their drinks. He set the tray on the low marble-top table.

"You 'ave spoken with Señor Noldes?" Pablo said.

"Yes," Gin said, looking up at the high, shadowy ceiling. "I don't know whether the man's just stubborn or if he's in shock. I'm not sure he believed me. But we called Dallas and tried to reach Quillan Davies. He wasn't in his hotel room."

"You left a message?" Tina asked.

"Yes, and Noldes wants to contact Cameron in London, but he'll wait till morning. I think the chairman believes there's some mistake." She glanced at Pablo.

Pablo smiled and shrugged. "Experts 'ave made meestakes before. You will 'ave to see. You cannot simply go on what I say."

Nobody said anything till Tina blurted, "What were you doing in the Western Gallery anyway? You said you were going to the john."

"But, my dear, I was unable to locate it."

Gin stared at the flocked green wallpaper.

"Strange, no, thees painting up there?" Pablo hiked his head back toward the hill the museum sat on. "An almost exact copy."

"Aren't all forgeries exact copies?" Croy asked.

Their voices flowed over Gin like voices from another room. She was too anxious to be attentive, but she was trying to go easy on the herbal tincture.

"Oh, no. Hardly any are exact copies," Pablo said. "Most in thees—what you call 'racket'—they try to come up with a 'lost' painting of some Master." He swished his cognac around in his snifter. Gin watched the light come down amber through it. "That way there are no duplicates floating around to cause trouble. What they often do is copy, as nearly as they can, *pieces* of the Master's paintings—a figure here, a few details of landscape there, all changed a little and rearranged and put together as a 'lost' painting."

He recalled for them a time when an anachronism gave the forger away. He had added an original detail of his own and put a turkey in what was supposed to be a medieval painting, though turkeys were unknown in Europe before Europeans landed in America.

"I can think of very few like thees one of yours," Pablo went on, "thees almost exact duplicate. Well, there was the self-portrait of Albrecht Dürer, a much-copied painter. He had trouble with forgeries in his own lifetime."

The bartender peered around the corner to see what they needed.

"Thees Dürer self-portrait was owned by the town of Nuremberg. It had hung in the town hall since the sixteenth century, until one day a local painter named Kueffner simply borrowed it and split the painting—it was done on limewood—by sawing parallel to the painted surface. Then he painted a copy of the portrait on the back half and appropriated the front half with the original portrait for himself."

"Clever," Tina said, his Tina, one arm up above her head on the velvet arm of the love seat. He would like to nibble that soft underarm, oh only a gentle munch.

"How'd they find him out?" Croy wanted to know.

"They noticed no-thing," Pablo said. "Thees forged portrait, you see, had the seals intact on the back of the panel, where they had always been. But I believe they must never 'ave looked at their masterpiece. I 'ave seen both the original and the fake, and I cannot imagine anybody believing it the same painting. The forgery is nothing—a thin, pale, characterless thing, while the original it springs with life."

"Then," Gin said, opening her eyes, "he didn't get away with it!"

"Ah, Ginnee, the forger, this Kueffner, got greedy. When nobody noticed the fraud, he offered the painting for sale. It wound up in the Palace of the Elector of Bavaria. When the Nuremberg fathers heard of it, finally they grew worried. Only then did they look at their masterpiece. But according to the laws they had there at the time, since the painting had been legally purchased by the Elector of Bavaria, the town of Nuremberg could not get it back."

"So he *did* get away with it!"

"I suppose one must say that he did."

"Back in a minute," Croy said, and headed for the men's.

The conservator lay back with her head on the arm of the velvet love seat, looking, Pablo thought, like a painting herself. He laid his hand on Tina's, but she shoved it away. "How is a forger different from a philanderer?" she asked.

Pablo said, "Is this a riddle, Celestina?"

Gin closed her eyes, pretending to be elsewhere.

"They both tell a kind of lie, don't they?" Tina said.

"I 'ave never lied to you."

"No. You just didn't tell me the truth."

"Out of fear and cowardice."

"Fear that this Indian would have your scalp."

"Tina, please understand. What began as a leetle flirtation had become my life."

"Oh, please," Tina said, "no Latin dramatics."

"I speak only the truth."

"*Now*, maybe. Anyway, it was never possible. I live here and you live in Mexico City."

"How you would love Mexico City," he murmured.

"That's a word you use loosely."

She's learning, Gin thought.

The bartender set a tray of nachos on the low marble-top table. Returning, Croy stepped over her and fumbled in his pockets, but the bartender said he would put it on their tab.

"One thing is clear," Pablo said. "Your forged Rembrandt could not 'ave been painted between last night, when the original was there with Ginnee's pencil mark upon it, and this morning when it was not."

"No," Tina said. "It would never have dried."

Gin squirmed where she lay, half under the coffee table. "Tito Gonzales doesn't believe in the pencil mark."

Croy said, "Obviously the fake was ready to hang. All the forger had to do was make the swap sometime last night or early this morning."

"Yes, thees thief must 'ave planned it for some time." Pablo reached down and patted Gin's upthrust knee. "I am certain I am right, Ginnee, but you must, of course, subject the painting to scientific tests. Major museums 'ave their laboratories."

"It'll have to be taken up with the trustees. On my own I can't do anything," Gin said.

"I would be in the same sheep at the *Museo*. But, my dear, you must do something quickly, while the Rembrandt may still be in the country, though of course it could have already flown away."

Gin's heart did a skip. "Out of the country!"

"Oh, my dear, it makes legal steps much more complicated. And also if perhaps they have stolen the painting for a specific private collector, most likely he is in Europe or Japan.''

"And in that case, the painting will simply disappear, to surface generations hence, if at all." She fished out the herbal tincture and squirted a dropperful into her Drambuie. "What about customs checks?"

"Easy to evade. Thieves paint over valuable pictures with acrylics and pass them off as modern art."

"So," Gin said, "things have to move very fast."

A phone rang distantly. The bartender stuck his head in the room. "Tina Martinez?"

Tina leapt up. Soon she was back. "He's alive," she said. Pablo crossed himself.

"They did a CAT scan and then rushed him to surgery for some kind of emergency procedure to relieve the pressure on his brain. Tito thinks they bored a hole . . .''

Gin shuddered and tossed down the rest of her drink.

They parked the rig under the olive tree and Tina offered coffee. But while the others moved toward Tina's studio, Gin slipped away in the dark, pleading a headache.

She cut across the parking lot, a barren space under olive trees, ducked under an arch, and skirted the goldfish pond where soon they must rescue the fish and bring them inside for the winter.

The light from Magda's kitchen window fell over the path. She stepped into the flower bed and peered inside. Magda was ironing. A pot of beans simmered on the stove. She could smell them before Magda opened the door.

"They've kept you up late. You shouldn't serve such good booze," Magda said.

Everything about their sweet, spacey landlady was on a grand scale—she was six feet tall (taller with her hair piled up and cascading down her back), with a large bosom and small waist cinched with a red Guatemalan belt. She went barefoot summer or winter, or wore only Birkenstocks.

Everything about her was outrageous—her size, her hair, her bangles (big-looped and beaded earrings dangling to her shoulders), her philosophies—Christian one day, Zen the next.

The remains of a fire glowed in the small adobe fireplace set counter-high in the wall near the table where, from the look of things, Magda'd had someone to dinner. Probably her friend Elsie. The window seat was full of cushions, the floor was brick, and the counters Mexican tile. Red chili *ristras* hung from the vigas.

Magda's favorite colors were pinks and reds and browns, and they were everywhere, from the brick floor to the dark vigas overhead. Her windows were outlined with stained glass she'd made in some summer workshop, even the big one where she liked to sit near the idle loom left over from another abandoned enthusiasm.

Gin took the lid off the pot and sampled the beans with a wooden spoon. "Um, almost done."

"They ought to be. They've been cooking all day."

Magda had the television on low while she ironed—a small set on the kitchen counter. Gin stood with the spoon in hand, watching four smiling presidents—Nixon, Ford, Reagan, Bush—lined up in front of the Nixon Library.

"Look at that," Magda said. "They're all tall, dark-haired, white men. Just goes to show."

"What we need is a short blond black woman." Gin aimed the remote and fired. Bull's-eye. The sound went off but the presidents went on smiling, talking, saying nothing. "That was the tragedy of Jimmy Carter," Magda said. "He only had half the presidential qualifications."

Magda Sanchez looked naked without her arms full of bracelets. They lay in a heap on the counter beside the pots and pans waiting to be washed. But she always wore cotton, and cotton had to be ironed. "And besides," she claimed, "I like doing it. It's my meditation."

"What's up, dearie? Something wrong?" She shook the steam iron to check how much water was left. The ironing board overflowed—yellow cotton with a small flowered print. Magda's fiesta dress. Fiesta would start at the end of the week, on Friday night, with the burning of Zozobra, Old Man Gloom, in Magers Field. Then parades on the plaza, and music, and Indian traders touting rugs and pottery and jewelry, and tourists tourists everywhere. They came, these gringos, from all over the country, because, Gin thought, they made no fiestas of their own, only football parades.

She spooned a bowl of beans and blew on them to cool them—a mix of three or four varieties, very flavorful.

"Shoo, Pussyfoot," Magda said to her cat. Pussyfoot, an enormous tortoiseshell, was asleep in the rocker on top of a pile of laundry. "Just dump him on the floor."

But Gin sat on the window seat, and Pussyfoot, one of four, stayed where he was. The other three were a Siamese, an Abyssinian, and a Manx—Gingy, Phaedra, and Max, respectively.

"What's the matter?" Magda said. "You look bushed."

Between spoonfuls of beans, Gin told her. She mentioned the value of the Rembrandt and Magda hiked her eyebrows and glanced at her with eyes colored green by new contact lenses. "Sums like that and my mind goes blank. I can't even think them. I don't even try."

Gin sighed, picked up Pussyfoot, moved the laundry to the loom, and settled in the rocker still warm from the cat. It was true. Money meant nothing to Magda. If it had, she would long since have done what she sometimes threatened to do—deck herself out in all her gold jewelry (twenty years in New Mexico hadn't converted her to turquoise and silver) and march herself down to the bank for a loan to turn her scruffy old compound into condos that would support her in style. She often told her tenants when they gathered, as they often did, here in her kitchen, "Learn from the animals. That's what they're here for."

"I wonder if that's true?" said Croy, who could be so literal-minded.

"Hush," Tina said, "we'll never know, so let her rave."

"Learn what?" Croy always finally took the bait.

"All you really need is enough to eat and a roof over your head—and, if you can't grow fur, something to throw on your back. All this striving and achieving makes for a restless heart. Take Pussyfoot there." Or Max. Or Gingy. Or Phaedra.

The cats, except for the Abyssinian, a gift from Larry-the-last, had presented themselves at her doorstep. The lessons from them were frequent and varied.

"Pussyfoot," Croy would point out, "never ratted in his life. He's got you."

And Magda would laugh like liquid silver and the conversation take a leap that they couldn't follow. "Larry always said when I wanted a garden—" Larry Sanchez had been her most exasperating husband—" 'You don't need a garden, you just need to know somebody who's got one.' He was right. I never had a garden of my own, but we were inundated with fresh vegetables from all his kith and kin. We canned all summer. What we couldn't can, we dried."

Larry was the laziest of the husbands.

"Laziness is the root of genius," Magda told them. "Where do you think all these modern inventions came from?"

The modern inventions—in Magda's case not entirely modern as she bought them out of the *Thrifty Nickel*—were her many laborsaving devices—her washer and drier and toaster and juicer and can opener and hair drier and popcorn popper. Reuben, both potter and putterer, kept them in working order.

As Pussyfoot settled in Gin's lap, Magda said, "Worry never furrows that cat's brow. See what happens? He loses one seat, he finds another."

"We're unlikely to find another Rembrandt and this could mean my job. If I can't pay my rent, it'll affect you, too."

"The domino theory," Magda said. "On television they always ask who stands to gain?"

"Who wouldn't gain from fifty million dollars." No, not that much. A thief would have to sell on the black market. They might even cut it up to make new little Rembrandt's and sell them separately. They did that sometimes. But this was a pretty small painting.

"Maybe Reuben did it," Magda said. "It'd be just like him."

"Oh, come on."

"Just to prove he can."

"Be serious, woman."

"Well, it *is* a shame, isn't it? Here's Rembrandt, too dead to benefit from all those millions, yet so poor when he died he couldn't afford a marker for his grave."

"Is that true? How do you know that?"

"I take courses. I read books."

"No kidding!" Gin said. "Not even a marker for his grave?"

"So it says in one of your brochures."

Gin snorted. Pussyfoot gave her a look out of golden eyes and resettled himself.

"Reuben can hardly afford his materials," Magda said, turning the fiesta dress, shaking the iron again. "Yet one day Reuben's work will be worth lots of money."

Maybe, Gin thought. If he ever got it together and stopped throwing temperamental tantrums.

"But who'll get all that money?" Magda uncapped her water bottle, poured a little into the steam iron, and waited. "Not Reuben, poor boy—he'll be long dead. That's how we treat our artists." She bent to the fiesta dress and began on another skirt panel.

"Not always," Gin said. "In Caesar's time"—(which Caesar? She couldn't remember.)—"somebody called Polyclitus got a hundred talents for a statue of a boy binding his hair. That was about six thousand pounds of gold."

"Was that when they went in for little boys?"

"That was the Greeks."

"Reuben is so discouraged he breaks up his statues and tosses them out. His trash is mountainous."

"And morbid," Gin said.

"Have you no faith in our mad genius?"

"I have faith he's mad."

"Well, if Reuben's your forger, you're in luck. He wouldn't do it for money, just for a lark—to prove he can. Your Rembrandt would be safe."

"It wasn't Reuben."

"Why not? He told me he was painting you a surprise."

Gin stopped rocking. Pussyfoot leapt down, disgruntled. "Are you serious?" Reuben had been in the museum last night, helping unload Benito's paintings, an act of altruism foreign to his nature.

Magda shrugged. "Is it a crime to copy a painting?"

"Only if you pass off the copy as the original."

"Lots of painters paint like somebody else," Magda said. "Is that forgery?"

"What forgery is now, it wasn't always." It was all non-sense about Reuben, of course. Just Magda's way of bringing his plight to her attention, which their landlady had been doing regularly ever since Gin landed the museum job. "A long time ago people didn't even sign their work."

"You mean once upon a time? You're talking down to me, Ginevra."

"It's the *intention* to deceive that makes it a forgery, and even the intention counts for nothing unless money's involved."

"So," Magda said, "the whole idea of forgery is based on commercial considerations."

So Tina had said this morning. "I suppose." Gin put her feet on the ottoman and settled her empty bean bowl on the floor beside the rocker. Pussyfoot moved over to sniff it, then hunkered down, wrapped his tail around him, and began scouring the bowl with his quick pink tongue. "The thing's a catastrophe."

"A friend of mine once worked as a disaster expert," Magda said. "Earthquakes, hurricanes, *tsunamis*—you name it, he was there. I asked him how he dealt with disasters. He said you set up a large desk and sit behind it and point out the way to the bathrooms."

Gin snorted.

"You'll feel better once you've sorted it out," Magda said.

It was true, she was a sorter. She'd always hated things in a jumble. As a child she'd eaten from a divided plate—meat in one compartment, spinach in another—and separated her marbles according to color and subdivided by size.

"What you need is a good night's sleep."

How could she sleep? But the soft glide of the iron over Magda's fiesta dress was soothing, and Pussyfoot was back purring in her lap.

In the small hours of the morning, she woke with a start, still in the rocker, the moon shining in her face and a tall figure moving stealthily toward her from the doorway.

The scream died in her throat. It was Magda's fiesta dress on a hanger hooked to the lintel, moving in the breeze from the window. Magda had thrown an afghan over her. She stumbled with it as far as the window seat and dropped again,

Pussyfoot leaping out from under her and making for the rocker. She tugged the afghan up to her throat and fell asleep again smiling. That's what you could learn from Pussyfoot: how to play musical chairs.

12

THURSDAY

This had to be it.

Gin pressed the button that rolled down the window—the rig had once been a fancy automobile—and stuck her head out to check the bank of rural mailboxes again. Right. There it was. Waldheimer. She tossed down a shot of the herbal tincture to quell her anxiety and turned off the Old Santa Fe Trail up the long, winding drive through piñons.

She had wakened at dawn in Magda's window, dragged herself half-asleep across the compound to her own place to await the chairman's call, and opened her door to a gale. The rear window, which she always kept closed, was wide open, the curtains billowing. She was suddenly wide awake.

The bathroom door was closed. She made herself open it and look around. That left only the closet. She drew a breath, opened the door, and stuck her head in. Nothing in there. Maybe the wind . . .

She crossed the room and closed the window and, turning, confronted something new and strange. On the wall over her couch bed fluttered a big sheet of foolscap full of bold, bright colors.

She caught her breath and laughed with relief.

What in Benito glowered, here exploded. Fireworks in every direction. This was Reuben's surprise, his comment on the opening. A spoof of a Benito Montoya painting that proclaimed: Anybody can do this, this is nothing, it's easy. She had to admit it was very good. But damn Reuben anyway. He'd given her a scare. She left the picture Scotch-taped where it was, threw herself down, and promptly fell back to sleep.

Lloyd Noldes's call came at seven. He had reached Cameron in London, this mythical Cameron, the Anglophile, the real director, whom she had never met but who held her future in his hands. For Quillan Davies had made it clear the day she was hired that hers, like his, was an interim appointment. "If you do well," he'd said, with his meager smile, "I'll recommend you to the permanent director." It had sounded like a promise but she'd taken it as a threat.

On transatlantic telephone with Lloyd Noldes, Cameron had laughed at the idea of theft and forgery until he learned Esperanza-Ramos was in town.

"But couldn't the switch, if there was one, have happened anytime in the last three centuries?" Noldes had asked.

"No way," Cameron told him. "The Metropolitan authenticated the paintings while the museum was being built."

Noldes had asked her to meet him for breakfast at Tia Sophia's, just off the plaza.

The waitress stopped beside them and refilled their coffee cups. The chairman waited till she was gone. "I want you to go see Perdita Waldheimer," he said. "Don't mention any fake painting. We don't want to upset her, she's getting up in years. Just get the provenance and bring it in so we can have a look."

A waste of time. The missing pencil mark proved when the painting had been stolen. But she suspected the chairman put no more stock in the pencil mark than did Tito Gonzales.

"Why me?" she said with a touch of panic. The board chairman seemed to fill the booth. It felt crowded. A spike of blond hair standing up at the crown of his head reassured her that upon rising in the morning he had to get his hair under control like everybody else. "I really ought to be at the museum. It's closed this morning at the request of the police. They'll be all over the place."

"I'll get up there myself," Noldes said.

She wished he'd go see the benefactor instead, but something about the way he avoided her eyes suggested he might be afraid of Perdita Waldheimer. That made her even more reluctant.

"I don't know the first thing about her. I know she built the museum and endowed it. I know she's very rich, and I hear she's quite old, but—"

"She was Charley Burrell's woman," Noldes said. "Burrell was an Englishman. Fought in the First World War and never went home. Lived in Paris with artists and writers during the twenties. Pal of Leo Stein's, Gertrude's brother. Brother and sister lived together before Alice. Alice B. Toklas." His features drew into a smirk. "They bought all those paintings, you remember? Well, Charley Burrell bought paintings, too. Sometimes on Leo's advice. Sometimes when his painter friends needed to pay their rent. Anyway, he acquired the Picasso, the Juan Gris, and the others. Not the really old ones, but those from the twenties. You know the ones I mean. How he ended up in Tesuque, I have no idea."

She sipped her coffee. It scalded her tongue and she winced. "Why on earth does his widow have the provenance?"

The board chairman frowned. He'd asked George Cameron the same question.

"Oh, come on, old fellow," Cameron had answered—he went in for anglicisms—"she gave us the paintings, let her keep the scraps of paper if she wants to."

"I don't know," he said to Gin. "It ought to be in a safe somewhere. I guess George humors the old girl."

Why not? Gin thought. She built the museum and endowed it, and stocked it with millions of dollars' worth of paintings. That warranted a little humoring.

"But there must be copies," Gin said.

The director thought there *were* copies around somewhere. The chairman shrugged. "His late assistant . . ."

That would have been Gin's predecessor, whose main interest had reportedly been not art but slalom racing.

"Perdita wasn't his widow," Noldes said. "They never married." That smirk again.

She looked away. "Was he a painter?" she asked. "Charles Burrell?"

"He was a wastrel, from all I've heard. Never did much of anything but play around. He was what they used to call a remittance man."

"What does that mean?"

They settled on her again, those cold eyes. "It means the family gave him an allowance. In fact, they paid him to stay away from home. Some old respectable family, I guess, and Charley the black sheep."

"You knew him?"

"No." His mouth did a faint ironic twist. "I never had the pleasure. He died some years ago."

That much Gin knew.

"Perdita's family was in railroads, like the Vanderbilts." Noldes contemplated the cup in his hand. "She was a wild girl, they tell me. Family sent her out here to a dude ranch up around Cimmaron to get her away from some Russian prince after her money, though a lot of American million-aires wanted those titles in the family. And what did she do but hook up with Charley, out here playing the cowboy."

He moved his elbow to let the waitress refill his water glass. "The family disowned her, but relented when they began dying off. After she got hold of the family fortune they built a mansion up off the Old Santa Fe Trail."

"What's she like?" Gin asked anxiously.

"Just a nice little old lady now. You don't have to tell her anything. Just get hold of the provenance and bring it to town."

A hairpin turn and the rig slowed alarmingly. Then the gears ground into low. It was only recently that she had ever seen an original provenance—the history of a painting, in-cluding all the hands it had passed through down to the pre-sent day. For a Rembrandt, the provenance could be quite long. Or very short if the painting had been held, say, in one family for years. In that case, it might even be shorter than one of the Western Painters—a Mollhausen's or a Moran's. Moran was her favorite. His paintings of the mountains and the wilderness were so alive they could make you sick the camera had ever been invented. They documented Indians in the same way the old masters documented *their* times. He wasn't a copyist any more than Rembrandt was a copyist.

Then photography forced artists into impressionism and self-expression so as not to be "representational"—that dirty word. Nowadays not even photographers claimed to be that.

A turn in the drive gave her a sudden view of the desert to the south, blue volcanic cones jutting up like breasts. She loved Matisse, Cézanne . . . Still, art had come to rely entirely too much upon invention. She would put her money on discovery—which might one day again give art some reference outside itself.

A dog's deep-throated barking. The chairman had telephoned Perdita Waldheimer to expect her. Her imminent arrival was being heralded, though still no sign of a mansion.

The gears hiccuped into low and the rig went on climbing—past an empty stable with stalls for horses, an empty corral, then a whole bank of hutches of some kind. Then to a frenzy of vicious barking she arrived.

An impression of tiered adobe masses, of levels rising against the timbered foothills, windows gaping and black, the sun as yet behind them, but Gin was entirely focused on the canine in the drive—mottled gray, coyote-ish, growling deep in its throat, functional-looking teeth bared.

It dawned on her slowly that what she was looking at in a red dog collar—heavy-browed, ears pricked forward—was a wolf. This was the home of the nice little old lady?

The wolf made several low, slow, catlike moves toward the car. She threw the gears into reverse and backed, ready to turn and speed away, when a voice called sharply, "Nemo!" The wolf turned, docile as a house pet, and wagged its long brush of tail.

Somewhere a window closed. Across the raised brick terrace the front door opened—tall and carved, with a big brass knocker. A figure appeared, small in that expanse, an old man thin and bent as a ginseng root, all in black with a high, winged collar. A butler. Far out!

But it was a woman's voice that cried "Nemo!" again from the depths of the house. And the wolf ran up the terrace steps, skirting the old fellow in the doorway, and disappeared inside.

She got out and closed the car door—gently, so as not to disturb the sudden quiet broken only by the cry of a piñon jay.

She approached the house, mounted the steps, crossed the brick terrace, and opened her mouth to say hello. But the old man bowed stiffly from the waist and, turning, muttered, "This way, mum." A British accent. Too much.

He led her across a tiled hallway, up several broad steps, and into a drawing room. It ran the full width of the house, its two ends great expanses of glass framing, to the east, the mountains rising sharply behind the house, and to the west, over the top of the low piñon forest, the desert with its low volcanic hills and in the distance what might be clouds but could be the Sandias.

"Good morning, my dear." The clear, low-pitched voice startled her, the voice that had called off the wolf who now lay like the Sphinx in the glow from the fireplace, his tongue lolled out in a grin. He eyed her with his ears tipped forward.

"Oh," Gin said, "I'm sorry. I didn't see you."

Perdita Waldheimer sat in the shadows, obscured by the light from the expanse of glass behind her, where she could see her visitor before being seen.

"Sit down, my dear."

It was more a command than an invitation. Gin glanced at the household pet.

"Nemo's harmless," Perdita Waldheimer said.

The benefactor glided toward her with a small, whirring sound. Nemo got up and moved toward his mistress, who parked her wheelchair beside a small drum table near the fire. She dropped a hand on the wolf's broad head.

The old man came and stood by the door.

"Yes, Jack," Perdita Waldheimer said, "bring us some coffee. There's a good fellow."

Gin glanced toward him and Perdita Waldheimer chuckled a surprisingly throaty chuckle. "Don't mind Jack," she said. "He only plays at being a servant. Otherwise he wouldn't know what to do with himself. He was Burrell's batman." Perdita Waldheimer put the accent on the *Burr*, and the '*r*'s were guttural. "After that, Charley was stuck with him for life. I inherited Jack.

"Come closer." She reeled out pince-nez on a delicate silver chain and settled them on her nose. "Let me see you."

Gin drew a chair nearer the fire. She wanted a better look herself. The bright morning window backlighting Perdita still obscured her face.

It had once been handsome. Gin saw that immediately. Was handsome still. The features precise—sculpted nose, firm mouth—and behind the pince-nez the eyes were very blue. Heavy hair, cut short and falling in choppy waves, a bit of pepper mixed yet with the salt.

"Miss . . . Prettifield, is it?" the benefactor said, glancing at a note she'd written to herself on the back of an envelope and stuffed in the pocket of her cashmere cardigan. "An Indian name?"

"Actually . . ." Gin said, and explained about her great-great-grandfather Andre Beauchamp.

Perdita Waldheimer laughed—not politely but with pleasure. "So George Cameron is in London. I'm not surprised. He ought to move over there. Now what was it you wanted? Oh, yes. The Rembrandt provenance."

She reached slowly, painfully, with a trembling hand, to the drum-top table beside her, on which rested, in addition to the lamp, a magnifying glass, a telephone, an address file, a vase of yellow roses, a small flashlight of the kind backpackers use to minimize weight, a box of nougat candies, a Chinese lacquer saucer full of plastic vials that looked like prescription drugs, and a packet of papers in a rubber band.

"This is my filing cabinet," Perdita Waldheimer said, indicating the jumbled tabletop. "It's here somewhere. I really should let the museum have these. Might not be safe, keeping them here like this." She took up the packet of papers in the rubber band. "But it's hard to let them go. I like reading them now and then."

She smiled across at Gin, who began to relax.

"Here it is," her hostess said, flipping through the papers, stopping, pulling one out. "The Rembrandt." She offered it with that trembling hand on which the rings were loose, and diamonds sparkled in the firelight.

Gin leapt up and took it and settled back in her chair as Jack brought in a tray with a coffeepot, thin china cups, a cut-glass bowl piled high with whipped cream, and a fifth of Irish whiskey.

He set the tray on the cluttered tabletop and started to pour, but his mistress fanned him away. Unsteadily she poured herself coffee, added a splash of whiskey, and topped it with a dollop of whipped cream. "I like a bit of stimulant after breakfast," she said. "They tell me it strengthens the blood. I know it strengthens nerve."

Nerve for what? For getting through the day?

Jack offered Gin the tray. She poured herself coffee and helped herself to whipped cream. But whiskey at ten in the morning?

"Allow me," Jack said in a wavering voice from the height of his thin, luminous face. He had to be well over ninety.

He poured the whiskey while surreptitiously she examined the room in which Spanish *santos* hobnobbed with Hopi kachinas, and a heraldic shield on the chimney seemed at home with *mimbres* designs on the hearth.

"Thank you." Gin unfolded the provenance.

"Go ahead, read it, my dear, though you may take it with you if you like. I've no objection. Take them all. These are only the provenances of the four old masters, of course. The others are in a safe-deposit box at Noldes's bank, but Cameron and Noldes know all about that."

With trepidation Gin sipped and put the cup down beside her on the hearth. She began to read.

Provenance of small landscape similar to *The Polish Rider* and painted close to the same date, around 1660. Sold at auction to satisfy the artist's debts. Purchased by Italian family, hung in their villa from 1669 to 1748. Sold to French dealer, who resold it in 1759 to Sir Joshua Reynolds (1723–1792), a collector of Rembrandt's work and largely responsible for bringing him back into favor. Presented by Reynolds to the fourth Earl of Tor (1717–1799) c. 1777 in appreciation for commission to paint the earl's family and enjoying a summer at Mousehole.

The second page, attached, gave the provenance in its usual form.

Collection: the Princippi Antonio Rinaldi, Rome, from the
             artist to satisfy his debts. Died 1675.

             His son, Bassanio (1655–1710), who went to live
             in Sicily c. 1680.

             Giulietta (1701–1779), daughter of Bassanio,
             who married the Frenchman Count Pierre
             LaPerouse (1677–1725), and thence by descent
             to a member of the family. Sold to dealer said
             to be Cutron, Paris, c. 1748.

             Acquired by Sir Joshua Reynolds (1723–1792)
             c. 1759.

             A gift from him to the fourth Earl of Tor (1717–
             1799) c. 1777.

             Acquired by Charles Burrell in 1936 and from
             him by bequest to Perdita Waldheimer of Santa
             Fe, New Mexico.

             A gift to the Waldheimer Museum in Santa Fe,
             New Mexico, 1979.

A skip of over a hundred fifty years between the fourth
Earl of Tor and Charley Burrell. She bent over the prove-
nance and read it again while Perdita Waldheimer's eyes
bored into the top of her head.
   "I envy you," her hostess said.
   Gin sipped her Irish coffee.
   "Reading it through, I mean, just like that," Perdita said.
"I don't regret growing old but for my eyes and my knees."
   Jack returned with thin wheat crackers and a wedge of
Camembert on a board.
   Perdita cut into the soft cheese, steadying the knife with
one hand on top of the other. "At my age you may as well
eat what you want when you want it." She poured herself
more coffee, splashed it with Irish whiskey, and added an-
other dollop of whipped cream.

Gin smiled. "You still seem young."

"I still *feel* young, but one's body lets one down, and none too gently." She smeared a wheat cracker with the Camembert and passed it to Gin with a trembling hand, a surprisingly intimate gesture.

Gin took the cracker and stuffed it in her mouth. Delicious.

"Now, my dear, what is it you want to know?"

"Well," she said, "the provenance only says, 'Acquired by Charles Burrell in 1936.' How did he acquire it? Did he buy it from this"—she glanced at the papers—"Earl of Tor? And what is this"—she glanced again—"Mousehole?" Did it really say Mousehole?

Perdita Waldheimer smiled and hummed a little hum that perhaps she herself did not hear.

"Mousehole," she said, "is a small point of land a few miles from Penzance, not far from Land's End, which is the westernmost point of land in England, there where the English Channel runs into the Atlantic."

Gin watched her hostess reach for a package of Gauloises and fit one with those trembling fingers into the gold tip of a very long holder. She wanted to leap up and help. "Keeps the smoke out of my eyes," Perdita explained.

"A strange name for a place," Gin murmured.

"Oh, I don't know," the benefactor said. "I suspect a mousehole is a sea cave—one of those indentations in the coastal cliffs disclosed at low tide and hidden when the tide is high. You've seen them, I'm sure, if you've been to Britain."

Gin nodded that she had. The honors' tour. They'd bummed around England, Ireland, and Wales with backpacks in the rain.

Perdita held a lighter to the Gauloise and blew out a cloud of smoke.

Gin searched vainly for a way to rephrase the question her hostess had ignored. "Perdita is an unusual name," she said.

"I was named for Shakespeare's Perdita in *The Winter's Tale*," the heiress said. "But Burrell called me Perdie, though I've never been Perdie to anyone else."

Small wonder, Gin thought. She was not a woman to whom one easily applied diminutives.

Perdita Waldheimer picked up something from the jumble on the drum table and handed her a snapshot in a leather frame. "That's Burrell and me."

Gin bent over it and peered at two blurred figures in the old photo—a man and a woman in high-crowned, wide-brimmed hats and fitted knee boots laced up over those cord pants that flared at the thighs, leaning against a touring car. The background faded away to white, they could have been anywhere. Their faces were shaded, they might have been anybody.

"You can't tell much from that old thing," Perdita said crossly. "That's a portrait of him—there, by the entry—when he was older."

Gin looked. It was a friendly, open face, a face that you found immediately familiar, like someone you'd known somewhere but couldn't quite place.

"He was in the First War," Perdita Waldheimer said. "The Great War as we called it—though what's great about any war, I'll never know. As I said, Jack was his batman. They were in the Argonne Forest, the only two of their group to survive. Jack was not seriously wounded. He played dead and lived, though they fired into the bodies littering the field, the damned Germans, the *Boche*." She spoke with such vehemence it might all have happened yesterday.

"When night fell, Jack wandered all over the blighted wood, turning up the eyes of corpses to the moon, until he found Burrell. He carried him for miles—stumbling, starving—till he came upon a farmhouse where people were hiding in a root cellar, coming out only at night, terrified of the Huns.

"Burrell was unconscious for a month, and when he woke up he was utterly changed. They say it can happen in a coma. From a British officer all spit and polish, he'd turned into a renegade. Toward the end of his life, he grew interested in some crackpot theory about Walk-ins: you die and another entity comes into your body and you wake up as someone else altogether. The idea, I gather, is that these . . . Walk-ins . . . are coming to save mankind. Teachers, you see,

from some higher level of being.'' She laughed. ''The closest Burrell came to being a teacher was the way he had of
debunking foolishness.''

''Fascinating,'' Gin murmured. In the guise of straight-
ening her skirt over her knees, she snatched a look at her
watch.

''He came out of the coma a different man. He would
never kill again. Nor be killed if he could help it. He saw the
whole thing as an idiocy of the human spirit surviving from
Neanderthal: fight, kill, rape, burn, bomb, pillage. He was
through with all that. He didn't look for his outfit, he just
got up and walked away from the war.''

''You mean he deserted?''

''Call it what you like. He came to his senses.''

Gin nodded approvingly.

Perdita sighed. ''Boys will be boys. Can you imagine
women fighting a war? Try telling a bunch of women that
another bunch, across the Channel, are their mortal enemies
that have to be killed, and they must dress up in monkey suits
and go shoot them, maim them, cut them to pieces, destroy
their homes, their pantries, their kitchen gardens, their towns,
their children . . .''

''I see what you mean.''

''If all males came to their senses as Charley Burrell did,
there'd be the end of the foolishness.'' She reached for the
photograph and while she looked at it, frowning with dissatisfaction, Gin snuck a squirt of the herbal tincture into her
Irish coffee.

''This . . . Mousehole, is it in Cornwall?'' This could lead
to how Charley Burrell had come by the four old masters.

Perdita nodded. ''The ancestor of the earls of Tor was
related to the Killigrews of Cornwall, who managed a pirate
syndicate. I suppose piracy is a natural profession for an
island people. They operated out of Pendennis Castle and
Arwennecke in Cornwall. Both are near Falmouth.''

Gin sipped her coffee, relaxed, almost mellow.

''Lady Killigrew,'' Perdita said, ''was the directing genius. She was assisted by her brother-in-law, Peter, a pirate
in the Irish Sea, and they operated in Cornwall, Devon, Dor-

set, Wales, and South Ireland. Their kinsman, the ancestor of Tor, was their factor in Devon.''

''Just like a legitimate corporation.''

''Everybody who was anybody in Cornwall in the seventeenth century was a pirate or a wrecker. A wrecker was a salvager of wrecked ships. And when there weren't any wrecks, he wasn't above arranging a few, helping some poor vessel onto the rocks by means of misleading lights, and doing away with survivors. Sir John, Lady Killigrew's husband, was appointed Commissioner for Piracy in 1577. That is, he was appointed to suppress piracy.'' Perdita Waldheimer chuckled.

Gin heard herself giggle.

''Exactly, Miss Prettifield. Like appointing a wolf to guard the sheep.''

''Oh, please. Call me Gin.''

''Very well. Gin. And you must call me Perdita. This factor in Devon was, you see, the first earl of Tor.''

The room was getting warm. Gin made herself concentrate.

''Well, he wasn't any earl then—just a pirate like the rest of the cutthroats. But he got rich off the loot and bought himself a title. Oh, nothing much, he was only a squire. Are you all right, my dear?''

''Oh, I'm fine.'' But she couldn't stop nodding.

''His descendants took the monarchist side during Cromwell's reign,'' Perdita said. ''And when the Stuarts were restored, the current Sir was rewarded with the title of Earl, and lands in Devon and Cornwall. A sizable domain. And hence Mousehole Castle, Cornwall, built by the third earl.''

How all this connected with Perdie Waldheimer and Charley Burrell Gin had no idea.

''Bushmill's,'' Perdita said.

''I beg your pardon?''

''Bushmill's distillery.'' Her hostess pointed to the bottle of whiskey on the tray. ''In Northern Ireland, the oldest distillery in the world. It was taken over last year by a multinational conglomerate. Tells you what's happening all over. It made the Irish very sad.''

It made Gin sad, too. She could have wept.

"Have you seen Mousehole?" She thought she was being crafty. She was looking for some connection of all this to Perdita.

"I have." Perdita Waldheimer crushed out the Gauloise and carefully chose a nougat and offered the box to Gin, who brushed it away like so many gnats.

"The point of land near Mousehole is gorgeous," Perdita said, "when the weather's right. It's a rocky peninsula looking out to sea. But it's gray and cold when the fog comes in. Mousehole is east of the Eddystone Light. You've heard of the Eddystone Light."

Perdita sang out in a voice surprisingly lusty,

"My father was the keeper of the Eddystone Light

"And he slept with a mermaid one fine night.

"And from this union there came three,

"A porpoise and a porgy and the other was me."

As Perdita kept time with a fist on her knee, it seemed no more than polite for Gin to do likewise. Then suddenly the song ended, leaving her with a fist she didn't know what to do with.

Perdita laughed. "When Burrell had a few, he'd recite that at the top of his lungs. If I was waiting up for him and he was unsure of his reception, he'd start in before he hit the door, knowing it would soften me up and give me a laugh."

"And who—I mean how—I mean, your Charley, the changed man, how did he get the Rembrandt? And Tor. What *is* this Tor? I understand Mousehole, I think, but—"

"A tor, my dear, is a geological formation. It's a little hill. There are lots of those in Cornwall. Hence the earls of Tor."

"Oh, of course, I see. Goodness, I'd better be going," she said, putting the Rembrandt provenance in her purse. She had to get back to town. She was due shortly at Josie's on Marcy, to meet the chairman for lunch.

Perdita handed her the packet. "Take them all," she said. "You might as well. You should have had them long ago." She leaned forward, patting her wolf on the head, and got slowly to her feet. She picked up her elegant black cane with a gold head and, taking Gin's arm, walked slowly with her to the head of the three broad, low stairs in the hall.

"Come again, my dear," she said, patting Gin's hand, looking up, for the assistant director was much taller. "I've liked our little visit."

"Oh, may I, really . . . come again—to see you, I mean?" She knew she was chattering, but she seemed unable to stop.

The benefactor patted the assistant director's arm. Again that little hum from somewhere high in the back of her cranium. Steadied by the cane, she stood watching Gin descend. Jack held the door. "Good-bye, mum," he said. "Do come again. We enjoy a lively visit."

"Oh, I will," Gin said, and turned and gave Perdita a wave. She thought of blowing a kiss but was uncertain of the propriety.

She flew down the winding drive. It was like a roller coaster, but as it was about to dump her out on the Old Santa Fe Trail she slammed on the brakes, got out, and fanned herself with the hem of her shirt. She needed to clear her head. A pickup passed, its bed full of Spanish workmen. They called out to her and waved and whistled, and she waved after them, smiling. Such friendly fellows, such a pretty day.

The air was resiny. A piñon tree beside the road was full of nuts. She took off her denim jacket and laid it on the ground, then grabbed a branch and shook it. Piñon nuts rained down. She gathered them up in a bundle and walked back to the rig, where she sat for a while, cracking the soft mahogany hulls between her teeth, marking with her eye the location of the tree. She and Magda could come back for the harvest.

Now straighten up, she told herself. It was almost noon. Before driving into town she had to go by the hospital and check on Raoul Query. Then lunch with Noldes. He'd hoped to get Pablo to join them. Then a quick visit to her office to check the mail and off to Benito Montoya's studio, where the pod was invited this afternoon for the "visit to an artist's studio" promised by their tour brochures. An assistant director's job was never done.

The sky was very blue and the mountains in a haze. She

felt clear and ready for anything. The herbal tincture was a marvel.

13

After Perdita's, straight to the hospital and the Intensive Care Unit. Raoul Query was still on the critical list. Her conscience smote her. She'd hardly given him a thought since last night. Tentatively she pushed in the door and was startled by the uniformed guard inside.

The officer, a plump young woman with curly fair hair, said, "You can't come in here, miss."

She hated being addressed that way. Across the uniformed shoulder she glimpsed the nurses' station in the center of the unit and patients' cubicles around the outside walls, in one of them a youngish man, probably an accident victim, with half his face scabbing and crusted, eyes closed, an IV bottle dangling overhead.

The guard was apparently guarding the cubicle to Gin's left. A small anteroom separated the ICU entry from ICU-3. Through the glass, she saw Raoul Query with his head swabbed in white. She felt a surge of pity for the man lying there alone, a stranger in a strange town.

"I have orders to allow nobody entry but the attending medical staff," the officer said.

"Yes, of course," Gin said. "How is he?"

"Are you a member of the victim's family?"

She hesitated, looking past the guard at the nurses' station, a lopsided triangular island in the center of the ICU. There were two nurses at the desk. One was annotating a chart. The other stared across the room at her.

"No," she said, "I'm from the museum where it happened."

"Information can only be given to members of the victim's family," the plump officer said.

"But he doesn't have any family here that I know of."

The policewoman looked straight ahead and said no more. Not knowing what else to do, Gin backed into the hall and let the door close.

"Miss Prettifield?"

She turned. It was one of the poddies, the one with the hint of a hump. "I'm Hanna Enright." The woman put out a hand. She had nice eyes and a smile that made her younger than her short gray hair implied. "I told them I was his sister, so they let me go in for a minute."

"Have you seen the lieutenant? Has he any idea what happened?"

"If he does he isn't saying."

Hanna Enright opened her purse, looked inside, and closed it again. "There's been some dissension in our group."

Telling herself it was none of her business, Gin asked, "What about?"

"Oh, just some feelings. I've gone into all that with the lieutenant." Then she explained what Gin already knew, that the lovely Ellen had married first Raoul Query, and then Victor Weldon.

Gin said, "I can see how that might cause mixed feelings in the group."

"Yes, well, it wasn't that exactly." Hanna Enright wandered over to the tall corridor window. Outside in the small roof garden, a patient's family was spreading a picnic lunch on one of the round stone tables. "Ellen was the heart of the group. She was extraordinary."

"How do you mean?"

Hanna Enright turned back from the window. Her look focused somewhere beyond Gin's ear. "Oh, she was funny, subtle, intelligent, a wonderful listener, marvelous friend. There's not another like her. Not anywhere." Her voice trailed off. She looked at Gin. "Ellen had cancer. The doctors had given her up. It was . . . disturbing." Her voice peaked and broke on the word, which hardly described the naked pain on her face.

Gin looked out the window to where a child stood on a

stone bench and poured lemonade from a thermos into a
paper cup. Embarrassed, she was wondering where exactly
Hanna Enright had been the night before, when she
screamed. In the corridor? In the Gallery of Western Art?
She turned back full of questions she didn't know how to
ask.

Tears had surfaced in Hanna Enright's eyes. She pulled a
crumpled Kleenex out of her pocket and blew into it. "I'm
sorry," she said. "I must be coming down with something."
She looked for a place to dispose of the Kleenex, and, not
finding one, stuffed it into her pocket. "I really must be
going. I'm meeting the group for lunch." Before Gin could
say anything, she turned and hurried down the corridor, leaving the assistant director certain that not two but three members of the pod had been in love with lovely Ellen.

With a parting glance at the closed door of the ICU, Gin
headed toward the exit past the X-ray Department.

"Parvenu!"

Gin whirled. "Elsie!"

It had been their standard greeting since the night they last
played Password in Magda's kitchen. An inveterate worker
of crossword puzzles, Magda's best friend Elsie Cooper had
come up with "parvenu" and Magda had bounced a rolled
newspaper off the top of her head. "Parvenu! How am I
supposed to know what that means?"

Elsie, with cropped brown hair, was as small and spare as
Magda was large and opulent. "What're you doing here?"
she said. "Are you sick? Hurt? Any broken bones?"

"No. I'm fine." Elsie was an X-ray technician. The hospital was her bailiwick, and she knew everybody from Maintenance to the president.

"What brings you up the hill?" Elsie asked. "Got a
minute? Follow me."

Once in the lounge around the corner, Elsie lit a cigarette
while Gin told her about Raoul Query.

"Oh, sure," Elsie said. "I was on call last night. They
beamed me up here three times, last time at four A.M. Guy
went to sleep with his cruise control on. He had my sympa-
thy. I was on cruise myself by then. How's Query doing? I
took lots of pictures."

"They won't tell me anything," Gin said. "I'm not a relative."

"Oh, shit." Elsie crushed her cigarette out in the sandbox and marched back to the ICU, Gin trailing at a distance and waiting outside.

"Still unconscious," Elsie said, returning, "not responding to the drugs."

"That sounds bad."

"It's not good."

"How long do you think before he'll . . . ?"

"No telling. He could start responding any time now. Or he might not. In that case . . . They find out who hit him?"

"I don't know. I don't think so."

Elsie hiked her head hallward. "C'mon. Things have quieted down here since last night. I'll show you the pictures."

Gin followed down a short corridor with a mural of the Albuquerque hot air balloon festival on the wall, then through a door with CAUTION: RADIATION AREA in big red letters, and into a room out of *Star Trek*. She eyed the booms and monitors and dials, everything in gray. What looked like a TV screen hung on an arm from the ceiling. In the place of prominence, like the altar in a space-age temple, a long, gray elevated table.

Elsie beckoned her behind the lead wall partition where she hung up a series of X rays like clothes on a line.

"There he is." She thrummed a finger across several transparencies.

Any way you looked at it, it was a skull.

"See? Here, look." Elsie pointed. "That's an epidural hematoma."

Even his skull was handsome. "You're talking to a parvenu, you know. You might have to draw me pictures."

Elsie laughed her hoarse, short bark. "Okay. Listen. A hematoma is a bruise—blood puddling where the blood vessels have been smashed. Got that?"

Gin nodded.

"Okay. Look." A blond young man greeted Elsie and passed through a door into an inner sanctum behind them. Elsie made three short parallel slashes with her pencil on a memo pad. "The first's the skull, second's the derma, third's the film around the brain. A subdural hematoma comes between the skull and the derma. That's not so bad. We drill holes through the skull and the blood spurts out, releases the pressure. See? Patient comes around."

"But you said—"

"He's got an epidural hematoma, and that's more serious. It means the puddle of blood is between the derma and the brain. Now we're in delicate territory."

Gin said what she'd been afraid to say last night. "I guess somebody tried to kill him?"

The young man came out again, and before the door closed you could hear voices beyond it.

Elsie shrugged. "Somebody hit him one hell of a blow over the head with a not-so-blunt instrument. And heavy, from the look of it. It struck pretty deep. One sixteenth of an inch deeper and . . ."

Gin was looking at a panel of red and amber lights on the console beside them, thinking: art forgery, theft, attempted murder. How many people had known the director would be away and the museum left in the hands of a parvenu? She felt the vein worming its way down her forehead.

"That lieutenant . . . What's his name?"

"Tito Gonzales."

"He was here at the crack of dawn. I showed him these. Told him what I'm telling you. The doctor could tell him more."

"Did he talk to the doctor?"

Light flashed off Elsie's glasses. "I'd think so, sure," she said with her Texas accent. "But the doctor's gone by now. He was on duty all night in the ER. He's home asleep, lucky dog."

"Do you think . . . Is he going to make it?"

Elsie shrugged. "They might have to go in again, do some more drilling to relieve the pressure."

Gin shuddered.

"Too bad. Subdurals are routine procedure these days."

A light was flashing. Footsteps hurried down the hall. "Tell you what, gimme a call later. I'll find out what I can and let you know."

"You're a peach, Elsie."

"I've always been told I'm a nut." Elsie held the door for an orderly pushing a gurney. A young man with a badly barked cheek grinned up at them, embarrassed to be caught flat on his back. "Crap," Elsie muttered. "Cycle accident. If the child from twenty to forty would lay off his toys, my job would be easier."

From the hospital straight to Josie's on Marcy Street for lunch with Noldes and, she hoped, Pablo—two meals alone in one day with the chairman might wreck her nerves.

She stuck her head inside. They were in the first booth, too engrossed to notice she was late. They both did a little hunched half rise off the booth's benches, clutching their napkins.

They had enchiladas and she had tamales. She only half listened while, as males will, the two sparred politely—Pablo with charm and persistence and all that expertise, Noldes with his cold eyes and the weight of his physical presence. On some far back burner of her brain she considered apricot pie for dessert.

Pablo: Perhaps it was best to send thees painting immediately to the Metropolitan Museum in New York City to 'ave it vetted.

Chairman: You can't turn over to UPS an artwork valued in the millions.

But of course not, nor would they take it, Señor. However, eef I am right, and weeth all due humility I believe that I am (chuckle), you would be entrusting something worth a great deal less. I might, if you like, take it with me to the Dallas conference and convey it to Señor Davies, who might then take it with him to the Metropolitan in New York.

The chairman looked doubtful.

A deep Latin sigh. But it is essential that something be done. Even a little time lost can make all the deeference.

Gin was struck suddenly with an idea of her own. She was delighted by its clarity and simplicity. Would it work? If it did, it could cut through all this red tape.

"How is the old girl?" Noldes asked, turning to her, prodding her into saying something. The waitress brought a carafe of ice water.

Gin found it hard to reconcile Perdita Waldheimer with ''the old girl.''

''Let's have the provenance.''

She dug in her purse and handed over the packet. He thumbed through, took one out, and unfolded it. But her silence apparently made the chairman uncomfortable. He trained his gaze upon her. ''You meet the wolf?''

''Yes. Nemo. Very well behaved. For a wolf.''

''Well behaved my ass. He took a pants leg off my wife.''

She visualized Mimi Noldes with her bouffant hair and one pants leg ripped off at the knee. She smiled.

Lloyd Noldes watched intently. How seriously should he take these two?

''It seems desirable to do something with all deliberate speed,'' Pablo was saying.

Gin agreed.

The chairman said to her, ''Have you tried to reach Davies again?''

Pablo turned to her. ''I will go with you to telephone.''

14

There was still a police car nosed into the piñons at the end of the parking lot. Juan opened the door for them.

The museum had been closed all morning while the police searched the building and grounds, interested only in such things as The Weapon. She suspected Tito no more believed the Rembrandt was forged than did the chairman of the board. But now, except for the Gallery of Western Art, which was cordoned off with a band that read CRIME SCENE: OFF-LIMITS, the museum was open to the public.

When Pablo headed for the East Room, she glanced into the Gallery of Western Art. Tito Gonzales was walking slowly around, as if looking at the pictures, one hand in his trousers pocket, the other squeezing his chin.

She hurried to her office and called the hospital, but an angiogram was in progress and she couldn't get through to Elsie, whom she urgently wanted to talk to. She tried Davies's Dallas hotel. All circuits busy. Waiting, she shuffled restlessly through the mail. A gift catalog from the Museum of Fine Arts, Boston (save for Olivia); a letter from the curator of the San Francisco Museum hoping to have the Waldheimer represented in an O'Keeffe retrospective (landscape with skull); letters to forward to Cameron in England and one to hold for Davies, scented (she sniffed), from a place called St. Ives. She turned it over and inspected the small colored stamp on the back. It looked like a coat of arms. A woman. She felt instantly hostile to that letter. Two letters from galleries about the Helen Hardin show she was planning for the spring (one enthusiastic, the other quibbling); a request from an heir for comparative values for a Frederic Remington watercolor; a note from a Ph.D. candidate asking whether they'd yet read his article on the German Impressionists. Cameron had agreed to do it then forgotten all about it.

She dialed the hospital again, with the same results. While she waited she turned on her computer and wrote to the San Francisco Museum curator that the interim director was out of town but expected back soon; to the quibbling gallery, answering questions about shipping; to the heir, saying the last Remington watercolor that had come to auction had sold for two hundred and fifty thousand.

She signed the letters and tried phoning the hospital again. Angiogram still in progress and, though the circuits had cleared, the Dallas hotel line was busy. She went to the East Room and found Pablo bent over not the Rembrandt but the Turner.

"Extraordinary," he said.

"It's early. He was still under the influence of Poussin and Lorrain."

Pablo said, "Yes, but the style, my dear Ginnee."

She looked, but saw only what she had always seen.

Pablo brought his shoulders up around his ears in a Latin shrug. "It is a kind of anomaly, Ginnee. Don't you see?"

He took the packet of provenances from his inside coat pocket and shuffled through them rapidly. "Ah!" He read, " 'View of Mousehole Castle, painted in 1792 at the request of the fourth Earl of Tor when Turner, seventeen, was on a walking tour during his summer holiday from the Royal Academy, where he was a student.' "

Mousehole. Tor. Here they were again. What did this mean? Gin braced herself with a hand against the wall. She let her breath out slowly, feeling a weird combination of fear and excitement.

"Very well executed," Pablo said, taking down the Turner and eyeing it. "Look at the authority of the brush strokes. What verve! What style! Only a real artist could do this, perhaps not even Señor Joseph Mallord William Turner when he was only seventeen."

She sank slowly onto the wooden bench and clutched the edge. Now she saw it—hints everywhere in the brush strokes of impressionistic gambols. Not the Turner, too.

Pablo raised his shoulders in a helpless shrug that reminded her of Quillan Davies. "What we 'ave here is apparently an early painting in the late style." He rehung the painting on its hook. "But obviously Señor Turner did not paint in the late style until later."

She got up and turned dizzily in a circle, scanning the Matisse, the Braque, the Cézanne . . .

"No-no-no," he said. "I 'ave looked at them while you were in your office. They are fine. They are all okay. You 'ave my word. They are the real thing." He took her by the shoulders and turned her to the Dürer drawing.

"This, too," he said. "Quite authentic." He moved up close to the drawing and spent some minutes looking. He shifted the papers in his hand till he came to the provenance, and read aloud, " 'Early drawing of a group of animals, done probably about 1502. Drawing came to light in the personal effects of a ship's captain whose vessel 'ad been wrecked on the Cornish coast. Apparently part of the pirate's (wrecker's) spoils after the ship was lured to its death by false lights set out by mooncussers. Last owner, the Earl of Tor.' "

There it was again.

Pablo looked up from the provenance. "What do you theenk is a mooncusser?"

Gin said, "They were the wreckers. I guess they cussed the moon because it meant their false lights wouldn't work, the shore and the rocks could be seen by moonlight from on board the ship."

He read on, " 'A small water stain in the upper left-hand corner of the drawing probably resulted from this wreck.' "

She stood up and moved with dread to the Dürer. But there was the water stain, just as the provenance said. Shaped rather like a sea turtle. "Is it . . . ?"

"I theenk there is no question that the drawing is authentic, Ginnee."

The stain brought that dark night two hundred years ago into the room with them, the vessel bearing this very drawing moving inexorably toward the rocks, the captain as yet unaware he was going to his death—if not in the wreck itself, then at the hands of the wreckers. Gin put a finger to the water mark, then drew it away. A miracle that the drawing, by then already two centuries old, had survived.

"Imagine," she said. "It's five hundred years old." People had kept it, hung it in their rooms—and in ships' cabins— looked at it, treasured it, for all that time. How many generations had lived and died during the life of that simple drawing of a fox, a rabbit, and an owl in a hollow tree? How many hands had it passed through, preserved because people loved art, or liked animals, or hung on to their possessions?

"Do you know Dürer's writings?" Pablo asked.

"I've read his poetry."

"A true man of the Renaissance. An intellectual as well as an artist."

"I've seen prints of his tarot card drawings."

"Oh, yes, the *tarocchi*."

"He went to Italy when he was—what? Twenty-three or four?"

"Yes, and kept going back. Not unusual for a European painter at that time. They loved the warmth, the light. He once wrote a friend before returning to Germany, 'How cold I will be away from the sun.' It was on that first trip that he came across engravings of the *tarocchi*. He based about twenty drawings on them. Amazing things, precise reproductions of the human body. Figure drawings, actually. It was about 1492, I theenk.''

''About the time your Columbus discovered''—the Sioux in her smiled—''America.''

''Not *my* Columbus, Ginnee. I am more Aztec than conquistador.''

She moved with trepidation to the Van Dyck and made herself ask, ''What about this one?''

Please, she prayed. But what her heart hoped, as she stood there looking, her intelligence slowly denied. There were the rough textures of Van Dyck, and the dark, warm colors, but she sank with foreboding onto the bench while Pablo examined the painting.

''The canvas is old,'' he said. ''But forgers go to great lengths to find authentic canvas. Usually they paint over old paintings that have no value.''

She was holding her breath.

Finally he said, ''I know very little about Van Dyck.'' She suspected what seemed very little to Pablo might be a great deal. ''Though next to Peter Paul Rubens he was the finest of the seventeenth-century Flemish painters. They were different, though. Rubens's glazes were like enamel, but Van Dyck's were like this, rough. Rubens's lines flowed, but Van Dyck's were abrupt.'' He shrugged.

''Was he ever in England?'' she asked. But before Pablo spoke, already she guessed the answer.

''Yes,'' Pablo said. ''Charles the First knighted him and gave him an annual salary. And Van Dyck, for his part, created our image of what English society looked like before the 1648 revolution. His work in England was principally portraits, of which thees, judging from the clothing our nobleman is wearing, must be one.

''What's thees?'' he asked, pointing to a squiggle in the bottom right-hand corner of the painting.

''I don't know,'' she said. She'd taken it for some kind of emblematic signature of the painter.

He straightened and laughed. ''Why, it looks like a mouse.''

Gin's arms were cold, and the cold was spreading to her shoulders. Hugging herself, she moved closer. It was indeed a mouse—head down, tail up—on the painting's pale ocher background.

"The little creature seems to be running down a wall," Pablo said.

The portrait was of a handsome, blue-eyed nobleman, self-assured, clearly privileged, an open, friendly, familiar kind of face, very contemporary, though the strong chin was embellished by a Van Dyck beard.

She took the provenance from Pablo and read without surprise: " 'Portrait of an ancestor of the earls of Tor, painted in 1633.'

"The mouse," she said. "Mousehole was the castle of the earls of Tor."

Pablo chuckled. "We have discovered a little joke of the painter Van Dyck. You must see that thees elucidation is added to the provenance. To explain to future generations the little mouse."

He turned the painting over and touched the back. "The threads of the canvas are uneven, unlike canvas woven on a modern loom. We could get an analysis, but I do not doubt its age." He rehung the Van Dyck on the wall.

"I have an idea, Pablo," she said. And briefly she explained. "Do you think it'll work?"

A smile slowly surfaced on his face. He grasped her by both shoulders. "But Ginnee, it is a stroke of genius."

She looked at her watch. "Oh, God, I've got to get to Tesuque." The pod would be there, and the pod was in town only till Saturday morning. When they left Santa Fe, would the forger leave with them, taking the paintings along? They were staying for the Friday night burning of Zozobra and the onset of Fiesta.

"It may be to our advantage," Pablo said, "that the thief, whoever he may be, still theenks he's gotten away with it."

And maybe he has, Gin thought with a sinking feeling in her pit.

She dropped Pablo on the plaza. He would go to Yucca

Federal and ask Noldes for permission to try her plan. Then she rushed home and took out her raw silk best blouse, *tsk*ing that she'd forgotten to rinse it out the night before, cursing Juan for the streak of dirt at the waist where he'd trapped her against Tina's worktable. She drew from the pocket the scrap of paper retrieved from the basement floor, which turned out to be an old customs mark from the back of the Remington, with half his name on it. Tina again. She reminded herself to remind Tina to reattach it. Tina could get fired if she didn't clean up her act. Then how would she pay her rent?

Then back out Washington and Bishop's Lodge Road to Benito Montoya's in Tesuque.

The rig navigated with difficulty the several right-angle turns on the narrow Tesuque road. It was like driving a Cadillac in an English village—blocking traffic, sawing back and forth to get round a corner. She'd done nothing but hurry all day.

She had been to Benito's once before, arranging for the show, picking out the paintings. A number of drives led down to the river. Benito's had no name on the mailbox. She thought she had found it, came to a dead end, backed and turned and tried again.

This time there were cars parked in the yard—one of them Ted Torrence's Cherokee. She pulled up under a cottonwood blazing gold in the falling sun, peered in the rearview mirror, and steeled herself to enter the sprawling old adobe. Her grandmother had claimed you could read character by looking at a face. Could you tell a thief? Her grandmother probably could, but Gin didn't think she had the knack.

15

If there was one thing she couldn't stand it was walking into a room full of people. Why were they all looking at her? Or was it her imagination? She smiled tentatively, reached up and tucked a tendril of hair behind her ear.

Mrs. Trowber raised a hand and waggled an eager little wave.

They were all there except Raoul Query—Alice Maynard, Victor Weldon, Eric Albin, Hanna Enright, Sheila Wadsworth, Will Nevil the commander, and, of course, Mrs. Trowber—Toby—and Ted Torrence.

Nice to see Benito in his own space, happily at home in an apron as spattered as a de Kooning, pleased at their questions, animated, expansive. It was a large studio with good light, its walls covered with big white foam core panels. He brought out paintings one at a time from a sort of anteroom and held them for his guests to view. The smell of coffee came from another part of the house. His wife would be serving refreshments. Maria Montoya was a beautiful woman—oval-faced, dark almond-shaped eyes—who said little but smiled awkwardly, as if the language being spoken in her house was unknown to her.

The house and land had been in her family for generations. Benito was fixing it up, doing the work himself as his paintings sold and there was money for materials. On her way in, Gin had passed a ladder to the roof—not a picturesque Pueblo Indian ladder made of cedar poles, cross pieces tied with whang, but a functional aluminum extension ladder. Why hadn't Benito's wife been at the opening? They had no children to keep her home.

Ted Torrence watched Gin enter. He didn't much care for

the assistant director. His taste ran to clever women, women of the world as once portrayed on the silver screen by Bette Davis or Joan Crawford. They grabbed you by the arm and called you "dulling." Such women, he admired. Ginevra Prettifield would never be one of them. She hadn't the gift. And her clothes were awful.

He sprawled back on the cot, glad to let Benito take over. These tours wore him out. But they beat working for a living. You gave up a few weeks out of the year, called your soul your own, and got your own work done. He didn't pretend to greatness. His work was frankly decorative, he'd be the first to admit it. It sold very nicely to people trying to match up their couches. That fellow Albin—Eric—wanted to take slides back with him, drop them off in Honolulu with friends of his, a couple of fellows who ran a shop on Kalakaua Avenue in Waikiki. Albin had invited him over, as a matter of fact. It might be fun, if Herman had no objections. Serve Herman right if he went over there and stayed.

One more day to go—Bandelier in the morning, shopping on Canyon Road in the afternoon, and then Zozobra, the giant effigy of Old Man Gloom burned annually to launch Fiesta. Zozobra saved him having to plan the pod's last gala night in Santa Fe.

Alice Maynard, too, saw the assistant director arrive. Attractive girl if she'd do a little something with her hair. In a braid down her back it made her look about fifteen. The museum needed someone older, more socially experienced. How would it be to live in Santa Fe? The group was falling apart over this dreadful business. She'd told Hanna Enright it would test them and they'd come out of it stronger than ever, but to Hanna it had been Ellen who'd held them together. Annoying how they'd all found in Ellen some strange mystique. Had it been there, really? Eric said Ellen was just quiet and let everybody make her up, a vacuum they'd filled with their needs and longings. "When you come right down to it," Eric said, "there wasn't all that much to Ellen Query." They all still thought of her as Ellen Query.

Ellen hadn't made it with poor Raoul, though heaven knows he'd had eyes for nobody else all those years, and back then he could have had anybody. Alice herself had once found

Raoul attractive. But that was years ago. And then Victor had gotten to seem tormented during their marriage, so maybe Ellen wasn't a goddess after all. Of course there was Victor's business. Those damned Arabs. He said they took it as a point of honor to bilk you in some way. The man had depth. And last night—it gave her frissons to think of it—he'd held her hand and confessed to such despair. They were bound by some spiritual tie. She felt it, believed she had felt it all along (she hoped poor Ellen had never guessed), and she knew he'd felt it, too, those moments on the plaza, sitting on the bench, clutching her hand and asking for understanding.

Just look at Eric, not listening at all to what the artist was saying, fixed as he was upon Ted Torrence. In her experience, men always preferred the company of other men. Well, Eric could go hang himself. She'd been alone too long.

Hanna Enright, still nettled over losing control of herself earlier at the hospital, also watched the entrance of the assistant director. Sweet child, she thought. Raoul had taken a fancy to the girl. That was strange. She was nothing at all like Ellen. But Ellen had been too much for him. In the long run he'd been no match for her, though Ellen had turned back to him in the end. Why, Hanna couldn't imagine. Hadn't she realized Hanna had always been there for her? Weldon was not for Ellen, either, never had been. She'd taken his stolidity for strength, his boorishness for reserve. Purely a business mind. But Ellen had brought him into the pod. Now would they ever get rid of him? They would never have accepted him for anyone but Ellen. Without her they were a beached shell with the life gone out of it.

When Hanna Enright looked at the pod objectively—as she did more and more these days—she was led to wonder at the change in herself over the years. These were her closest friends. But how could it be? What had she in common with any of them? She'd been very shy in school, when they'd taken her up. Because they lived in close proximity, in the rumble-tumble way of children, more than anything else. She'd been the intellectual, as Raoul was the artist, Eric the aesthete, Sheila the clown. Their roles in the pod became their identities, really. And had they achieved any other?

Commander Will Nevil watched Gin covertly as she ranged

distractedly around the room. Strange, elusive creature with a kind of awkward grace. On the whole he liked Americans, though they insisted on touching you, a clap on the back or a hand on your arm. It always came as a shock. But he'd soon be back on board the good old *York*. Fine ship, good mates. He wished right now he could share a beer with the lot of them and have this business over. But he'd do anything for Bunny. A strange charade, the whole business. There was justice in it, oh, no question. And he liked these poddies well enough. And they'd been close to Ellen. It had taken all his nerve to look her up, and then to learn . . . He still dreamed about her. They were on the deck of a ship, together at the rail. She had a scarf around her throat, some filmy color, and the wind caught it and . . .

What rot. When he got back to Pearl he'd soon ship out. A cruise to Hong Kong and home by Christmas. He'd had his fill of this artsy business. Not his cup of tea. And speaking of tea, he'd jolly well love a cup. How long could this artist fellow go on talking?

Toby Trowber found it depressing, watching the little painter slowly realize that the questions were stupid or, worse, inane, and his answers, gently nudging the visitors in the direction of sense, taken as too grand, too serious, too passionate. Watching him grind slowly to a halt, all passion draining out of him, brought Mrs. Trowber down. She wanted to go to him and turn him away, say something intelligent, let him talk really about the work, speak with all the eloquence of which he was evidently capable. It would all be lost on her. She knew nothing at all about painting, she only knew what she liked.

She decided suddenly to buy a painting. She liked them, really she thought she did, and she had more money than she knew what to do with. It might be a good investment. Such a sweet little wife. They ought to be having babies. She'd have to speak with Ginevra Prettifield.

Eric Albin was glad the private showing was over. Nice, of course, to be able to say you'd been. Montoya was making a name for himself. He had talent, but what a Götterdämmerung. He wondered what Ted Torrence painted. He would like to see. And he had brought along photographs of his own jewelry designs. He could show them to Torrence and get his opinion. They could get together, just the two of them. Pod members were clearly getting on each other's nerves. Why else would Weldon . . . ? The man was a brute. No wonder poor Ellen did away with herself. If that's what really happened. He'd never have thought she had the nerve, swimming out in the dark that way. (Little mouse feet ran up his spine.) Grand, though. In keeping with all the notions they'd built up around her, as people did around lovely women. And she had been lovely. If he'd, say, been born a woman, he'd have wanted to look like that—even to the gray streak lately appearing in her hair. Often she'd said to him. "You're the only one that makes me laugh. And laughter's the only answer for it." For what? he wondered.

He heard Sheila talking in her tiresome way to the Trowber woman. "Are crimes getting worse? You'd think it, what with all this devil worship—which I find quite boring, as if the imagination itself lacked subtlety—and that horrible Dahmer affair . . . But serial killers are nothing new. It's just that now the media brings them into your living room. There was a bandit from Columbia . . . I'd do a book on him, but the drug situation won't allow me to go down there and do the proper research. He'll have to wait. They called him Sparks *Rojas*—Red Sparks, I guess that means—and he killed at least six hundred people. Some sources put it higher. He was caught in the early sixties."

Sheila used to be fun, downright comical, though she hadn't known it. They all used to play volleyball, usually after sundown when they had the beach to themselves except for people walking their dogs. Sheila, all arms and legs, flailed around, batting any old way. Exhausted, she'd leap up in the air and land sprawling. She used to be a hoot.

"But at present I'm working on John Murrell."

The Trowber woman murmured a question.

"He worked the Natchez Trace in the 1830s, taking advantage of slaves. He'd find a big, strapping fellow working in the fields and, pretending to be an abolitionist, lure him away on the pretense of leading him to freedom. Pretty soon he'd claim to be out of money and talk the slave into letting himself be sold. He'd sell the poor slave and off they'd run again. A few repeats of this charade and the slave would get suspicious. So Murrell killed the poor fellow and found himself another. He killed so many people Mark Twain christened him a 'wholesale rascal,' unlike Jesse James, who was only a 'retail rascal.' ''

Ellen had found Sheila amusing. Their families had been close. They'd played together as children. But Sheila seemed to suffer not at all over poor Ellen's death. He hated these people who were always saying it was for the best. She no longer depended on any of them for emotional support. That was supposed to be a strength but he found it grotesque. He could never be like that. Relationship mattered to him. They were a family. And families hang together. You can't like everybody in a family, can you? You know each other too well.

Ted Torrence yawned and smiled across the room at him with a kind of complicity, and this pleased Eric immensely. Here came the tea and coffee. The wifey passing the tray was nice. If he'd been born a woman, he'd take those eyes. He'd do something different with the hair.

Almost with consternation, Gin found herself sitting on the edge of the sofa beside Victor Weldon, and when he turned without interest to look at her, heard herself saying inanely, "Have you enjoyed your afternoon?"

His hair, torn as always by raking fingers, and his anguished eyes, conveyed contempt for her pleasantry. He said, "I know nothing whatever about art. It's a subject that interests me very little."

This rude honesty, far from putting her off, won her respect. "Then you must have found the week quite boring."

"On the contrary," he said.

She waited for some elaboration, but none was forthcoming. There was something brutal about his scarred and rumpled self as he sat there, hands hanging limply between his knees. The clothes of convention fitted him poorly. Maybe he saw through veneers and found preferable whatever lay beneath.

She couldn't think of anything more to say. She rose from the couch, stood for a moment, then moved toward the others while Victor Weldon watched.

Awkward girl, he thought, and corrected himself. Nowadays you had to say 'woman' for everything beyond the onset of puberty. Had she wanted something of him? He could never tell. There were cues he didn't pick up. He often felt he was watching life through a closed window, seeing lips move but unable to read them, watching expressions change too quick to make out.

What was he doing here? Who were these people? He'd inherited them from . . . But he wouldn't think about Ellen. He both admired them and held them in contempt. Admired them for their grace, their ease with one another, and felt contempt for their shallow emptiness. Art. He knew nothing about it. He studied pictures for clues and found none. There was the world, why paint bits of it? These other fellows, this Montoya, painted pictures of nothing at all. He half suspected it was an elaborate joke at the expense of those not in on it. Ellen had been in on it, but she took it all seriously—painting, music . . . Why had she married him? Had she taken him for some alien potentate only to discover he was just a stranger in a world of strangers? This little colony of friends isolated themselves from strangers. And now he had inherited them. He didn't trust it. He could do something for them. That was all it was. They needed him. He had become a necessity. That gave him power, but did he want it? No, he wanted Ellen. Ellen. It seemed to him she was all he had ever wanted in his life. And sitting there on the cot he bent his head and let his face contort into the shape of agony.

Toby Trowber, holding a cup, sidled up to Gin. "What do you hear of poor Mr. Query? I've sent him flowers, but I understand he's still unconscious."

"Yes," Gin said.

"It's very serious, then?"

"I'm afraid so. The police have a guard there around the clock. They must think it's attempted murder."

"Oh, dear." Ought she to speak? Mrs. Trowber wavered, but Bobby wouldn't have. He'd known the difference between right and wrong. But just one more day and she'd be flying home to San Francisco and to Pooley, her little aging cockerpoo, so sensitive he read her mind. Still, wasn't it her duty, after what happened to poor Raoul Query?

When Gin turned away to find a phone, Mrs. Trowber caught her by the arm. "Crime crime crime," she said, startling the assistant director, "it's all these people think about. Miss Prettifield, if anything happens—anything out of the ordinary, like something awful, criminal, I mean—I want you to know I had nothing whatever to do with it."

Gin looked at her.

"I didn't mean to do it," Toby Trowber went on, drawing her aside and lowering her voice. "Oh, all right, I did mean to. I eavesdropped. Last night. At the bar."

What on earth was the widow talking about?

"They were all talking about something Mr. Query had done. Someone thought they ought to call the authorities, but somebody else said they had to keep it to themselves."

Something Query had done? The forgery had been done by a gifted painter. Raoul Query was a painter. His work was in a gallery downtown for anyone to see. She'd seen it herself and admired it, not prejudiced at the time by knowing the artist was handsome and charming. But had it verve? Had it style? It was careful work, a good surface, nice treatment of light, the work of someone who liked to paint and was good at it, but not obsessed, not like Benito. Still . . .

"And then there was something about money," Toby Trowber said. "Getting a lot of money." She watched Gin closely for any sign of disbelief, any telltale clue that the assistant director thought her a babbling fool. "The sum mentioned was quite large, in the millions."

Gin's mouth opened but she didn't know what to say.

"Miss Prettifield . . ."

"Call me Gin. Everybody does."

"I'd like to see you sometime tomorrow, Gin, if that's possible. To talk. I want to buy a painting. One of Mr. Montoya's."

The pod was scheduled to spend the morning at Bandelier and be back in town for lunch, so they set a time in the early afternoon. People around them were saying good-byes, pleading early dinner reservations. Victor Weldon was already out the door. Maria Montoya stood there looking be-

wildered, holding a tray full of empty cups. Gin asked to use
her telephone.

"There's an extension in there," said the painter's wife,
pointing. "Benito uses the storage room as an office. It'll be
a little quieter."

Gin went through a door into a long narrow space, airless,
windowless, with paintings stacked face to the wall. She
pulled the phone toward her across the desk and dialed. While
it rang, she eyed the overhead racks and reached for what
looked like a watercolor, unmatted, bright. She hadn't known
Benito did watercolors.

As she pulled it down, something fell out of the rack to
land face-up before her on the desk. Startled, for a moment
she'd no idea what she was looking at. Then, while the voice
at the other end of the line repeated, "Hello? Hello? Is somebody there?" she gently replaced the receiver in its cradle
and stared at what, as if of its own volition, had wafted down
to her—a copy of a Modigliani drawing, unmatted, in pastels
and colored ink.

"What are you doing!"

Benito, undone and black of face, took the drawing from
her hands and shoved it back in the untidy rack. "This is
student junk."

"I didn't know you gave classes," she murmured.

"I was the student, and he—" he brought himself with
effort under control. "The fool thought the way to develop
talent was to turn it into some kind of copyist."

"Excuse me," she said, and moved away, leaving him
trembling with—rage, or fear? For here was a work with all
the verve, all the style you could hope to find, this Montoya
Modigliani.

16

It was half past eight when she parked the rig in St. Vincent's Parking Lot #2 outside the main entrance to the second level. The hospital, built on a hill with both first and second floors opening at ground level, had a curious shape, roughly a triangular frying pan with a squat rectangular handle. She'd come up here looking for Elsie. Probably a futile effort, but she was in a state of anxiety that compelled her to do something even if it was futile.

The afterglow on the west horizon, visible from this eminence, had long since faded. The lights along St. Michaels Drive and Cerrillos Road ignited the cloud cover brought in by dusk. New Mexico needed rain. It always needed rain. But this thin cloud cover would be burned off by the rising sun tomorrow and there'd be another blue-gold perfect day.

That was the trade-off—rain for sun. New Mexicans wouldn't survive in a sunless place, but perversely—or perhaps consequently—they were always on the watch for rain-bearing clouds. Something told Gin—perhaps her Sioux ancestors—that whenever there's an imbalance of sun and rain, attention turns skyward in search of whichever's in short supply.

It was past visiting hours but the woman at the information desk hardly glanced up. Gin crossed the dark brick floor of the waiting area furnished with banks of red upholstered Siamese chairs, passed the rest rooms, and followed the corridor toward the ICU. She hesitated outside the door. Beyond the big windows, the roof garden was deserted. A man slept with his chin on his chest in one of the chairs in the waiting room. The smell of coffee wafted into the corridor.

Footsteps approached down the hall. She moved into one

of the Plexiglas telephone nodes and pretended to look up a number. A nurse passed into the ICU. An officer still guarded the door to the isolation cubicle where Raoul Query lay, a different officer, a muscular young man with hair long on his neck.

She'd put her foot in the door, meaning to speak to him, when the door jerked out of her hands. Tito Gonzales looked down at her as if trying to place her.

"I came to see how he is," she said.

He glanced toward the bed in the isolation room and grunted noncommittally. "Who's been in here the last hour?" he said to the young officer.

"Only hospital personnel, sir."

"How do you know? How long were you in the john, huh? How long'd it take you to get a cuppa coffee from the waiting room?" He said to the charge nurse—handsome, blond, mid-to-late thirties—who followed him into the corridor, "I want to talk to the other nurse again," and she went back to the nurses' island in the middle of the unit. "What hospital personnel?" he asked the officer.

"Only the other nurses, sir, and one of the orderlies."

"Is something wrong?" Gin asked.

The lieutenant didn't answer. He moved toward ICU-3 and she followed.

Raoul Query was as white as the sheet covering him. The veins at his temple read like a road map. Wherever he was, it was very far away. Gauze swathed his head, leaving his face exposed, a face strangely composed, invulnerable. His left arm was strapped to a board, and a tube fed into it from a hanging bottle. Even the hand looked patient, tolerant, raising no objections at all to these ministrations. A transparent mask covered his nose and chin—oxygen, she supposed, surprised by a surge of feeling. The palm of the hand lay with the fingers half curled—long, sensitive fingers. She put her own curled hand into the open palm and got no response.

A machine beeped regularly beside the bed where a needle drew an illegible scrawl. She withdrew her hand, glancing to see if the lieutenant had noticed. He might have, he avoided looking at her.

The charge nurse returned, accompanied by a younger nurse. In a cubicle across the room, an old woman—eyes closed, thin eyebrows flexed over them like the wings of a bird—groaned in her sleep.

Tito Gonzales turned from looking at something on the table beside Raoul Query's bed. "Let's go over this again," he said to the young nurse. "Just start from the beginning."

The young nurse looked up at him and down. The charge nurse gently prodded, "Chavez?"

Nurse Chavez, with a helmet of neat, straight hair that Gin envied, said, "Well, as I said before, ER called that they were sending a patient up."

"One they never sent."

The nurse frowned and shook her head.

"But you thought you had another patient on the way so you had some things to do to get ready, that right?"

"Yes."

"How long were you out of sight of . . ." He motioned to Raoul Query without looking at him.

"No more than two or three minutes."

"Okay, so you were over there in the corner cubicle getting ready . . ."

Nurse Chavez said, "And I heard the door open. I thought it was the stretcher from ER, so I went on with what I was doing. Then I heard the monitor go off and I rushed back here and the O$_2$ Sats. were at seventy."

"What's that again?"

"They should be at ninety," the charge nurse said. "It meant he wasn't getting oxygenated."

"He wasn't breathing?"

"Just barely," Nurse Chavez said. "I immediately gave him a shot of Narcon."

"About what time this happen?"

"It was ten past eight."

Gin glanced at the wall clock. It was only eight-thirty. The lieutenant must have already been in the building.

"And this Narcon got him breathing again okay."

Nurse Chavez nodded without looking at the lieutenant. Her face was flushed—with annoyance, Gin realized.

"And nobody ever brought that other patient from ER."

"They said nobody from down there called. They couldn't account for it."

Tito nodded. "Was it a man or a woman's voice?"

"I told you I'm not sure. Whoever it was just said, 'This is ER. One's coming up.' "

The lieutenant touched the tube leading from the suspended bottle. "What's this?"

"He's getting Decadron intravenously," Nurse Chavez said. "It reduces swelling of the brain and nervous tissue. In cases of head trauma it's a usual precaution."

"What's this?" He touched a tube.

"Hyperalimentation. Sustacal. Nourishment fed through a tube in the nose leading into the stomach." Her tone suggested annoyance. Apparently she'd been through all this before.

The lieutenant looked at her with surprise, as if he'd caught that, too. Hands in his pockets, he touched his toe to a tube leading from under the sheets to a bag hanging from one of the bed rails. "What's this thing?"

"A Foley catheter," Nurse Chavez said firmly. "It's attached to—"

"I know what a catheter is," the lieutenant said.

Gin thought Nurse Chavez smiled. "We measure the input against the output," she said. "That's very important."

The lieutenant hiked up his trousers by the belt and cleared his throat. "Okay, so when you checked, all these things were fine. Nothing wrong with any of them."

"That's correct," Nurse Chavez said.

"Everything was right except the—"

"Except the epidural in his back. The tube had been removed."

"And the doctor put that in himself?"

Nurse Chavez nodded. "The anaesthesiologist, when the patient was in OR. It feeds Fentenol into the patient at the rate of 4 cc.'s—"

"Maybe instead of dialing 4 cc.'s you dialed 40," the lieutenant said.

Nurse Chavez flushed.

"That possible?" Tito Gonzales asked.

"That's not what happened."

"You're sure about that."

Her head came up and she looked at him with flashing eyes. "I'm positive."

Gin watched the lieutenant process that information. She asked, "Does that mean whoever pulled that thing out of his back knew what he was doing?"

Tito gave her a look that said he could handle the questioning.

"It would appear so," the charge nurse said.

"You check all the medication that comes in here against the chart?" Tito asked Nurse Chavez.

"Yes. I'm required to. It's regular procedure."

Tito turned to look out the window. "Who sets that dial?"

Nurse Chavez said, "I do."

"And you haven't changed it since he come in here last night."

"No." The edge in her voice was sharp.

The charge nurse said softly, "Chavez is a very competent nurse, Lieutenant."

"I wanna talk to the orderly that was in here."

Nurse Chavez looked at her superior.

"The guard said an orderly came in here," the lieutenant repeated.

The charge nurse said, "We don't have orderlies. Someone may have come to take out the trash." She walked over to a metal stand supporting rings from which hung white plastic garbage bags and shook her head. "This hasn't been emptied in the last hour."

"Whoever comes in to pick that up, what's he wear?"

"A scrub suit," she said.

The lieutenant went back to the isolation cubicle, where he could be heard questioning the guard.

The guard's voice rose defensively. "It was just a guy in one of those hospital suits."

"Ever see him before?"

"He was swabbing the hall awhile back."

"Sure it was the same guy?"

Silence from the guard and a rumble from the lieutenant. "Are you even sure it was a *guy*?" He came back from ICU-3. "Who's the doctor in charge?"

The blond nurse frowned. "That would be Dr. McIver. He's on for Dr. Ramirez."

"I wanna talk to him."

The charge nurse went out the door. Nurse Chavez returned to the patient.

Tito Gonzales walked back to the corridor, running a hand through his hair. He wasn't sure he was cut out to be a cop. He sometimes wondered if he would have fared better in local politics or the armed services. He knew he wouldn't have made it selling cars or insurance. He thought he'd made lieutenant because to hide his uncertainty he acted every inch a cop. A man in a bar once asked him didn't he know the way to *become* something was to act like you were already it? "Man, that's how you made lieutenant," the fellow said. And Tito had grunted, "Hell, I oughta start acting like captain."

Inside ICU-3 Gin laid her hand on Raoul Query's arm and was surprised to find it flesh, it looked so much like marble. It was cold. She nudged the covers up around it. "Has there been any change?" she asked.

"Yes," Nurse Chavez said softly, bending over him and looking intently at his face. "He's starting to respond to the drugs."

Tito Gonzales stuck his head back in the door. "What brought you up here tonight?"

Gin hesitated, then told him only one of her reasons, that she had wanted to check on the man lying so quietly there on the bed.

"You telephone up here a while ago?"

"No. I came by at lunchtime, but I haven't checked on him since."

"Know anybody who did?"

She tried to think. "Mrs. Trowber might have. She told me a couple of hours ago that he was still unconscious."

"She say anything about him responding to the drugs?"

Gin shook her head. A voice on the intercom, blurred by distance and the closed door, paged the doctor.

Presently the charge nurse came back. "I'm afraid Dr. McIver is not in the building."

The lieutenant went back to the anteroom, where he could be heard instructing the officer on duty.

"How long before he'll come around?" Gin asked Nurse Chavez.

"You can't really tell. It shouldn't be long."

Gin wondered how long was long.

"Will that be all, Lieutenant?" the charge nurse asked, putting her head in the door. Tito nodded and the nurse returned to the nurses' station.

Gin could hear the lieutenant berating the young officer in a whisper. "And that means *without exceptions*. Anything happens, you know how to reach me."

"Yes, sir," the young man said. He had very dark hair and skin that mottled easily.

Gin stepped into the anteroom. "You've no idea how it happened?"

You could see he was worried, but the lieutenant only shrugged. "It was probably an accident and they're covering."

She could understand Nurse Chavez's annoyance. The lieutenant looked back at the young officer, who wouldn't look at him. "Come out here," he said. The young officer stepped out of the anteroom like a soldier in a drill and stood in the corridor with his feet apart and his hands behind his back.

"Go find yourself a cotton suit," the lieutenant said. "I want you to sit in there at the desk with the nurses. Anybody you don't know comes in this room, I want you to nab him, see? I don't care if he's the surgeon general, get him, find out who he is. Got that?"

The young man's jaw muscles worked, but he nodded. While the lieutenant went on talking, Gin slid away.

Down the hall in radiology, at the desk across from the balloon festival mural, she asked for Elsie and was told that Elsie had been called back up the hill to do an emergency heart catheterization, which was still in progress. Gin wandered down the hall and lingered a moment, but the box above the door read ROOM IN USE, DO NOT ENTER, and the red light was on. No telling how long Elsie would be.

Heading toward the entry, she was sorting again. Whoever

attacked Raoul Query at the museum had come back and tried to finish the job, once he—or she—learned Query was responding to the medication. And whoever it was seemed to know what he was doing.

Or it could have been an accident.

She conjured up Nurse Chavez's face, an intelligent face, full of assurance, and decided it was no accident.

In the parking lot, she ran into Victor Weldon getting out of the pod's rented station wagon. He had seen her before she noticed him.

"I see you beat me back to town," he said, slamming the car door behind him.

"I've just come from the ICU," she said, detouring across the lot toward him. "He's better. He's responding to the medication."

He straightened from locking the car. His eyes were shadowed and she couldn't see them. "I was delegated to come see how he was. Still in a coma, eh?"

She nodded.

Victor Weldon watched his toe edge a candy wrapper toward the curb. "I never liked the man."

She was surprised. Perhaps he needed to make this confession. It reminded her of the death of an uncle when she was fourteen. She had despised him for always grabbing at her when he thought no one was looking. She'd been glad he was dead, and then felt guilty.

"But I never wished him ill."

A car came up the hill and turned into a parking space, lighting his face for an instant. He was looking at her with those suffering eyes, the marks on his face like scars from ancient battles.

"Well," he said, "no point in going in. You've told me all the nurses would tell me."

She felt his eyes as she crossed the asphalt to the rig. She thought of the beautiful Ellen. Hard to imagine a woman who would fall in love first with Prince Charming and then with Hamlet.

17

She parked under the olive tree and sat a moment, noting the lights in Reuben's place. Tina's windows, and Croy's, were dark. It was Reuben and Dolly's night and that meant spaghetti. Suddenly ravenous, she took the keys from the ignition, stowed them under the seat, and made for Reuben's studio.

It reeked of tomato sauce and garlic. They were all there, even Pablo and Magda. Dolly, in a soft, pink short-sleeved sweater and miniskirt, waved her to the stove with a smile brightened by contact lenses. "Help yourself." Her dimples dimpled. In case I'm angry at Reuben, Gin thought. She hadn't seen him since he'd hung the cartoon Benny Montoya on her wall. "It may need heating up." Dolly turned on the burner under the pot.

"Thieves and artists." In the middle of the room, Reuben, pacing, threw her a glance. "We have a lot in common."

Tina and Croy sat on cushions on the floor, backs against the white adobe wall, Magda and Pablo on stools at the counter.

"We satisfy society's need for illicit adventure. A society in which we have no legitimate place."

"How can you say that, in a town full of artists and galleries?" Tina asked without a trace of irony, goading him.

"*Picture* stores. *Decorator* shops." He paused in front of Pablo, who was pouring Magda more wine. "And critics, like Jehovah, separate the sheep from the goats." His voice was always a surprise—high-pitched, a little reedy.

Croy said, "Artists are *supposed* to suffer." His rationalization for the writer's block.

140

Reuben whirled on him. "So we record life as alienated because we live alienated lives."

Magda said, "There, dear, one day you'll get your recognition."

Aside from the ridge that jumped up in his jaw, Reuben ignored her. "In a corrupt society artists become hypocrites and opportunists."

"All societies are corrupt," Croy said.

"I am neither a hypocrite nor an opportunist," Tina said.

"No," Reuben said, "you're a kept woman. Land of your own out at the pueblo, government health care—"

"Like to swap places, gringo?"

"A reservation for artists!" Croy said. "There's an idea whose time has come."

"Make it a natural preserve," Reuben said, "with moats and islands and a few discreet signs: Please don't feed the minimalists."

"Right on," Croy said. "Let them go hungry."

Pablo laughed and Dolly made the mistake of joining in. Reuben sent her a look and she wilted onto a cushion on the floor, tucking her knees under her.

Magda smoked and drank wine, amused by her errant child's performance. "Come, pet," she said, "you're the host. Eat your dinner. Where are your manners?"

"Manners," he mocked, and Tina said, "Reuben doesn't believe in manners."

"But, dear," Magda said lightly, "we rely on those little boundaries that keep us from imposing ourselves upon each other."

His fists clinched and unclinched in the pockets of his baggy pants, his painting pants, spattered with color.

"Tell us, did you take the Rembrandt?" Magda asked offhandedly. "It would ease Gin's mind if you owned up."

Reuben sneered. "I wouldn't bother with the Rembrandt. Now the Turner's a different story."

Gin's fork stopped halfway to her mouth, dripping spaghetti into her plate. Pablo glanced at her and said, "But my dear fellow, no one can claim Señor Turner was ignored in his lifetime. All the Western world admired his work."

Reuben said, "They admired it so much, when he died

they stashed it in basements where it was ruined by flooding. *Now* one of his sketchbooks just sold for eight hundred and fifty thousand dollars. They passed over Turner while he was alive and knighted hacks. They couldn't forgive him for being a barber's son. The man was a genius.''

Croy said, ''I think his work prophesied the Second Coming—impressionism, abstraction expressionism, action painting . . .''

''That is entirely true,'' Pablo said.

Reuben whirled on him. ''But with a difference! He never turned his back on nature. It's what he was trying to paint, and he painted it, by God, with the atoms split and showing.''

He ranged restlessly, barefoot, aped by his outsized shadow on the walls. ''Turn your back on nature, you're reduced to idiocy.''

''I'd be hard put,'' Tina said, ''to locate in nature the origin of *your* paintings, Reuben, though you claim they are landscapes.''

Reuben shrugged. ''Who has eyes to see, let him see.''

''You can't deny,'' Croy said, ''that color is part of nature.''

''For God's sake, I'm not making rules,'' Reuben muttered, with a dismissing flip of the hand. ''I'm describing what I know. Here!'' striking his breast. He swooped up the jug and held it over his shoulder like a wineskin, aiming at his mouth. What missed spilled down his T-shirt in a pink cascading stain.

''Well, scientists haven't turned their back on it,'' he said, squatting, setting the wine jug firmly on the floor. ''That's why they get all the grants and endowments.'' He fell flat on his back and stretched out his legs with the wine jug erect between them.

''Whoever did those''—Pablo caught himself—''thees Rembrandt copy is a damn fine painter.''

But Reuben didn't rise to the bait. ''What's forgery anyway?'' he asked the ceiling. ''Warhol reproduced ad nauseum the commercial artist who did the Campbell soup can. But that wasn't forgery, was it. Oh, no, that was genius.''

Croy said, "I guess if you copy a work but don't sign the original artist's name, it's not forgery."

"Right," Tina said, "it all goes back to what's in a name."

"Let me tell you," Gin said. "Millions."

Tina said, "A Rembrandt by any other name would smell as sweet."

Croy rocked back and forth on his cushion. "No other artist could produce a Rembrandt."

"That is not true, my friend." Pablo reached down and plucked the jug from between Reuben's legs and replenished his glass. "In Rembrandt's time, a painter named Ferdinand Bol painted a Rembrandt that was so wonderful everybody said if Bol had not owned up, it would have been taken for one of the Master's finest works."

Croy persisted. "Well, but he copied Rembrandt's *style*. The *style* was Rembrandt's, and this Bol guy stole it."

"Crap," Reuben muttered, "everybody steals from everybody."

"If Rembrandt hadn't come up with it, somebody else would have," Tina said.

"You mean," said Dolly, readjusting herself on her cushion as Reuben reached back and pulled her bare foot toward him, "something like the hundredth monkey?"

"*But,*" Croy said like a raised finger, "there always has to be that first genius monkey who washed his yam in the river. Without him, there'd have been no progress—if it *is* progress. Look at it this way—having to wash your yam . . ."

"Hear, hear," Reuben said.

". . . having to wash that yam in the river could be a handicap. If the river changed its bed, the whole troop might have to travel miles to wash their yams. In which case, the dullards who'd never learned to wash their food would have an advantage in the survival of the fittest."

Magda got up and turned on the stereo and shoved in a tape of Vivaldi. "De Chardin said that something once known by one member of the human race would eventually be known by everybody."

"Look who's into de Chardin," Reuben teased.

Magda put an arm through Pablo's. "They think people over thirty should be put out to pasture."

Pablo lifted her hand and kissed it.

Gin mopped her plate with the last of the garlic bread and denied herself another helping of spaghetti. She had begun sorting things out. Who had phoned the hospital to be told Raoul Query was on the mend? Any member of the pod could have done it and told the others. And Perdita Waldheimer must know how these old masters—Dutch, Flemish, German, English—how these separate islands had come to be joined in their nether parts to that bleak Cornish headland and the earls of Tor.

She handed her plate to Dolly, who was neatening up, took the phone around the corner and flopped with it on top of everybody's jackets on the unmade pallet bed. She dialed, only to learn there'd been a five-car pileup out on I-25 and Elsie and the other X-ray technicians could be working through the night.

18

At the other end of the hall from the X-ray rooms, where doctors, nurses, and technicians worked urgently over the accident victims, Nurse Chavez, who had just come on duty, muttered disapprovingly at the noise down the corridor, adjusted the pillow under the patient in ICU-3, and froze.

It moved again, the index finger of the hand attached to the wrist strapped to the board. Feebly, as if trying to beckon. She turned and rushed to the door so fast it slammed into Officer Capra's arm. Officer Capra hated night duties, particularly this night. He felt like a fool—out of uniform, dressed up in cotton scrubs and sitting there in the nurses' station. He was sure he was in the way and the nurses were laughing at him. So he'd gotten up and walked over to ICU-3 just as the nurse came bursting out.

The intercom began paging Dr. Ramirez.

* * *

Like a string.

A guitar string?

No, more like a whisker.

The fingertip tested. And tested again while the ripe orange sun fell out of the sky and splashed into the sea, sending colored ripples all up and down the horizon. In his dream he mixed the colors along the line that always receded as you approached.

Such things struck him as wonderful. If you tried to reach it—walking on the water, or out in a boat—would it keep moving, always, miles from where you stood? He was no scientist.

But his father was.

He frowned and it hurt. He might have cried, but he mustn't cry, for someone was there.

Who's there?

She said, "I have to talk to you."

What's all that noise?

The Pacific was not peaceful tonight. It was angry. It struck at the rocks, poured over the reef, and flooded the tidal pool.

"You'd better not swim," a man's voice said.

"I've been out in worse."

She'd trained years ago for the Olympics.

"I really wish you wouldn't," said the voice he recognized as his own.

Ellen said, "I'll do a few laps in the tidal pool. It'll be quite safe."

Quite safe. The ocean? Oh, you are wrong.

In his childhood there'd been a high-arced bridge that let sailboats go under. It crossed a sound to a barrier island full of seabirds' nests, where his father made notes about eggs and hatchlings. His mother gave them leftover bread to toss to the gulls, wings beating as they hovered, screaming. They caught the crumbs midair or alighted noisily around his feet. A child's voice, thrilled and terrified, and the beating wings and cries of the gulls.

Look, Rory, look! What did I tell you! Some have black legs, and some have yellow. Do you see that, Rory?

I see it, Dad! I see it!

And the tips of their beaks hooked cruelly.

To get to the island humped with dunes, dune oats bent landward before the wind, you had to cross the arcing bridge. Something terrifying about that bridge. What was it now . . . ?

I'll stay in the tidal pool, she said.

Protected, she meant, by the reef. But the reef was nothing. The ocean poured over. You could see if you looked.

He always looked. The Chevy coupe that was older than he topped the arc of the bridge. As it dipped down the other side the ocean rose. Much higher, it seemed, than the arcing bridge that the boats went under. Huge. The biggest thing in the world. The land was nothing, and all the fishermen's shacks and cottages, the little boats.

What held the ocean in its shores? Not those little dunes.

The biggest thing in the world. A restless giant, held in check by what?

By God, he thought, and said a prayer as the aging Chevy coupe dropped off the sailboat bridge and rolled to a stop across the oyster-shell road and parked out of the wind behind the dunes that now seemed mountainous. He ran away from his father and plowed to the top, sinking to his ankles in the sand.

And Ellen said, "I'm leaving . . ."

Don't leave me, Mother! he cried out. Oh, God, it hurt.

Ellen said, "You hurt me so, I had to punish you."

He wanted to shut her up. So white in the dark, the ruffled surf.

"See that?" Nurse Chavez said to her superior.

"Yes, I see. He's coming around."

"I've paged the doctor."

Her superior smiled. "No hurry," she said. "Let the doctor make his rounds. It may take hours. It could even be tomorrow."

Tomorrow, tomorrow, echoed down hushed corridors of his consciousness. Tomorrow she'd be all washed up. On the windward coast. Tossed by a warming sea while he twiddled his thumbs.

But it wasn't a thumb that twiddled while the nurses watched. It was the index finger of the hand on the board. The charge nurse said, "They'll sometimes get these neurological twitches. It doesn't mean a thing."

But was it really like a guitar string? No, it was more like a whisker. No, a card, the edge of a card!

A joker?

A Jack that cried.

No card has ever been known to cry.

This card cries. It cries for justice.

"Look at that," Nurse Chavez said.

"What's he doing now?"

"He frowned and it hurt. I saw him wince."

Her superior gave a superior chuckle. "Gas pains," she said. "They'll get them every now and then."

"You mean," said Nurse Chavez, not without irony, "like a baby's smile?"

"Something like that," said her superior, and tucked the covers neatly under Raoul Query's heels and turned and went out, leaving the young nurse hovering hopefully over her charge.

19

FRIDAY

The wolf was howling. *ah-ooo, ah-ooo*. It filled her with what? Dread? Loneliness?

The rig rounded the last curve in the long, winding drive through the piñon woods and there he sat, beside the broad steps rising to the terrace, throat up, mouth pursed to the blue morning sky. Howling for his breakfast? For his lost wild freedom?

She'd heard that wolves howl when somebody dies. But wasn't the man in the ICU out of danger now? She slammed the car door. Nemo bared his teeth and growled. She ignored his threats in hopes they'd go away. The wolf stopped howling to watch her hurry across the drive and run up the steps. She pressed the bell.

Jack took a long time coming. When finally he opened the door, she asked, ''What's he howling at?''

The fragile old man stepped out on the flagstone terrace and peered down his blade of a nose at the wolf. ''Well, miss, I can't honestly say. He's like that sometimes. Madam thinks he's calling for a mate. But we read into animals so much of what's actually human, don't you think.'' He smiled at her.

She smiled back, thinking: Why not? We're *all* animals. Of course we have the same feelings. She looked down at Nemo, who looked up at her. Did Perdita howl in her silent breast for Charley? ''How is Mrs. Waldheimer?''

''Jack!'' came Perdita's voice from inside the house. ''Who is it?''

Gin hadn't phoned. She'd meant to, from the hospital. But one pay phone was out of order and the other taken by an excited young man telling his in-laws—apparently at great distance—that the baby had finally arrived. She had stopped by the hospital to check on Raoul Query and been told that one of the ICU nurses thought she'd seen him gesture in the night.

''Gesture?''

''Yes. Of course it's hard to say what it might . . .''

He was still unconscious, but his vital signs were strong. She'd looked again for Elsie, but the little Texan was at home—asleep, most likely—after the five-car smashup on I-25 had kept her on the hill all night.

''Well, well,'' Perdita said when she walked in. ''Good morning, my dear.''

''I apologize for just showing up like this.''

''As you see, I'm always here.''

The benefactor sat this morning in her wheelchair drawn up to the Louis Quinze desk. She had been writing in a ledger. She had on a green plastic eyeshade of the kind once worn by stationmasters, the pince-nez perched low on the bridge of her nose.

"I don't usually—I mean, I do know better."

Perdita put up a hand. "Tut, tut, pour yourself coffee, dear."

Gin looked at the coffee tray on the desk. There was the whipped cream and the Irish whiskey. Did she imagine Perdita's smile?

"Tell me what propels you out here so early in the morning."

"I truly am sorry to barge in like this," Gin said, helping herself to coffee, hesitating, then adding a dollop of whipped cream, passing up the Irish whiskey. "But I do need to talk to you."

"Have you had your breakfast?"

"Actually, I haven't."

"Jack, are there any more croissants?"

Jack disappeared into the hall and, apparently, to the back of the house and the kitchen, where soft female voices warbled.

Perdita Waldheimer laid down her pen and wheeled herself from behind the desk, heading for the fireplace. Though the day was warm, a piñon fire burned, filling the room with its aromatic breath.

"At my age," Perdita said, "one needs a fire to warm the blood."

This morning she had on another cashmere cardigan, this one dark greenish blue. She took off the pince-nez, gave a gentle little yank, and the spectacles reeled back to the silver disk attached to her shoulder. She had on camel's hair slacks today. Gin thought how nice she looked, but hesitated telling her. Her mother said people took patronizing liberties with their elders.

She sat on the edge of the chair, still holding her coffee cup, exactly where she had sat before, the fire burning between them.

"It was cold last night," Perdita said. "How is it out this morning?"

"Warm again. Very nice."

"Are you returning the provenances?"

"No, I—They're in the archives. Not copied yet."

"Well, keep them, keep them, I've no more use for them."

"I've come . . ." Gin started, then paused to sip nervously from her cup.

"Yes, dear, what is it?" Nemo wandered in and crossed to his mistress and sat down. Perdita leaned forward and patted her wolf on the head, whereupon he yawned contentedly, emitting a shrill little sound.

"I was wondering after I read all the provenances . . . I mean, when I left you yesterday morning I'd only read the Rembrandt. . . ." She heard her voice trail off. "Well, anyway, I came back to ask you—I mean, I couldn't help wondering, once I thought about it . . ."

"Yes, dear," Perdita Waldheimer prompted.

"I wonder how it came to be that all four of the old masters were in some way connected to Mousehole Castle and the earls of Tor?"

Perdita Waldheimer chuckled. She got slowly to her feet, took the elegant cane leaning against the hearth, and slowly crossed the room to the large glassed-in bookcase while Gin watched anxiously. She unlocked it with the spindly-looking key that apparently hung on a ribbon inside her blouse. She took down a heavy tome.

Gin leapt up and rushed to take the volume from her trembling arms.

"Burke's Peerage," Perdita said. She allowed herself to be led back on Gin's arm across the room. Ignoring her wheelchair, she dropped into a handsome recliner that lowered her back and elevated her head, which was shaking badly. She laid it against the headrest and closed her eyes. "Look under Tor, dear."

Gin dropped into her chair and opened the heavy volume on her lap. She flipped back and forth, turning pages.

" 'Tor,' " she read aloud, " 'eighth Earl of. Captain Charles Owenby, eighth Earl of Tor. August 10, 1895, at Lizard Head. Eldest son of seventh Earl of Tor and his Scottish wife, Jocylyn Burrell . . .' " Burrell. She looked up.

"Yes, yes, dear, go on," Perdita said, without opening her eyes.

" 'Married Betty Campbell, 1915. Succeeded to title on

death of his father in 1919. No progeny. Died 1975 in USA. Family residence: Mousehole Castle, Cornwall, built by third Earl.' ''

When Gin looked up, Perdita's head still lay against the backrest, but her blue eyes were bent upon her visitor.

"I see," Gin said. "This means . . . Does this mean . . . ?"

Perdita chuckled. "Yes, dear. Charley Burrell was the eighth earl. He went by his mother's name to avoid confusion should his nephew succeed to the title, you understand."

Gin looked down at the book open on her lap and read aloud, " 'Married Betty Campbell, 1915.' ''

Perdie Waldheimer nodded. "That's why we never married. Lady Owenby so liked being Lady Owenby. The family supported her claims, of course. After all, I was an upstart American. Those descendants of wreckers and pirates wanted nothing to do with a daughter of robber barons."

The patroness reached to the cluttered drum table and carefully chose a nougat from the box. "At some point," she went on with a smile, "Lady Owenby got herself pregnant, perhaps as a means of producing a ninth earl. But as Charley'd been home only once since he married her—all in a rush, on impulse you see, when he was on leave in 1915— and she'd been shooting in Scotland at the time, he hoped a divorce or annulment might come of that. But she wised up and had a miscarriage—or, I suspect, an abortion. Canny old girl, I gather." Perdita shrugged her shoulders in the handsome heather cardigan. "Whose it was, we never knew. Some suspected the gamekeeper, but of course that was inspired by D. H. Lawrence." She chuckled.

"Mr. Burrell was the Earl of—"

"Oh, call him Charley," Perdita said. "Everybody did. Yes, dear. Charley was the eighth Earl of Tor. When I met him I was eighteen and he was thirty. And wild. With a wife in England who wouldn't give him a divorce. My family had a fit. But that was it. Once I laid eyes on Charley Burrell, I'd met my fate."

"And the paintings?" Gin prompted.

"Yes, the paintings. Charley stole them, of course. From Mousehole Castle."

"Stole them!"

Perdita Waldheimer laughed delightedly at the shock she'd dealt. "Oh, just the old masters. He brought the others—the Miró and Juan Gris and all—from Paris when he came to America. But he had to steal the others from Mousehole— the really old ones—the Rembrandt, the Turner, the Van Dyck, and the Dürer. They were his, of course. He was, after all, the earl. But there might have been challenges— whether they belonged to the estate or to the Earl of Tor, you know, though nobody cared about the old things. So he by-passed that altogether. He left behind the land, the fortune, the title, a castle *full* of old masters. He took with him only those four paintings."

"Why those particular four?" Gin asked. Probably be-cause they were the most valuable.

Perdita smiled. "I'm glad you asked, my dear. The rea-sons may tell you a bit about my Charley. You see, when he was a child, he once lay in bed for half a year, an invalid after a fever." She ran her finger along the edge of the little lacquer tray full of vials. "In those days they didn't have these miracle drugs that keep you alive, sometimes too long. The lengthy confinement was hard on a child, you know, though his mother, whom he adored, did everything in her power to make it easier. It was she who hung the little Rem-brandt landscape in his room—just something for him to look at. It was the last thing he saw when he fell asleep at night and the first thing he saw in the morning. He came to love that painting, made up fantasies about it, put himself into it. Have you seen *The Polish Rider* at the Frick? Strange . . . The same landscape, really. Well, when Charley—a grown man by then—was traveling cross-country from New York to the Coast, and saw New Mexico, it was the landscape of his childhood dreams—of that strange, unlikely Rembrandt. Without a moment's hesitation he got off the train and never went any further west. So you might say it was Rembrandt who brought him to Santa Fe."

Gin saw a young Englishman in belted tweeds stepping off the iron horse into the enchanted landscape. "And the Turner?" The painting of the castle on the headland by the sea. But she thought she knew the answer. She was feeling sentimental about Charley Burrell.

"That's easy, my dear. It's a painting of Mousehole Castle, Charley's ancestral home. He loved that place, though he didn't want to live there. Turner sketched it one summer when he stopped there on a walking tour. He was a young man then, pretty much unknown, and once he returned to London he did the painting from the sketch. He presented it to his hosts."

Perdita offered her a nougat and this time Gin took one, her mind busy sorting, sorting . . .

"What about the Dürer?" she asked.

"That time when he lay abed for months?"

Gin nodded.

"His mother made up stories for him about Dürer's animals, the ones in the drawing, the hare and the owl and the strange little creature. Charley was just a little boy then. He'd always loved those animals." Perdita fitted a Gauloise into her long holder. "So—yes, he took them."

"Why the Van Dyck portrait?"

Perdita chuckled, drew on the Gauloise and exhaled, enveloping her head in smoke. "The Van Dyck portrait. That's the Tor ancestor who made the family fortune. The pirate, I mean. The family always told Charley as he was growing up that he was the spittin' image. You can see that for yourself." She nodded to the portrait of Charley, and indeed Gin saw the resemblance now—the smile, the eyes, that air of assurance. She had thought the portrait of Charley familiar the first time she looked at it. "So he stole that one as sort of a joke," Perdita said, "a portrait of himself in drag."

Sorting, Gin got up and stretched. Her head back on her neck, she found herself looking at the frescoed emblem on the fireplace chimney.

Perdita said, "The arms of the earls of Tor. *'Sable per chevron or and gules crowned tor proper.'* Charley loved to reel that off." Perdita crushed her cigarette in the silver ashtray. Her head settled back against the chair. "That's a blazon, dear. Heraldic descriptions are called blazons. *'Sable per chevron or . . .'* Let's see. *Sable* is the ground, and *per* means the shield is divided—into a chevron, you see. *Or* is of course gold—that's the top half—and *gules*, or red, is the bottom. *'Crowned tor proper'* means there's a small hill in the center—that is, a tor. See it there?''

"Yes." Gin frowned up at the shield, gold at top, red at bottom, with the little squiggle, like an inchworm, that was the hill in the middle.

She turned her back to the fire, held by the room, the depth of the carpet, the carved corbels. She smelled something cooking. Somewhere in the back of the house a woman laughed, probably a cook. Perdita seemed to be nodding with her head on her chest.

Jack came to the door and peered in at his mistress. Gin picked up her backpack. He held a long, thin finger to his lips. She tiptoed across the rug and plucked the croissant from his tray as he let her out the front door. Nemo wagged his tail and followed her to the rig. The visit had been rewarding. She'd learned more than she'd hoped to learn.

20

Now if this were *her* house . . .

Toby Trowber had loved playing house as a child, and playing house with Bobby after she'd grown up—arranging things, redoing rooms, planning the den, the nursery. Later, when they'd given up hope of a child, she'd turned it into her sewing room full of flowered chintz.

Now if this were *her* house . . .

While Gin sat in Perdita Waldheimer's drawing room, Mrs. Trowber was sitting at the back of a cliff dwelling on a ledge cut into the tuff, as the ranger at Bandelier called the soft rock of the cliff.

Cut in with what? she wondered. Sharp rocks, probably. But the ceiling low over her head was smooth, and black still from the smoke of their fires after a thousand years, just think.

You'd always have to crouch in here, you could never stand up. You could stretch out your arms and touch the sides. Not a lot of space, but you'd probably spend most of your time outdoors.

There were no doors.

Out*side*, then.

Into the rounded walls the Indian housewife had dug several niches. What had she kept in them? Her jewelry perhaps. Made out of bone and turquoise. Would she let her children play with the beads?

There was another niche closer to the floor, this one quite large. She kept her herbs in there, Mrs. Trowber decided. Medicinal herbs.

This niche was deep. She bent and stuck in a hand, touched something, thought of scorpions, and jerked it out, then bent down and peered. Nut hulls of some kind, all in a pile. The lair of a small desert fox who hulled seeds and nuts in his den. She smiled. As a child she'd carpeted her dog's house and made him a little pillow.

The cave mouth framed the distant mesas and the sky. Down below was the river. The Indian housewife had to lug her water all the way up here in an earthen pot. Or maybe a basket. Did she carry it on her head? Some Indian baskets were still woven tight enough to hold water.

Now if this were *her* house . . .

Bobby, dressed in skins, muttered a curse as he tried to light the fire there in the pit dug in the middle of the floor. He wouldn't have made a very good Indian, not without his fire starter. She'd always been scared he'd burn the house down.

But *she* would have made a very good Indian. She'd peered with interest at the *metates* at the Wheelwright Museum. She would have liked kneeling right out there on the ledge in front of her cliff dwelling, grinding corn with her *mano* and gossiping with her neighbors. She wondered about the real estate of it all, whether you might expand your house to *two* rooms as your family grew, perhaps joining them together by digging through a wall.

How on earth would they sleep in this little space?

In good weather they could sleep outdoors—out*side*—maybe in a brush arbor down by the river.

Would that be safe? Hadn't they dug these rooms high up in the cliffs to be safe from enemies? The cliffs faced south. These were solar homes. They would catch the sun and hold the warmth when the sun went down.

What about cold nights?

You'd hang skins over the opening.

Then how would the smoke get out?

Early in the evening they'd have a fire. Then when the fire had burned to embers, she would let down the furry curtain and they would curl up together and the whole cliff room would be warmed by their body heat.

Hearing voices, she peered out over the ledge. The Indian mother must have leaned out this way to look for her little boy. He'd be down there playing in the willows by the stream with all the other Indian children. There, she saw him—tall for his age, obviously the leader. She took a deep, prideful breath. The boy's limbs were long and lean, and his cheeks the color of mango skin.

Voices again, below on the path. She drew back into her cave to let them pass, unwilling to abandon her Indian life for the tour that had become so problematic.

But they didn't pass. They stopped in the bend of the path below and their voices drifted up. Two of the women—Hanna Enright the little cripple, and Alice Maynard the little fool. At first Mrs. Trowber didn't catch what they were saying, only their voices muffled by the intervening ledge or dispersed by the breeze that stirred the willows down where the Indian children played.

". . . if he dies, we can put the whole awful thing behind us. This trip . . . supposed to get over it . . . think about nothing else. After all, it's probably a just retribution."

"Nonsense, what happened to Ellen was an accident." Now Mrs. Trowber could hear them quite clearly. Either they'd moved nearer or the wind had died. Yes, the willow tops were still. "I believe what he told the police is exactly what happened."

"Oh, come on, Hanna," Alice said. "She sends him back

for her sweater, but when he returns she's not there and he doesn't even *look* for her? Just leaves her sweater on a rock, gets in his car, and drives all that tortuous way back home? It doesn't make sense, after he'd driven two hours to see her on that twisty-turny Hana Road.''

Hanna Enright said, "That dislocated shoulder. She must have died in terrible pain . . .'' There was pain in Hanna Enright's voice.

"Yes, what *about* that shoulder?" Alice said. "And those awful bruises?''

"Perhaps she fell from the cliff, and the tide—''

Alice Maynard snorted. "If she fell from the lava cliff there'd have been gashes, not bruises. And why did the body wash up where it did, against all probabilities what with the tides . . . ?''

"She left *everything* to him.'' What was it in Hanna Enright's voice? Disappointment? Bitterness?

"Exactly,'' Alice said. "There's your motive.''

"Why should she have done such a thing?''

"It's unheard of,'' Alice said, "leaving everything to a divorced first husband. But she wasn't herself. We all knew she *wanted* to die.''

"Raoul said she phoned and asked him to come.''

"We've only his word. Why would she have done that, if she meant to kill herself?" Alice laughed scornfully.

"If she meant to kill herself,'' Hanna said, "after leaving everything to Raoul . . . It's almost as if she *meant* to implicate him in her death, get him out there, provide a motive. But that's diabolical. Ellen wasn't diabolical. He didn't *know* he was her heir, after all.''

"So he says. I think knowing he would inherit a fortune, Raoul lent her a helping hand.''

"Then it was a mercy killing.''

"Oh, don't be naive, Hanna.''

"This isn't real. It's your own scenario.''

"Or maybe they swam out together, the sea was rough, she started to go under and cried out for help, but Raoul . . .''

"You're making this up. You don't *know*. Nobody knows.''

". . . but at the last minute she changed her mind and

fought for her life. And he—What else could account for those bruises, that dislocated shoulder?''

''The buffeting sea. She was in the water overnight.''

''Poor Ellen, pleading, reaching, begging him for help, and the sea—''

''*Stop it, Alice!* Ellen had enormous courage, the courage to take things into her own hands.''

''Poppycock! You've always romanticized her. She was as terrified of dying as anybody else. Not all the Zen in the world could save you from that.''

''You were always jealous of her, Alice.''

''I haven't a jealous bone in my body! It sickened me to see you worshiping at her shrine.''

''I don't know what you're talking about!''

''Oh, yes, you do.''

''What about *you*? *You're* in love with Victor Weldon. I heard the door—that *whoosh*ing sound—and I heard something else, something familiar that I couldn't place when the lieutenant questioned me. But later I knew what it was . . . It was high heels tapping in little short steps. You were the only one of us in heels that night—no doubt to charm Victor. Sheila and I knew we'd be walking up the hill to the museum so we both wore flats. I heard you, Alice, leaving the building a fraction of a second before I found Raoul lying there on the floor with that Mexican fellow kneeling over him.''

''Don't be silly. Twenty women must have worn heels to the opening.''

''But only one of those women went out that door.''

''What about you, Hanna, if you're so busy accusing everybody else? What were *you* doing in that gallery? We've only your word that you *found* him on the floor, that you entered *after* the Mexican fellow. Maybe you'd stepped behind one of the statue pedestals.''

Voices called along the cliff above the dwelling where Toby Trowber sat—Sheila and Eric Albin. Then footsteps sliding, a shriek of laughter—that was Sheila—and Eric's voice. ''Where *is* that guide? The surly fellow left us up there in hopes we'd kill ourselves. He hated the lot of us on sight, you could see it in his face.''

The commander called something from higher up and they

urged him to hurry down. In slacks today, finally. Mrs. Trowber had lived long enough in a port city to know that most naval officers got out of uniform the moment they had a little leave. But not Will Nevil. That uniform was his identity.

"Righto," he called back cheerfully. Then gravel sliding, and one of the women yelped. The naval officer laughed. "Bit of a near thing." Then they joined forces with Hanna and Alice and headed back toward the parking lot.

Toby Trowber shrank against the wall of the cliff dwelling. Indian children no longer played in the willows along the river. The Indian housewife was dead a thousand years. In another thousand there'd probably be no river, only a dry arroyo where wind blew the scurrying sand.

The ranger stood below with his hands on his hips, scanning the cliffs for the missing tourist. The others were safely inside the visitors' center.

Mrs. Trowber stood up beneath the smoked ceiling of the cliffhouse and tugged at her skirt, which had hiked up at the back. She crept out onto the ledge deserted now by all her happily chattering Indian neighbors grinding corn with their *manos* and *metates*.

She looked at her wristwatch, so tiny she could hardly make out the time anymore without her glasses, and rimmed with diamond chips, a present from Bobby on their twenty-fifth anniversary. Squinting, she held her wrist as far away from her as she could and made out the spidery hands. Quarter to eleven. Plenty of time to meet Gin Prettifield before lunch.

She waved to the ranger from the ledge. "Yoo-hoo!"

He saw her but did not respond. He turned on his heel and let her get down to the path as best she could. She'd gotten up there on her own, hadn't she? He liked his job, but oh, these tourists. Indian summer brought more of the intruders, but then winter and snow and the whole quiet canyon to himself.

21

In another half hour it would be noon. Hard to believe. Awake at seven, Gin had phoned Jean Medows, knowing the horsewoman rose much earlier on her Galisteo ranch. The secretary of the board sometimes spelled her at the museum when she needed to get away. It always worked out very well. Mrs. Philipson, something of a snob, approved of Jean Medows, who ran in the best crowd, drove a Jaguar, and gave lavish, rowdy parties in her rambling old adobe hacienda.

The secretary was every inch the horsewoman—short, light brown wavy hair that, graying, managed to look palely freckled like her face, canny blue eyes, fair skin, square, competent-looking hands, and a thin, mobile mouth with vertical creases that made her upper lip seem strung on a drawstring of good-natured amusement. In her fifties, she was slender as a girl.

She had, she said, to be in town for a Zozobra party anyway, so she'd agreed to come in and "sit the museum." Her bookish husband would meet her at the museum at five. He could come into town early and park in the museum lot as there'd be no parking anywhere else and the traffic would be too heavy out the Old Taos Highway and Bishop's Lodge Road to drive anywhere. They could walk down the hill to Magers Field for the spectacle.

Gin promised to be back at the museum before noon for her appointment with Mrs. Trowber. That would let the board secretary off in time for lunch.

On her way back to town she stopped at the hospital. Raoul Query was still unconscious. Elsie was off for the day. She stopped at the pay phone downstairs but she didn't have a quarter. She glanced at her watch and, on a quick decision, got in the rig and drove down St. Michael's to the Casa Allegre neighborhood.

Elsie opened her door in jeans and sweatshirt. From the back of the house came the sounds of televised football.

"C'mon in!" Elsie said. "They're on the three-yard line!"

Gin followed the stovepipe jeans and Clark oxfords back to a den with a deep-pile, powder blue carpet where the televised crowd broke into wild cheering. Elsie stood jack-knifed in front of the set with her hands on her knees. One of the teams was the Houston Oilers with little derricks on their helmets.

"C'mon!" Elsie said to the Texas team.

The ball was snapped and handed off. A pileup on the goal line, but the tailback flew over the top for a touchdown.

Elsie waited in suspense for the extra point. There was the snap. And the kick. The crowd roared.

"It's good!" Elsie cried, pounding a fist into her other palm, falling back onto the couch. "Want some coffee?" Her eyes were still on the screen. "It's already made."

The teams lined up in the middle of the field. The kick went deep, received on the ten-yard line. Up to the fifteen, the twenty, twenty-five . . .

Elsie was up off the couch. "Get 'im! Got 'im! Good!" The runner was nailed at the twenty-four.

"I'll get it," Gin said. "Want a cup?"

"They won't get anywhere. Only a few seconds till the half." Elsie looked up. "That's okay, I'll get it."

"Don't move," Gin said. "Let me." She went to the kitchen, found cups, poured coffee, and came back as the fullback ran the ball through the middle.

The small Texan grabbed her head in both hands and groaned. "Look at that! Hole big as the Holland Tunnel, you could drive a bus through there!"

First down. Ball on the forty. The whistle blew for the half and the teams trotted off the field.

"Whew. That was close. Coulda been a touchdown." The announcers came on and Elsie turned the sound off.

"How come they're playing football on a Friday morning?" Gin asked.

As it turned out, they weren't. Elsie'd had to work on

Saturday. They were watching the VCR. Elsie sat back on the couch, putting up her feet. "What's up?"

Gin set her cup on the coffee table and outlined the plan she'd tried out on Pablo.

Elsie eyed her, running it through. "I don't know," she said. "Might work, might not. But, shoot, it's worth a try." She glanced at the halftime show on the silent tube. "Meet you on the hill—say, 'bout five o'clock. They got a heavy schedule up there till then."

When she walked into the Waldheimer, the gift shop was crowded, Olivia looking nervous. An art teacher led her sixth-grade class through the gallery of Taos painters. Mrs. Philipson was watering plants in tubs in the large west window at the end of the corridor.

Pablo's voice resonated from the Frida Kahlo Gallery. "Diego Maria Concepción Juan Nepomuceno Estanislao de la Rivera y Barrientos Acosta y Rodriguez." The name rolled off his Latin tongue.

She heard Jean Medows say, "You're pulling my leg."

"No. I swear. Diego Rivera's full name. Impressive, no?" Jean Medows laughed her gruff, low laugh.

Gin peered in and Pablo, beside a large surrealist portrait, probably a self-portrait of the artist, raised his eyebrows questioningly. She nodded. He smiled.

"Was the hummingbird meant as a symbol of herself?" Jean Medows asked, looking at the painting of a crucified hummingbird garlanded with thorns.

Pablo shrugged. "*Es posible*. The lady had thirty operations in her lifetime. She was always in pain—from a metal rod thrust into her in a bus accident."

Into her vagina, Gin thought with a wince.

"Even before that," Pablo said, "her health it was not good."

"Weird stuff." Jean Medows looked around the gallery at the paintings. "But I like it. All that green!"

"She was a surrealist," Gin said, "while Diego and his friends were doing political murals."

"Yes, but a dedicated Communist," Pablo said. "It ees known that she had an affair with Leon Trotsky." He looked boyish today in a gray V-neck pullover and flannel slacks. "She was included in the Paris show of 1929."

"The one with the *Nude Descending Staircase*?" Jean Medows asked.

"That was the 1916," Pablo said.

The walls of the gallery were hung with lacerated self-portraits, people growing from trees, vines growing from people, death, pain, *retablos,* Christ suffering, martyred, fawns pierced with arrows, papier-mâché skeletons . . .

Pablo said, "Diego Rivera was of 'ees time, but Frida soars above time and politics."

"Not politics," Gin said. "Her politics brought her down. She went to a protest of U.S. actions in Guatemala and caught pneumonia and died at forty-seven."

"Yes, Ginnee, you are right. The museum is fortunate to have these paintings. Frida has been declared national patrimony, you know."

"What's national patrimony?" Jean Medows wanted to know.

"It means," Gin said, "her work now in Mexico can't permanently leave the country. Not since 1985."

"And consequently," Pablo said, "the value of the paintings in thees room is very great and bound to go higher—the value, that is, of all the Kahlo paintings on the international market. The world is infatuated with our Frida, perhaps for all the wrong reasons—the feminists and the political left, and all those who like their pictures to tell a story, particularly a story of the world's cruelty."

"And Diego Rivera's," Gin said.

Pablo chuckled. "But she was a better painter than the great Diego. It is for her art she should be known and enjoyed."

"They hang junk on their walls to enjoy," Gin said, "and buy art for investment or to impress other people."

Jean Medows laid a freckled hand on Gin's arm. "I have something to show you." She led Gin out of the gallery, leaving Pablo behind.

As they passed the reception desk, Gin smiled at Mrs. Philipson, but Jean Medows paused and asked, "Everything

all right today, Regina?'' And Mrs. Philipson raised wor-
shipful lavender eyes.

Nobody in the Montoya show, but as usual the O'Keeffe
Room was busy. They flattened themselves against the wall
as a teacher herded her noisy class down the corridor.

Jean Medows closed the office door behind them, went to
the desk, opened the top drawer and took out a Ziploc bag.
"Know what this is?'' she asked, holding it up by two fingers
as if it might be contaminated.

Gin pursed her lips, though she'd never been able to whistle. "Where'd you find this?''

"In the bed of my pickup. In the hay. Wednesday night
on our way to the opening we had to stop by the feed store
and pick up a few bales to tide us over. Our delivery had
been held up. This morning the stableboy swept out the truck
bed and found it.''

Inside the Ziploc bag was the Apache woman's arm, and
the arm was attached to the hand holding the burden basket.

"The baggie was my idea. I thought there might be fingerprints. Though of course Francisco had his hands all over
it.''

Presumably the stableboy.

"It's worth a try,'' Gin said, dialing Tito Gonzales. The
statue might be repairable. She'd have to ask Tina.

"Whoever attacked Raoul Query with the statue must have
pocketed the broken arm, then tried to toss it down the hill
in the *chemiso*,'' Jean Medows said. "Only my pickup happened to be in the way. Oh, and there was also this.'' The
board secretary opened her large glove-leather shoulder bag
and took out another plastic bag. "I've no idea if it means
anything, but it was in the truck bed, too, down between the
bales.''

Gin opened the bag and shook out bits of paper onto her
desk. "Looks like a torn calling card,'' she said. There was
a small stylized crown in one corner, like the crown on a
playing card.

"What's a kahuna?'' Jean Medows asked.

"I think it's some kind of Hawaiian priest or healer.''

"Well, this is the card of a kahuna. There's a penciled

message of some kind on the back. It's been ripped in two, then ripped in four, but Francisco found only three pieces."

With the tip of the letter knife from her pencil mug, Gin nudged the bits till roughly their edges fit.

Jean Medows looked over the assistant director's shoulder. "I wouldn't have given it a thought," she said, "but for the address."

Gin touched the button beneath her desktop and a moment later Juan appeared.

"We have to search the grounds for the rest of this card," she said. Juan peered over her shoulder at what lay on the desk. Jean Medows told him where the pickup had been parked.

You could read the name, a Hawaiian name, and a post office box in a place called Hana. Gin tipped the pieces face-down with the edge of the letter knife and shoved them together again. The message read, ". . . office on Oahu called to confirm your doctor's appointment." The date of the appointment was almost two months ago, in July.

"I guess it landed among the bales," Jean said. "The missing part may have blown off as we drove home."

A curved ink stroke was all that remained of the patient's name.

Gin nodded. "But it may be in the parking lot, or the courtyard, or down in the piñons."

Juan shrugged. "The police have searched all over the place. You expect me to find a little thing like that?" He gave Gin a hurt look. "Ask me for the moon," he muttered.

Gin bit her lip. "I want that piece of paper, Juan, if it's anywhere to be found."

As the guard went out Pablo came in. Gin showed him the Apache woman's arm. "Can a bronze statue be mended?"

"Perhaps," Pablo said, "by a reputable bronze foundry."

"We have an excellent one out in Tesuque."

"But go at it minimally. Talk to the Walker Museum." They were frowning together over the pieces of the card when a timid knock came at the door. Jean Medows crossed and opened it. Toby Trowber stood there smiling apologetically.

Gin had forgotten about Mrs. Trowber. "Oh, Toby," she said, "come on in."

"I'll give Juan a hand," Pablo said, and sidled out behind Mrs. Trowber.

"I'm off for lunch then," Jean Medows said, and followed him out.

Gin closed the door behind them. Now she remembered. Mrs. Trowber wanted to buy a Benito Montoya. Any other time this news would have filled her with pleasure.

Mrs. Trowber clasped and unclasped her hands over the top of her girdle where the little roll bulged beneath her dress. "Oh, Miss Prettifield . . . Gin. I hardly know what I'm doing. The painting . . . I do—I want to buy one. But *first* I need your advice. Such dreadful things."

Outside the window, children spilled down the slope. One swooped to pick up a gum wrapper. Others careened among the piñon trees, playing tag. "Yes, of course," Gin said.

Outside a din of voices, and the teacher's shrill call.

". . . so I thought first I'd speak to you, and—"

Juan opened the door without knocking. In came an anxious young woman with short hair and glasses, ushering before her a ten-year-old with his shirt out and his hair in his eyes. His cheeks were red from wind or excitement, and he held something up in a grubby hand as he told the teacher over his shoulder, ". . . sort of halfway under one of those railroad ties where you park your car."

"I think we got it," Juan said.

The ten-year-old pointed at the guard and said to his teacher, "He said if you found it you'd get a dollar!"

"Tuck your shirt in, James," the teacher said.

"Yeah, but he said—"

"Wipe your nose!"

"Let's see, James." Gin rounded the desk.

James eyed her suspiciously and held onto the torn bit of card. Sighing, Juan dug in his pocket and counted out change.

Then while they all watched—Toby Trowber, Juan, the teacher, and James—Gin fitted the last piece to the puzzle on the desk. The message scribbled on the back of the kahuna's card was to Ellen Weldon.

Toby Trowber said, "Miss Prettifield . . . Ginevra . . . there are a number of things I really must tell you."

22

"We could CT it."

"Aw, c'mon," Elsie said. "How could we CT it?"

Elsie's colleagues were a dark-haired, pretty woman and a blond young man with longish hair. Their voices in the gray room came to Gin through a cloud of cotton. No windows. It might have been ten floors underground. She'd suffered from claustrophobia only once in her life—on a crowded elevator in New York City—but she felt a touch of it now.

A uniformed Brinks guard stood with his arms crossed and his back to the door, Cerberus guarding the gates. Lloyd Noldes leaned against a counter containing a bar sink. Tina stood close to Elsie while the technicians arranged what looked like a boom over the table. Magda was in the lounge reading *Good Housekeeping*. Pablo had stood the crates bearing the Rembrandt, the Van Dyck, and the Turner against the pale gray wall and disappeared.

"When I was in New York," the blond young man was saying, "we CT'd a painting by putting it on its side. You know, in cross sections. You could tell it'd been painted over. You could see something underneath the surface. Looked like a flower, like the painter made a mistake or changed his mind and painted over this flower, and the underlayer of paint was so thick it showed through."

"Let's try some tomo cuts," Elsie said.

Strangely detached, Gin helped Tina move the painting. Tina, when nervous, bit her lip. Her lip had been clutched between her teeth ever since they'd entered the room marked RADIOLOGY. She glanced at Elsie with a minimum of trust and rested *Barren Landscape* on the X-ray table.

They'd arrived at the hospital in a caravan, Magda's old

Dodge camper leading the way. As Gin had planned it, the operation would take four people. Which reminded her of all those jokes—how many painters would it take to change a light bulb?

According to Pablo, there were three forged paintings— the Rembrandt, the Van Dyck, and the Turner—so to be on the safe side she'd figured the operation would take one person to hold onto each painting and a fourth to drive the van. Magda would have to do that, as the gears required pampering and only she knew how.

But Lloyd Noldes looked at her like she might be insane and arranged through Yucca Federal for a Brinks truck. Soon after Quillan Davies called from Dallas, the bright red armored vehicle appeared at the museum.

When Pablo saw it he showed some artistic temperament of his own. "I see you do not take my judgment seriously," he said to the chairman.

"You can't expect me to allow paintings worth millions to run around town in a hippy van."

Pablo shrugged. "Forgeries have no value. Thees Brinks-manship draws attention."

"We don't want the thief to know we're onto him," Gin said.

But Lloyd Noldes's voice was steel. "If these paintings are forgeries, somebody already seems to know all about what goes on at the museum. I plan to ride shotgun with the guard."

Gin detected the slightest smile on Pablo's lips. "Certainly. Of course. As you wish," he said.

Then she and Pablo returned to the East Room where Tina, who arrived with Magda in the van, was readying the paintings for transportation, wrapping them, Gin was surprised to see, in bubble plastic and crating them separately.

"God, are you packing them for shipment overseas?"

"Now you suspect even *me*?" Tina said. "If anything were to happen to them, who do you think would be responsible?" She tapped the last of the crates closed with her hammer. "The crates were already here. They came back last month with the O'Keeffes we had on loan to Chicago."

"We've got to hurry," Gin said. "Elsie's fitting us in."

Lloyd Noldes, suspicious of the whole undertaking, had ridden to the hospital in the Brinks truck, and Lieutenant Gonzales had been persuaded to get permission from the hospital's president for the truck to stop at the ambulance entrance.

Sweating with anxiety, Gin escaped the windowless X-ray room by focusing on Quillan Davies's voice as it had reached her over long-distance.

She was just stepping off the elevator from a clandestine search of the basement when his call came through. He hadn't gotten their messages because he'd abandoned the dull conference for a side trip to the museum in Houston. He'd only called, he said, to check with her once more before flying on to New York.

"You're just trying to lure me back for Zozobra," he said when she told him what was happening. "Don't think I'm not tempted."

She was quiet for a moment, choosing her words before she spoke.

"Gin?"

"Yes, I'm here."

"I thought we'd been cut off."

"No. I was thinking. It would be too bad to miss the rest of your trip."

"Yours is the only opinion I'm interested in," he said. "What do *you* think? Is something amiss?"

"I think Pablo Esperanza's all wet," she said, keeping her voice low. "Maybe he's pulling my leg."

Silence at the other end of the line. A flicker landed on the parapet outside Quillan Davies's office, its red breast spot bright against the autumn colors. She'd taken the call in there for the sake of privacy. The bird looked at her, then gave the parapet one peck hard enough to convince its beak that this was not adobe and no fit dwelling for adobe bugs.

She heard herself say, "I think you should go ahead with your plans."

The large speckled bird flew away.

She could hear his breathing on the line. He had a way of clamping a telephone receiver between his shoulder and his ear, hands occupied with writing himself a note. She wanted to ask what he was doing. Then something clattered against the mouthpiece and she heard him suck in like a deep sigh over the phone and knew he'd been filling his pipe and lighting it.

"This Mexican gentleman—this Pablo Esperanza-Ramos"—he sounded as if he were reading the name off the conference program—"he canceled his address here at the last minute, claiming the authorities wouldn't let him leave Santa Fe. The planning committee was exasperated, you may be sure. He is known to have an eye for the ladies. So we had a substitute speaker last night. Dull chap, bless him."

She made sympathetic noises.

"Esperanza-Ramos sounds more like one of your American playboys than an art historian. Could he have reasons of his own for misleading you? Could there by any chance be a woman involved?"

"He claims he's in love with Tina."

"Uh-huh." A long draw on the pipe like something flying away through a wind tunnel. "And what of our conservator? Is she enamored?"

"She's not at the moment confiding in me."

"I see." A pause. "I know how fond you are of Tina, Ginny, but you've said she quite loses her head in amorous situations."

"She claims to be cured of that."

"Um." The meerschaum clattered against his receiver.

"Look, Quill, I think I'm capable of handling things here."

He chuckled. "I'm sure you are, my dear." She imagined him in a hotel room looking out over the Dallas skyline of J. R. Ewing. "Leaving you in charge was a stroke of my customary genius."

She smiled into the telephone. "Right," she said. "Let me prove it to you."

"Have you notified the police?"

"Yes, but they don't take it seriously."

He chuckled. "All right, tell me what I should do."

She took a deep breath, stepped up to the ledge, and plunged. "Put it out of your mind and go on to New York."

Elsie's voice brought her abruptly back to the present.

"No, come on, the scanner's out. Too much radiation. Let's go ahead with the tomo cuts. Hand me a cassette."

The young man handed her a large, dark gray flattish rectangle, which Elsie placed carefully on the center of the long padded table, also gray, where ordinarily a patient would lie.

This time the patient was the barren landscape Tito Gonzales had mistaken for Chimayo. With Elsie directing, Tina placed it faceup on top of the cassette. Elsie did something to the overhead boom and onto the painting fell a rectangle of light quartered by lines that crossed in the middle.

"Okay," Elsie said, "everybody behind the lead wall."

Gin and Tina went behind the wall with the technicians. Lloyd Noldes pushed himself off the counter with the bar sink and followed. But the Brinks guard hesitated at the door.

"C'mon!" Elsie said. "We got to hurry this up. An accident case or a heart patient could be wheeled in any minute."

A tall, graying man with a flat stomach, the guard still looked unconvinced.

"Look," Elsie said, walking out from behind the panel, "you can't stay there."

The guard looked at Lloyd Noldes, who nodded, then moved reluctantly behind the wall.

Elsie pushed a button. They watched the X-ray tube travel the length of the table and back.

"That's it. That's all she wrote," Elsie said, and went out from behind the wall to retrieve the cassette. "Here, Hank, get this developed."

"How long'll that take?" Lloyd Noldes asked nervously.

Elsie's throaty laugh.

"Ninety seconds," Hank said, and left the room through the door at back.

The Brinks guard returned to the entry door.

"Where's Pablo?" Gin asked. Tina shrugged. Gin said, "He ought to be here. He's the one who knows what to look for."

Elsie said, "We might get a good picture that still won't prove anything."

Hank returned, frowning. "Nah," he said. "We got nothing at all."

Elsie took the X ray, held it to the light, and shook her head. "Okay, so now what?"

"We could still try the scanner."

"C'mon," Elsie said, "that'd be way too much radiation."

"How 'bout the cath lab?"

"Forget it," Elsie said. "We need the smallest amount we can generate, with the longest exposure."

"That'd be an ordinary old cardboard X ray," the pretty woman said.

Elsie looked at her. A spurt of hoarse laughter, and, "You're right. All this advanced technology's just getting in our way."

"I don't think we've got any cardboards, Elsie," Hank said. "Haven't used them in God knows when."

"Sure we do," Elsie said. "Go look."

Tina chewed her lip. Gin leaned against the wall. Lloyd Noldes's mouth drew down at the corners. He turned to the Brinks man, looking for an ally in his disdain, but the Brinks man was as expressionless as a sci-fi robot behind his dark glasses.

The door behind the control booth banged open, startling the guard, who whirled around, unsnapping the leather flap over his gun holster.

"Found one!" Hank said, holding up a black cardboard folder with faint green crisscrossed lines.

" 'At's the ticket!" Elsie said. "Gimme."

Tina raised the painting once more. Elsie slipped the cardboard folder beneath it and adjusted the X-ray tube till it was about forty inches over the painting. "Okay," she said, "now everybody back here. C'mon, *c'mon!*"

This time the guard followed willingly. Elsie pressed the button and, while they watched through the window in the wall, the tube arced across the table and back. Elsie recovered the folder. "This time you'll have to take it to the darkroom, Hank."

Hank headed out the door into the hall.

"Okay," Elsie said, "now everybody cross your fingers."

A few minutes later Hank burst back into the room holding

the X ray with both hands head-high in front of him. "We got something!"

Elsie tore the transparency out of his hands and held it to the light. She gave a long, low whistle.

"What's there?" Lloyd Noldes tried to see.

"What is it?" Tina asked nervously.

Gin said, "Where for pete's sake is Pablo?"

"It's writing," Elsie said. "Under the paint. It's not English, but somebody's signed the painting *underneath the paint*. He signed the picture *before he painted it*! Idn' that bass-ackwards?"

Tina ducked under Gin's arm. "It's lead white," she said. "They used to use a lot of it."

"Yeah," Elsie said. "X rays pick up lead. What's it say?"

"It says," Gin frowned, translating from the Spanish, " 'From the hand of the . . .' Supreme? Matchless? No, 'From the hand of the *incomparable* Pablo.' "

23

Lloyd Noldes said, "Where's Esperanza-Ramos?" Then running feet and yelling in the hall. Tito Gonzales's voice shouted unintelligibly. Elsie said, "What's going on?"

Gin looked at Tina, questions rioting inside her.

The Brinks guard, pistol out, faced the door to the hall and backed into the room. Gin passed him, bursting into the corridor. She had to escape the windowless space. She needed air. She looked wildly up and down the hall. Where was Pablo?

Tito shouted from down by the nurses' station. "Get your security people up here!"

A flurry of nurses rushed the lieutenant. "This is a hospital!" one hissed.

Something touched Gin in the ribs. She jumped. The Brinks man, cautiously opening the door of the X-ray room behind her.

"Cover that outside door," Tito called down the hall in a gruff stage whisper.

An officious-looking nurse bustled toward him. "There are sick people behind those doors."

"Yeah, I got it!" The lieutenant pushed both hands downward against nothing but air. "Not so loud," he whispered hoarsely to nobody in particular, and said to the officer in the green cotton scrub suit who had been in the ICU, "get on the phone. Get some cars up here pronto!" He ran toward the elevators and Gin followed till he disappeared behind a door marked STAIRS.

Behind her the young officer hit the phone buttons and spoke tersely into the mouthpiece, calling all squads, ordering those in the vicinity of St. Vincent up the hill, requesting that traffic be cut off at all entrances to the hospital. "Get some men up here," he said. "We got an armed suspect in the building. Hurry! He's dangerous!"

Gin ran down the hall and burst into the ICU. The charge nurse looked up, startled. "What's happening? What's going on? That wasn't Dr. McIver!"

"Who?"

"The man in the suit and mask."

"Are you sure?"

"What doctor in Santa Fe wears a scrub suit? They all wear blue jeans," the charge nurse said. "And why wear a surgical mask in here?"

In ICU-3 the patient was not Raoul Query but an old man with gray stubble on his chin. "Where is he?" Gin demanded.

"We hid him on the floor an hour ago. The lieutenant's orders. His vital signs were good. What is it? Who was that man?"

"I wish I knew."

"Oh, my God," the charge nurse said, "the lieutenant left the guard *here*. In case . . . to catch whoever . . ."

"You mean he's alone?"

"Of course not. There's a nurse with him."

"Where is he?"

"We're not to tell anybody—"

"Where is he?"

"Upstairs. Pediatrics. Room 3232."

Gin ran out past the telephones in their Plexiglas shields, past the door to the waiting room, past the big windows to the patio roof garden and the doors to the rest rooms. She swung around the corner and punched at elevator buttons, but she couldn't wait. She yanked open the door to the stairs. The gray-blue stairwell echoed her climbing steps and Tito's booming voice from down below. Outside, squad cars raced up the hill with sirens blaring. She came out on the third floor and searched for the ROOMS sign with the arrows. There it was. Room 3232 was about ten paces away from her, to the left and diagonally across the hall. She rounded the corner and found herself facing a nurses' station a little way down the hall. She tiptoed across to the door of 3232, took a deep breath, and cracked it open.

It was a private room, dim with the blind pulled. The first thing she saw was Raoul Query lying there apparently asleep, eyes closed, breathing peacefully on his own, oxygen mask gone, a hanging IV still feeding into his arm.

The second thing she saw was Nurse Chavez. She was sitting on the toilet in the bathroom, one towel gagging her and another tying her hands behind her.

Then she saw the gun and the figure behind it in faded cotton scrubs and cap, a surgical mask hiding all of the face but the eyes.

A hysterical laugh clutched her throat. Did he think she wouldn't recognize those eyes? He had pulled himself into the corner where the bathroom wall hid him from the door. He reached quickly, grabbed her, and whipped her around facing away from him with her arm wrenched up under her shoulder blade. More than anything, she was surprised. The pistol jabbed her in the back. He took a fistful of hair and twisted her head sideways. Then while in horror she watched, he put the gun with what she thought must be a silencer against Raoul Query's head and gave her another jab, his eyes questioning if she understood. She nodded yes, she understood, she wouldn't scream, she wouldn't try to run, she would do whatever he wanted.

24

Magda wondered what she was doing there anyway. She had better ways to spend her time. First they wanted to borrow her van. Then they wanted her to drive it. Because of the gears. Her own personal shade-tree mechanic hadn't gotten around to that yet. Lately Reuben had been preoccupied. Then when she finally ground up the hill to the museum, they were loading the paintings into a Brinks truck, would you believe it?

So they didn't really need her after all. Except that they couldn't ride to the hospital in the Brinks truck, so they'd all piled into the van—Tina, Gin, and Pablo Esperanza.

She could have been home making chili for her poker club's Zozobra party. Or running the vac. Or washing the dishes of yesteryear.

She put down *Good Housekeeping* and picked up *Vogue*. She hated these shoulder pads. They would make her look like a hippopotamus. *Shoulder*potamus.

She tossed the *Vogue* aside and picked up a copy of *People* with Jacqueline Onassis on the cover. She'd heard Jackie had bought a house in Santa Fe. Gloria Vanderbilt, too. And Carol Burnett. And Oprah. Where was their sleepy little town? Gone with the wind.

There ought to be a reservation for the rich, too. They never took part in a community, contributed anything, did they? Just ran up real estate so that natives who owned homes couldn't pay their taxes and the ones who didn't could never hope to buy one.

She felt sort of sorry for the rich. Nobody wanted them.

Poor things, no wonder they jet-setted around the world with their own kind, paranoid about who liked them for themselves and who liked them for their money. Still—she flipped through pages of ads—she'd like to try it for a while, running around the world from one beauty spot to another, buying whatever tickled your fancy and never a thought to the price.

Pablo Esperanza came stealing down the corridor on tiptoe, looking over his shoulder, glancing down the hall toward the side exit. She got up to speak to him, but someone tapped her on the shoulder.

It was her late husband's second cousin.

"Jerry!" She was glad to see him. She'd always thought Jerry was the handsomest one in the family.

He had on the blue outfit of Maintenance, with his name stitched on the pocket. "How you been, Magda?"

She was about to tell him when a shout broke the hush of the hospital, then another, muffled this time. A nurse hurried down the hall past the lounge. Her late husband's second cousin muttered, "What's going on?"

A phone shrilled at the reception desk. The receptionist picked it up. Her eyebrows shot skyward. She said, "What's that?" She tapped the button several times. "Hello, hello?"

The police lieutenant came barreling in, grabbed Jerry by the shoulder, and told him to station himself at the entry and keep people from going out or coming in.

"Now, see here," the receptionist said, rising in her island, a pretty, middle-aged fat lady with her hair in a roll round her head. She came out from behind the counter.

The lieutenant said something to her and her mouth fell open. She leaned over the high counter, flattening her ample breasts on its polished surface, grabbed up the phone, punched buttons, and cried, "Code-Seven! Code-Seven!"

"Cheez!" Jerry said, and started off.

"What is it? What's wrong?" Magda cried, and he said over his shoulder, "Emergency!"

At the entry, he stopped a portly gentleman at the glass doors. The portly gentleman grew angry and red-faced. He said his mother was in there and he'd be damned if he wasn't going to see his mother.

Magda pulled herself together and hurried across the dark

brick floor toward Radiology. Elsie could tell her what was going on. She passed a large machine parked in the hall with BERTHA stenciled upon it. And passed a door marked STAFF, muffled yelps coming from behind it. "Open the door! Open this goddamn door, somebody." Magda hesitated, then shrugged and opened the door.

"Thanks," a young fellow said. "Goddamn bastard had a gun. Locked me in and stole my clothes." He brushed past her in his Jockey shorts. Behind him the closet was full of janitorial supplies—mops, galvanized buckets with wringers, bottles of liquid disinfectant, containers of powdered soap, cans of floor wax.

Magda shrugged and went on down the hall, only to be confronted by the Brinks man, his pistol out of its holster and stuck in his belt. In his tan khaki uniform, with the Sam Browne belt and wraparound dark glasses, he looked like some TV constable guarding the door.

Elsie burst out into the hall. "Where's Gin? What're you doing here, Magda?"

"I wish somebody'd tell me. Are they through with the paintings?"

"Hell, no," Elsie said. "Everybody's run off suddenly. I got to get these things done before we get a call from ER."

"Can I help?"

But the Brinks man stepped in front of her when she started in.

Elsie shrugged and gave Magda a look and went back into the lab. "Okay," she said, "let's get this show on the road." You'd think she had all day. She patted the X-ray table where another cassette lay in place.

Tina removed the Turner from its crate and positioned it on the table. Elsie adjusted the light with its cross hairs centered on an old-looking painting of an ocean and a castle. She didn't like the water. Gave her the creeps. As a kid she'd almost drowned in a cattle tank out on her grandpa's ranch. She shepherded everybody behind the lead wall and pressed the button. Tina Martinez removed one painting and set another in its place, and Elsie got them behind the wall again and took another picture. Hank rushed off to the darkroom down the hall and developed them, and they all crowded around while she hung them on the line.

"We got something every time," she said. "Looks like they've all been signed."

But the signatures were not where they should have been. Weren't paintings signed in a lower left-hand corner? The chairman bent closer, squinting. The careless white-lead scrawls showed *beneath* the paint all the way across the canvas. Noldes grabbed the X ray off the drying line and, frowning, followed with his finger the white lead underneath the painted portrait of the nobleman, lips moving as he read. " 'Gonzales.' Who the hell is Gonzales?"

He swung around to face them. "That the police lieutenant? Tito Gonzales? Christ!" he said accusingly. "What *is* this? What the hell's going on?"

25

When Gin was seven years old, the boys at the rancho down the road leaned a plank against the high first limb of a big cottonwood in front of their house and ran up and down it all morning like squirrels. She'd wanted to go up that plank but, though it had little cross battens nailed to it like the runs into chicken houses, that first limb was the height of a second-floor window off the ground.

Finally, amid taunts and dares, she made it up. It wasn't so bad if you crept on all fours, if you kept your eyes on the board rising in front of your nose and not on the drop-off to either side. But when she sat on the huge limb, ten times as big around as she was, looking down at the faces grinning up at her, her fingers dug into the bark—there was nothing else to hold onto, the next limb was way up over her head—and she froze. She couldn't move closer to the tree trunk.

She couldn't move at all. It was all she could do to breathe. She was young to feel like a helpless fool.

And that's how she felt this minute. She wanted to look at Raoul Query, touch his wrist, maybe feel a pulse. She felt the urge to examine the IV bottle and the tube leading to his arm. If she could move her eyes a fraction she could see out the window. But out there was only sky. They were on the top floor. But the hospital sat on a hill, and that made it feel still higher.

Approaching sirens distracted the masked intruder. Surely she could reason with him, if only she could find her voice. But in that mask, wielding that pistol, he shifted around the bed and looked out the window, the pistol resting against Raoul Query's throat.

In spite of the sirens and the stillness in the room, something happened, something changed, she was sure of it. Then she realized that Raoul Query's eyes were open. Only a slit, but open all the same. Did he know she was there? Please, she thought, let him close his eyes. It seemed dangerous for him to be conscious now.

Then voices, distant, down the hall. And pointing the gun at Raoul Query, giving it a sharp little kick to tell her to watch herself, he moved to the door and cracked it open and looked out.

"Please," she said, "listen—"

"I've got to get out of here," he said in a whisper, like talking to himself.

He came back and grabbed her arm and again put the pistol with the silencer to Query's head. The patient's eyes had closed.

"No!" she said. "Don't. You're making a mistake."

A whimper came from the direction of the bathroom. He heard it, too, and closed the door on the terrified nurse. "You are a nice girl, Ginevra. I would not choose to hurt you," he said.

She bit her lip and felt the worm crawl down her forehead.

He grabbed her shoulder and spun her around, the pistol cold in her back. "Open the door and tell me what you see."

She opened the door. Fifteen feet away, the nurse at the nurses' island bent over the desk. Only the top of her head showed. Gin willed her to look up, but she seemed to be writing. To her right where the halls intersected, something—a mouse?—scurried out of sight.

The gun jabbed, the familiar voice said, "What do you see?" Ten paces diagonally across the intersection of halls was the door marked STAIRS.

"Nothing. Nobody."

"All right. Do you know what's on the end of this pistol?"

She nodded, swallowing. Something was stuck in her throat. Surely she could appeal to him. If she could only find words, surely he would listen.

"If I pull the trigger," he said, "no one would hear." The pistol jabbed again. "All right, just walk now, stay ahead of me." He grabbed her arm and thrust her out the door. A moment later they were in front of the door marked STAIRS.

Could she run? Would he really shoot her? He was no criminal. But where would she run to? The nurses' station? A surge of adrenaline buoyed her. But he shoved the door open and pressed the pistol with the silencer into her side.

A jumble of footsteps echoed down the hall. Tito Gonzales's voice, but what was he saying? A groan of anguish came from the masked throat. "Come on," he said, pulling her by the arm through the door.

Before it closed, she managed to snag her heel on the sill, slip out of her shoe, and leave it behind in the hall with the toe pointing to the door now silently closing behind them.

A gigantic window on the landing lit the stairwell. Up they climbed. Like him she tiptoed. Another door led out onto the roof. Through its wire-reinforced glass top, she could see the sky. High up, clouds like cotton balls headed west, flat-bottomed as trees in a pasture full of cows.

He tried the door to the roof but it was locked. She was looking back down the stairs, listening for footsteps. Without turning he reached and shoved her against the wall. He aimed and fired. The bullet slammed into the door lock and ricocheted. He dropped the gun. It fell, bounded down the stairs, struck the metal banister, flew through the uprights, and came to rest on the landing below.

He grabbed his wrist. Bright blood spurted over the cotton scrubs. Big spatters splashed on the floor. She stared in horror. Her gorge rose and her hand fluttered like a fledgling to her mouth. There was something on the floor. A glob of blood, or a severed finger? She couldn't look.

Crouching, he went down the stairs in a rush and reclaimed the pistol, and she quick tried the door and it opened. He surged up the stairs after her.

Out on the roof, she put her back against the door and dug her heels into the gravel, regretting the shoe left behind. The gravel was sharp, her bare foot ineffectual. Four-foot parapets surrounded her, some of them around the opening straight ahead that must look down on the roof garden.

There was nothing she might grab to barricade the door. There was only herself, and he was much stronger. As the door gave behind her, she ran to the parapet and looked over at a lone woman sucking Pepsi through a straw at a stone table one story below. He grabbed her from behind. The woman looked up, surprised. He yanked her away from the parapet and struck her along the temple with the flat of the gun barrel. Her head reeled. She was aware of wind whipping her shirt, billowing it out behind her like a parachute braking a carrier plane, a cool wind in spite of the sun. The days were still hot, but fall had arrived.

He looked desperately around. Something—probably the elevator housing—jutted skyward, the size of a bungalow. There seemed to be two of them. The roof was confusing because of the hospital's irregular shape. Thick slabs of rubber matting made walkways over the gravel. Otherwise, except for various vents jutting up, there was only the sky and the mountains. The parapets were too high to see over unless you were right beside them. She thought there might be the roofs of lower floors below, but she couldn't tell, and she knew that, even given the chance, she'd be afraid to jump.

Guessing her thoughts, he shook her roughly, his eyes full of pain and rage. Blood spattered the roof gravel. The gun against her side, he held her to him with the injured hand and made for an outside parapet. Were they going over? Her heart pounded at her ribs like a prisoner at the bars. His warm blood soaked through her clothes onto her skin. Her temples throbbed like drumheads. Cars looked small on the acres of asphalt parking lot below. Uniformed police rushed out of the building, looking up. Her captor shouted over the parapet. "Now listen to me! I have a hostage. Don't come up here! I am warning you!"

A voice came through a bullhorn, one she didn't recognize. Where was Tito? "Come on down," the voice called. "The hospital's surrounded."

He swung around, surveying the roof. He looked up at the mountain as if to escape his predicament if only for a moment. She flashed on King Kong scaling the Empire State Building. Something like pity stirred in her.

Behind her a scraping sound. She cut her eyes as far as she could toward the door they had come through onto the roof. Nothing. The door stood ajar, as he had left it. He pulled her closer with his bloody hand and groaned softly. She looked down with horror at the mutilated fingers against her waist, at the blood all over her, splashing down her legs.

"Don't try anything." It was like a plea.

Then again a kind of scratching, like a mouse in the wall. She couldn't tell where the sound came from. She daren't look around. He swung her before him toward the door. He'd heard it, too. The gun wavered toward the stairs, but she wasn't sure it had come from there. He moved with her off to one side, where they would be behind the door if it opened. He would have the advantage of seeing without being seen. He could shoot first. How many shots were left in the gun? She knew nothing about guns. She thought it would hold a half dozen, fully loaded. One was already spent. That left five. Five people dead, one maybe herself. But he was losing blood at an alarming rate.

The soft scratching came again. This time she knew it behind her, but she willed herself not to turn. He still had on the surgical mask. Perhaps he'd forgotten he wore it. His face around the eyes was white. It was clear he was in great pain. Even in the wind, she heard each breath he took.

"Please," she said gently, "give yourself up. You haven't murdered anybody yet."

Laughter exploded behind the mask. Hunched there against the sky, he turned to her eyes appalled by such ignorance. The eyes spoke a simple truth she couldn't absorb, like a dream you can't hold upon waking. "What do *you*

know?'' he said, his voice muffled—by the mask, or by his
pain? She shrank away. And then, ''Murder breeds.''

That surprised her. Pleased her even. It was almost Shake-
spearean. It confirmed something she had sensed about him:
no matter what he was, he was not banal. Already he was
looking away, hunched there by the parapet, listening to sirens approach from two directions: up St. Michaels, down
the Old Pecos Trail. He was like some great, rough grizzly,
powerless before his tormentors.

Though her insides liquefied, there were things she had to
know. ''Just tell me,'' she said, ''please . . . What have you
done with the paintings?''

He peered over the parapet, his bloody hand, badly mutilated by the ricocheting bullet, burying itself in the cotton
folds of the scrub suit, while in the other the gun pointed at
her. He registered nothing but maybe the sirens dying, one
by one, at the entry below. Then dully, absently, he whispered, ''What paintings? What the devil are you talking
about?''

Stunned to silence, she took a moment to get her breath.
These extraordinary happenings—the stolen masterpieces,
the attempts on Raoul Query's life—must surely at some point
intersect. ''The Rembrandt,'' she said. ''The Turner. The
Van Dyck.''

But he wasn't listening. His eyes scanned her only as part
of the space in which he stood. The sun slid behind a cloud
and its last rays slanted in shafts toward them. Was his secret,
then, that explained the mystery—of what? of life, she supposed, quaking internally with laughter at herself—just this,
that he, not Raoul Query, was the murderer of the beautiful
Ellen? And if so, why? For money? For love? Or jealousy?
For the pain Ellen had inflicted of the acid of rejection? Had
he killed Beauty for at some point looking with loathing at
her beast, her Caliban?

A warm wave of nausea rose in Gin like a tide. And he'd
set out to kill Raoul Query. *How* was very clear: with the
blow of a bronze statue; with a deprivation of the lifesaving
drug; last, with a gun. Why had it become suddenly so urgent that he do it now, here in Santa Fe, when Beauty had
set out to sea in her fragile earthly craft some months ago?

The *why* was tantalizingly obscure. If she died now, she would never know.

The sound came again, the gentle scratching. He looked around fearfully, tried to move, stumbled, too weak to walk.

Seeing her chance, she fled around the corner of the stair housing and flattened herself against it, holding her breath, listening. He could come after her from either direction. If she could hear him approach, she might keep moving away, around corners, until help came.

She listened. Not a sound. Then the breath was knocked out of her and she went flying. Something landed on top of her out of the sky. She screamed. Pablo Esperanza grabbed her and slammed her facedown on the roof. She heard the bullet and blacked out gratefully recalling a soldier in some war movie saying, "You never hear the one that gets you."

26

Tito Gonzales already knew, by some galvanic epidermal response he could always count on, that the suspect was no longer on the roof. He had vamoosed, vanished. He was gone. So he felt like laughing at the uniformed boys slinking sideways, shoulders flattened to the walls, noses of their city issue .38s pointing skyward, pale wrists showing above the navy blue. Like a bunch of Hollywood extras, TV Blues, on top of St. Vincent slinking around the housings—what the hell were they? Air conditioners? Elevators?—doors like bulkhead doors, the doors in submarines, you had to step up and over to get inside.

He stuck his gun in his belt. "Get somebody up here knows the layout," he said to his sergeant, not looking at him, looking at the little buildings on the hospital roof, behind them whole undulating bands of aspens turning gold on the mountain under the royal blue of the sky. The wind tore at his hair.

In a minute they'd find out the suspect was not on the roof. While he watched, they crept around the housings, rushed corners, stormed metal doors. Some leaned over the parapets, searching rooftops of the floors below. One said something to somebody down in a rooftop patio and, reaching over, gave a hand up to another man in blue stepping over the parapet, not the blue of a cop suit, but the dark blue pants and light blue shirt of Maintenance.

The lieutenant strode over. "The hell you doin'?" he said, peering over the parapet. An extension ladder leaned against the wall below, giving access to the hospital roof. Up it climbed a large woman in a fiesta dress.

"Go back!" the lieutenant said, putting up a hand like a barrier as Magda reached the top of the ladder in her Birkenstocks, hair tumbling around her shoulders. "Will you please go back down?" Tito said in an outraged voice.

But Magda glanced behind her down the ladder, shuddered, and said she'd rather not. She gave her hand to the uniformed policeman, who smiled painfully at the lieutenant while Magda climbed over the parapet exclaiming at the view.

Tito Gonzales stared with his mouth open. He read the name on the maintenance man's pocket. "Dammit, Jerry," he said, pointing to the ladder, "where'd that come from?"

And Jerry told him about "this man" who said he'd seen the suspect take to the stairs in his surgical mask, with his gun and his hostage, and "this man" had requested the ladder so he could get to the roof via a route the gunman would not expect.

The lieutenant sighed his exasperation. "Was this man a cop?"

Jerry didn't know.

In a uniform?

"No. Like yourself," Jerry said.

"Who the hell authorized—Where is he? You know him? Ever seen him before?"

Jerry had not.

"And who is this woman?"

Jerry began explaining that it was his second cousin's . . .

"Never mind! Stuff it! Anybody come *down* that ladder?"

Jerry shook his head. "Nope. We were right down there all the time after we leaned it up against the wall."

"Who the hell is 'we'?"

Jerry looked uncertainly at the lady in the fiesta dress. "Well," she said, "I couldn't find out what was going on, so when Jerry ran by I asked him what he was doing, and he said he was getting a ladder, and I said what for, and he said if he knew he'd tell me."

While the lieutenant came to terms with that, one of the Blues yelled excitedly, "Here he is! Over here. I got 'im!"

The lieutenant spun around, confused—his radar was never wrong. But they were doing their thing again. Pistols out in front of them in both hands, they converged upon the rear of the stair-top housing.

He hurried over. The officer who'd yelled stood with his feet planted wide apart and his .38 out in front of him in both hands, pointing down at something the lieutenant could not yet see but that everybody else was staring at.

Gin had fainted twice before in her life: on one occasion, having barely escaped being run down by a Greyhound bus when she was ten; and on the other, when she'd left home to live on her own and, except for breakfasts of boxed cereal, eaten nothing but canned corned beef hash wrapped in flour tortillas for an indeterminate length of time. The doctor pronounced it malnutrition and sent Tina out for a steak. Rare. That was before her health-conscious days.

Coming to, looking up into the slanting barrel of a revolver, she marveled that everything came in threes. As she started under again, someone took her firmly by the shoulders and shook. "Ginnee, Ginnee."

She opened her eyes again. Now she realized that her head lay in somebody's lap, Pablo Esperanza's. He was sitting up against the wall of the stair housing in his socks. Elegant socks, dark silk with a hint of iridescence, no holes anywhere. She frowned, concerned over the whereabouts of his shoes, acutely aware of the gun still pointing at her.

"Where is he?" she asked.

"Shhh," he whispered, and said to the officer with the

gun, "My dear young man—" but the officer only shook the pistol at them, clearly meaning Pablo should shut up.

But Pablo said again, "My dear fellow, if you would be so kind . . ." And reaching up, to the officer's surprise he brushed the pistol aside. "Firearms can be so dangerous."

Lieutenant Gonzales rounded the corner of the stair housing, a maintenance man behind him. Other men in blue crowded around. The lieutenant saw Gin. "What the . . . ?"

She tried to smile.

"Ginnee was the hostage," the Mexican fellow said, lifting his shoulders in a shrug, lifting a hand and letting it fall, wearing socks but no shoes.

"Cuff him," the lieutenant muttered. But something was wrong. The young officer from ICU sprang forward, pulling handcuffs off his belt. But the lieutenant said, "Hold it. Wait a minute." Something didn't add up.

Magda peered over the lieutenant's shoulder, lifted a hand close to her ear, and waggled her fingers at Gin.

Gin said, "Hi, Magda."

"Can we can the greetings?" the lieutenant said. And to Jerry, "He have the gal with him when you saw him?"

"This guy?" Jerry said. "He didn't have *nobody* with him. He just wanted to get to the roof, so I—"

"Okay, *okay*."

"Please, Lieutenant," Pablo said, "hear me out. I can explain everything."

"I've heard that before," Tito muttered.

But he listened while Pablo explained that while bringing the paintings into the hospital from the Brinks truck he'd recognized someone he'd seen at the reception. The man was coming out of a supply closet in a scrub suit, putting on a surgical mask. "I feared, you see, that this fellow might be the assassin of my friend Raoul Query, so I escaped the X-ray room as quickly as I could and went in search of the man in the mask."

Pablo looked around at the faces of Santa Fe policemen. "I was looking for heem," he said, lifting his shoulders for emphasis, "when I saw heem head up the stairs with Ginnee." His shoulders sank against the stucco wall slashed now by afternoon shadow.

"So you borrowed . . ."

"The ladder," Jerry said. "I had to go get it."

Pablo said, "I thought 'ee would expect to be followed by way of the stairs."

Magda looked around her, nodding. That made sense.

"And then I held it for him so it wouldn't scrape against the wall and make a noise," Jerry said.

But, Gin thought, it had scraped a little. That was the mouse she'd heard, the mouse that paused and listened. And the mouse scooting round the corner outside room 3232 had been the toe of one of Pablo's missing shoes.

Pablo patted her hand. "The one in the mask, Ginnee, he raised the weapon to fire, so I had to launch myself off the parapet and strike you down."

"That's all right, Pablo. You saved my life."

Pablo squeezed her hand.

The lieutenant looked around the roof. The suspect was still at large. "What's behind the doors?" he demanded of one of the officers, but just then a helicopter approached and hovered like a dragonfly.

"What's behind the doors?" the lieutenant shouted again, but by then the helicopter had veered off so he felt like a fool.

"In there," an officer said, pointing to one of the doors, "looks like big tank vacuum cleaners set up on a concrete bank. You can see at a glance everything in the room. He's not in there."

"That's the elevator housing," Jerry said.

"How 'bout over there?"

"Air-conditioning."

"Not in there," the sergeant said.

"What's that one?"

"Machinery," Jerry said.

The sergeant shook his head. "We already checked. He wasn't there."

"What's that stack?"

"Air intake for surgery."

The lieutenant cleared his throat. "Okay," he said, "he's not on the roof, he's not in the housings, he didn't go over the parapets or down the ladder. So where the hell is he?"

Jerry caught his chin between thumb and forefinger and pulled at it thoughtfully. He began to nod. "I think I know where you'll find him, Lieutenant."

He led them back to the door marked MACHINE ROOM 4M06.

"They already looked in there," Tito Gonzales said.

But the maintenance man opened the door and stepped over the high threshold. One of the officers caught his arm and tried to stop him. The suspect was armed, after all.

But Jerry said, "It's okay. If he's where I think he is, he'll be harmless."

Unlike the other rooms on top of St. Vincent Hospital, Machinery 4M06 was dark, but the rectangle of light from the door revealed huge ducts, a giant turbine to their left, pipes everywhere. The air hummed with machine noise. They watched while the man from Maintenance stepped around a tall machine to the left of the door. Hidden in the dark behind the turbine was the outline of another bulkhead door. It opened to Jerry's hand upon total darkness. He unhooked the flashlight from his belt and aimed the beam downward, then turned to the lieutenant.

Tito stepped forward. Not three feet away, the floor fell off to a chasm. "I've yelled about this," Jerry said, "trying to get a railing in here."

"Cheez," the lieutenant breathed, stepping back. At the bottom of the shaft lay a figure he recognized from the opening two nights before.

Gin ducked under the lieutenant's arm. She gasped aloud. The surgical mask, askew, disclosed a pockmarked face. Neck twisted at an impossible angle, Victor Weldon stared up at them. The pale eyes looked alive, a little amused, smug at all the faces peering down at him two floors below. It was as if he knew a secret and could tell them if he wanted to, but he didn't want to.

27

Helicopter rotors beat overhead like the wings of a ptero-
dactyl, rousing the patient in 3232. He felt a wave of relief.
He opened his eyes expecting a twilight beach, not this white
room.

Somebody *tsk*ed. "They've been told not to fly over the
hospital." A disapproving sigh. "It's the governor"—a
woman's voice—"on his way to Albuquerque. A helicopter
in Santa Fe means either a prison break and they're overflying
the arroyos, or else the governor is on his way to the airport."

Did that make sense? He moved his head to see who she
was and his mouth gaped in a silent cry of pain.

"I can give you something for that," she said.

He shifted his eyes, careful not to move his head again.
Small, with dark, short hair. Not Gin Prettifield. But Gin
Prettifield had been here, hadn't she? The sound of the helicopter faded. He closed his eyes. They were back on the
black sand beach. "I'm cold," she said. She'd worn her
swimsuit though he'd cautioned her about the wind, and the
sun had already set. They'd watched for the green flash along
the horizon at sundown, but there wasn't any. Too hazy.

"I'll run back for your sweater."

"Raoul, I asked you to come because . . ."

She had asked him to come to the kahuna's compound, a
tortuous drive out the winding Hana Road. She had showed
him around. A steep forest path . . . a waterfall with a shaded
pool, people lying nude in the ferns. She smiled. She was
happy. "Raoul, I'm well. I asked you to come because . . .
the first to know."

"We just had a call from Oahu," the Hawaiian girl said.
She handed Ellen a card and he glanced at it. The kahuna's

card. She had scribbled the message for Ellen on the back, confirming a doctor's appointment.

"But I'm not going," Ellen told him. "I'm through with their poisons. I'll call and cancel." She put the card into her sunglasses case, and the glasses case into her beach bag.

"Ellen, are you sure?"

"I guess I won't go in after all. You're right, it's chilly."

"I'll run back and get your sweater."

While he trotted back up the path cut in the black, evil-looking lava and across emerald green lawns to the main house—a big, old Hawaiian house from the early days, wrap-around porches, wood bleached silver, roof shingles showing inside over the rafters where geckos lay in wait—above him, behind him, a helicopter's rotors beat the air.

As he ran into the house the helicopter landed somewhere behind him, beyond the dense foliage. In all that followed, he'd forgotten about the helicopter. No, not true. When he returned with her sweater and found her gone, his first thought had been, She's flown away.

"Here, swallow this. I'll raise your head."

Frowning, he opened his eyes. "Where am I?"

"I'm Nurse Chavez. This is St. Vincent Hospital."

She watched him attempt to nod and she felt his pain. "Don't," she whispered. "Just lie still." Along with her pity mingled relief—that he'd come back, he was alive. They taught you in nursing school not to get emotionally involved with your patients, for that way lies burnout. But for Nurse Chavez such considerations had long since flown out the window. He was helpless. He was in danger. He was handsome.

His eyes opened wide. "He hit me," he muttered, and lifted a hand toward his bandaged head. "It was the statue. I was so—*The card* . . ." That was it—the card he'd fingered absently as he sat on the reception desk in the museum corridor. He frowned. He'd had a dream about that card. Fingering the edge of it in the dream had been like plucking a guitar string. "I found it in my breast pocket," he said. "I wondered how it got there." He looked at her, frowning.

Oh, my God, she thought. He was delirious. Brain-damaged after all. Or reliving some fearful dream that had come in the coma, unable to distinguish it from reality. She turned to run for the doctor, but the patient grabbed her arm and held it in a grip surprisingly strong.

"I was in the corridor," he said urgently, "at the reception desk . . . I was about to sneeze. The card came out of the breast pocket with the handkerchief. The last time I saw that card, Ellen was putting it in her beach bag. What was it doing in my—Don't you see? Our jackets must have got mixed up at dinner. It was his blazer I was wearing."

He tried to lift his head but she restrained him gently. He gripped her with both hands, his eyes imploring her to listen, to understand, like—Who was it in high school lit? That old sailor. That ancient mariner.

"The helicopter! He was there, *Victor was there*, on the beach." He looked at her, pleading. "He often flies over from Oahu. She must have given it to him—the card—and asked him to cancel the appointment when he got back to Oahu. But he told us he'd last seen her *days* before . . .

"It all fits, it all makes sense," he said, lapsing back into the pillows. "Her doctor was on Oahu, and so is Victor's office."

Nurse Chavez eyed the call button lying on the bed. She could summon someone from the nurses' station, but the patient would not let go.

"He didn't, of course," he said bitterly. "Knowing about that appointment would prove he'd been with her on the Hana beach. The card in his pocket proves it."

He closed his eyes, exhausted, sweat beading on his forehead. Nurse Chavez was relieved.

But suddenly his eyes flew open. He lurched up out of the bed. "My God," he cried, grabbing her with both hands, almost dislodging the IV. It was all she could do to restrain him. She managed to reach the button and summon the nurses' station, meanwhile crooning to quiet him. But he wouldn't be quieted. "Her dislocated shoulder . . . those bruises . . . the body washed up in such a strange place, against all the logic of the tides . . ."

He tore his hands free and put them over his face. His shoulders heaved with sobs. He retched. Nurse Chavez grabbed the bedpan.

As a male nurse burst into the room, Raoul Query sub-

sided against the pillows. "Maybe he drowned her first,"
he whispered, "and that's why the dislocated shoulder—
because she fought him—and *then* got her into the helicopter. Or maybe he took her for a ride and, flying low over
the water . . . Those dragonflies have no doors. A sudden
tilt . . ."

Nurse Chavez visualized the horrifying scene. What did it
all mean?

He looked at her. "He thought I knew," he whispered.
"I showed him the card and told him we'd got our jackets
mixed up at the restaurant. I hadn't put it all together yet, but
he thought I knew."

She nodded, though she hadn't a clue what he was talking
about.

"He tried to kill me," Raoul Query whispered, "because
he thought I knew he'd murdered Ellen."

28

The paintings.

The voice in her head barely registered. In the chaotic last
hour, she had forgotten the paintings. Raoul Query's would-
be murderer was dead, but what had he to do with the stolen
masterpieces? She still had no idea.

The clouds had metamorphosed, by the magic peculiar to
clouds, into a herd of sheep stampeding toward the horizon
after the fallen sun. It was too late to get back to the museum
and release Jean Medows in time for dinner with her husband
and afterward Zozobra. The museum would be closed, traffic
thick. The burning of Old Man Gloom, heralding Fiesta,
brought out hordes.

She and Pablo stopped for a quick look-in on Raoul Query

while Magda stayed in the hall. ("After all, I've never laid eyes on the man.") There were two people besides the nurse in the hushed room. By the window on the other side of the bed, Hanna Enright held Raoul Query's free hand, the other still attached to the IV bottle hanging from its harness.

The second visitor turned as they entered. The commander, smiling his strange, chin-up smile. "I say," he said, "bit of a near thing, eh?"

She couldn't look the commander in the eye. Neither he nor Hanna Enright could know of the corpse on the roof, and the awful secret, which the lieutenant had cautioned them not to divulge, made Gin feel guilty. She focused instead on his cuff link. The commander was out of uniform for the evening's festivities.

The head of the bed was raised a little. Raoul Query lay swathed in bandages, but his eyes were open and very much alive. Pablo laid a hand lightly on his shoulder.

"Good of you to come," the patient said, looking not at Pablo but at her. In her shyness, her eyes again retreated to the commander's sleeve and the cuff link, jaunty red and gold.

Get back to the museum, the voice said inside her head.

"We're so relieved," she murmured, looking at Raoul Query's lips, the little mole. How awful, to stand there visiting while a man lay dead on the roof. She reminded herself what he'd been up to.

Hanna Enright said, "Will we see you at Zozobra?"

"There'll be a mob," Gin murmured.

"Well, old man," the commander said, "we'll be shoving off. Take care, old chap." He shot his sleeve and looked at his watch. The cuff link disappeared.

The small voice spoke more urgently. *Get back to the museum.*

The patient was looking at her. She forced a smile. "Get a good night's sleep."

"I've had a lot of sleep, they tell me."

The commander awkwardly patted the patient's hand.

Get back to the museum. Get back to the museum.

A CAT scan was in progress in one lab and a heart cath in another. Elsie was unavailable. Neither the chairman nor

Tina was anywhere in sight in the radiology corridor, nor were the paintings.

Gin hurried along the outside ramp with Magda and Pablo, toward the ambulance entrance. Below in the service parking lot an automatic vending machine truck backed up to a ramp near the trash compactor. Three motorcycles were parked near a stack of wooden pads. In Parking Lot #2 policemen had fallen into clusters, talking. Squad cars were pulling out. Magda's van was in the space next to the red Brinks truck, which at that moment was backing, ready to turn toward St. Michaels Drive.

Gin broke into a run. "Tina!"

The square red armored vehicle didn't stop, but as she watched its broad rear end retreat down the drive, Tina flew out of the main second-floor entrance and ran toward them. "Oh my God, are you all right? I just heard. Tito said—Who on earth . . . ? What did . . . ?"

Gin grasped Tina's arm. "What did the X rays show?"

"Oh, God," Tina groaned. Pablo took the opportunity to put an arm around her, but she threw it off. "You!" she said. "It was your name on the painting. It said Pablo . . ." But it was so confusing she couldn't finish. She said to Gin, "They're fakes. All three. And the forgers have signed every one of them."

Magda said, "Wow."

"My dear," Pablo said, but Tina pulled away from him.

Gin wanted to explain that Pablo Esperanza had nothing to do with the forgeries and besides had saved her life, but there was only time to say, "Don't be silly." Tito Gonzales had emerged from the main entrance, and the assistant director ran to meet him.

The lieutenant had to concentrate on the traffic, but he felt her copping glances at him. He didn't think she was admiring his profile. He thought she was wondering could she count on him. The lieutenant was wondering could you unload a round at somebody with a million-dollar painting under his arm.

The assistant director had come at him in a rush and he'd said, "Whoa. Slow down. Now give it to me again," and she took a breath and started over. Two of them, she said. He thought he could handle two of them. Depends what they were packing. What did the stiff in the hospital morgue have to do with it?

Attempted murder, suspect dead, no sense yet to any of it. So maybe she was right. What the hell. He'd give it a shot. The lieutenant glanced at her tense in the seat beside him. Nice girl. Too tall, but nice.

Roof lights flashing, siren wailing, the lieutenant tried to listen to what she was saying as they ran north on the shoulder of St. Francis past stalled bumper-to-bumper cars. He'd told Briggs and Peck to follow, but he'd lost their car in the snarl of traffic. He cut up the Alameda to Guadalupe, zigzagged till he came to Marcy and, because Washington was jammed, headed for Otero, nodding un-huh while she talked fast and breathy, he could almost feel it on his cheek. He crossed the Paseo where it narrowed—sidewalks full of people walking toward Magers Field—drove up the hill, and dipped down the drive to the museum parking lot, empty except for a yellow Dodge van, a silver Jaguar, and a green three-quarter-ton Ford pickup.

"Juan's," she said as they passed the truck. "The Medows'," she said, pointing to the silver Jaguar. That'd be the guard and the high society couple from Galisteo. But the yellow van was a stranger.

The museum was closed. They had to turn off the alarms before letting themselves in. Then they took it gallery by gallery. Nobody there. The lieutenant sighed.

He went with her down to the basement. He hated that. He hated dark, still, unused, unoccupied places. And they found just exactly what she'd said they'd find. He gave a long, low whistle. That proved it. The gal was right. Another crime on his hands. Trick was getting help up here. The Santa Fe police force was divided between the caper at the hospital and directing traffic all over the north side of town. Where were Briggs and Peck? Frozen in traffic like a ship in Antarctic ice.

"Whoa, what've we got here?" he said. Waiting in her office, the big window giving a view of part of the grounds.

"Oh, no," Gin breathed, and cursed a little under her

breath. It was Reuben, climbing the hill through the *chemiso* with a brown paper bag in his hand. She watched him approach the museum, try the big basement garage door and then the smaller door.

She had to get to him first. She started out of the office.

"Hold on," Tito Gonzales said. "Let's see what he's up to."

"I know what he's up to," she said.

Reuben went around the side of the building toward the front, and below them a figure in a red devil's outfit like a tapered suit of long johns attached to a devil's-head mask complete with horns, appeared among the piñons to the east.

"Whatta we got here?" the lieutenant whispered. Was this part of Zozobra, like the Little Glooms and the Fire Dancer, who finally torched the giant?

Gin didn't think so. Unlike Reuben, when the red devil bent to the basement door, he seemed to have a key. The door opened to his touch.

"Okay, that's one of them," she whispered.

The lieutenant's hand crept up to the bulge of his revolver. He took it out of its shoulder harness beneath his jacket and nosed it into his belt.

"Stay here," he whispered.

"No," she said. "I'm going with you."

"Aw, come on, you'll just be in the way. Let me handle this." He wished he could lock her in the office. He went out in the hall. He couldn't go down the elevator. Suspect would be waiting when the doors slid open. He was making for the stairs when she caught his arm.

He turned. The guy with the beard and the paper sack was at the front door, face pressed to the glass and shaded by his hand. He'd seen them. He said something, called something, his mouth moved.

But she was pointing to another guy—taller, skinnier—in another suit of red long johns with the red devil mask, who came tearing around the corner of the building. He ran over to the Dodge van in the parking lot, tried the door, then straightened—swearing, it looked like. The van was locked. He bent and peered in the window, yanked on the door. Almost tore off the handle. Then straightened with hands on

his hips and looked around. Then banged his fist on the roof,
lips moving, swearing to himself. Then he saw the bearded
guy at the front door, and the bearded guy had turned and
was looking at him.

The lieutenant wanted them both, wanted to walk out
calmly, gun in hand, and just take them where they stood.
But hold on. Not yet. There was still the devil in the basement.

If the lieutenant didn't know what Reuben was doing there,
Gin did. She had to get him out of the way or somebody else
might do it for her.

Oh, no! He'd put down his brown paper bag. He was stroll-
ing casually toward the red devil and the van parked next to
Juan's truck. He was saying something to the man in the
costume, offering to help. The red devil, hands out from his
sides like John Wayne in a western about to draw, stood
watching him come.

Reuben, come back! Get out of the way! Reuben!

But he couldn't hear her shouting inside her head.

"What's going on out there?" Tito whispered.

"It's a friend," she said. "He comes up here every year.
Loves the fireworks. It's a good place to watch. Usually I
wait for him, and he brings a snack."

"The paper bag?"

She nodded.

In the deserted building, they heard a noise.

"The garage door opening," Gin whispered.

The lieutenant had it now. The van was the getaway car—
a van because they had to carry the paintings. The devil in
the basement was the one who had the key to the museum
and knew where the pictures were. But now the devil outside
had locked his keys in their vehicle. A spurt of laughter escaped the lieutenant. He couldn't believe it. These creeps
were amateurs!

"Stay here," he said.

Torn, Gin looked at Reuben out there being helpful. He
walked over to Juan's truck and found something in the truck
bed—a piece of bailing wire. He was making a loop in one
end of it, poking it through what must be an eighth of an

inch opening at the top of the van window on the driver's side.

She heard the stair door open and softly close after Tito Gonzales. Then a whistle outside and the man in the red long johns and devil mask looked over Reuben's bent back and down the west side of the building. Was somebody there? Gin couldn't see. The tall devil lifted his shoulders and put his hands out in an elaborate pantomime shrug. He looked down at Reuben laboring with the twist of wire, peering in at the ignition where presumably the keys dangled, and shrugged again. Then he gave an exaggerated frown, "What?" and waited. Whoever was down the west side of the building, and she knew now who it had to be, must have been telling him in pantomime what to do, and the devil looked around on the ground, bent, picked up a rock, and as Reuben triumphantly fished out the car keys, raised it over his unsuspecting head.

She already had the door open. "Reuben!"

Startled, Reuben whirled and caught the arm raised with the rock. She couldn't have said what, exactly, happened next, but the devil was on the ground and Reuben glowering over him with the car keys still dangling on the hooked end of the bailing wire.

Around the corner of the building came the lieutenant, close on the heels of the second red devil. This one had a painting under his arm. Tito had his pistol out. He stopped and took up the stance he'd so recently smiled at on the hospital roof, gun out in front of him in both hands. "Stop or I'll shoot!"

But the man with the painting didn't stop and Tito was afraid of hitting the painting. The red devil snatched the keys from the wire in Reuben's hand and leapt in the van.

"Stop him!" Tito yelled, and Reuben lunged forward, but the open door of the wildly backing van caught him and knocked him down on top of the devil on the ground.

The van sped out toward Hyde Park Road, where the Brinks truck, blocking the drive, obligingly backed to let it pass. Sergeant Peck's patrol car swerved around the armored truck and into the drive. Tito ran after the van, Gin on his heels. "Get out!" he shouted to Briggs. "Get down there and hold the guy in the red underwear!"

The lieutenant leapt in the front seat next to Peck, Gin in the back. "Down the hill!" the lieutenant said. "After the van." The sergeant turned on the siren and waved the Brinks truck out of the way.

Up ahead the van was stopped by traffic at the foot of the hill. The man in the devil suit stuck his head out the window and the traffic cop smiled at him. "Oh, Lord," Gin said, "he thinks it's the Fire Dancer or something, he's letting him through."

The cop stopped traffic on Bishop's Lodge Road and waved the van across into the Fort Marcy complex. It sped up, swerved past the island in the middle of the drive, and turned the corner to the back of the sports complex.

The traffic cop waved the sergeant through as well, but when they got to the back of the building the yellow van stood in the middle of the parking lot with its door hanging open, and the man in the red suit was running across the arched wooden bridge spanning the arroyo, the painting still under his arm.

Gin leapt from the police car while it rolled to a stop, looked in the van but saw nothing, ran across the arroyo bridge and into the crowd that covered the baseball field. The sun had set. Twilight was growing dim. Zozobra, dressed in white, swayed over the crowd, eyes blazing red from the lights behind them. He lifted his arms and growled like distant thunder. The giant puppet, three stories high with a sound system behind him, looked and moved like something alive, part monster, part cartoon.

Children laughed and cried out to him. Toddlers looked, then buried their heads in their mothers' arms. People sat on blankets on the grass or stood in clusters, arms crossed against the twilight chill. They'd started coming in midafternoon to claim a spot on the grass of the baseball field. Evidence everywhere of picnics—coolers, thermoses, paper plates.

A politician shouted into the sound system, but you couldn't make out his words. Gin and the lieutenant climbed up on a picnic table and tried to spot the red suit. Behind them spectators shouted, "Down in front!"

Old Man Gloom hung from a pole on top of earth terraces like giant steps climbing the hillside toward Murales. Across the "stage" at Zozobra's feet filed conquistadores and señoritas, the fiesta court. A voice called out their names on the speaker system.

Gin caught sight of the red devil over toward the firehouse at the edge of the park, fighting his way through the crowd. "There!" she cried, pointing. They leapt down from the picnic table. The crowd behind them cheered and clapped. They ran along the path between the arroyo and center field.

"There he is!" Sergeant Peck shouted from the other side of the arroyo. They started up alongside the chain-link fence between the playing field and the fire station. Gin broke through the lines in front of the portable latrines and ran full tilt into a familiar figure eating a hot dog.

"Come help us!" she yelled.

Juan, clutching his hot dog, mustard on his face, ran along at her side.

The fiesta court filed back across to the bleachers and out of sight. Here came the Little Glooms, kids dressed in sheets, dancing like small ghosts around Zozobra's giant feet. Old Man Gloom looked down amazed, growling louder and louder while the little fiends danced.

The long desert afterglow had faded. It was finally dark. The crowd quieted. Zozobra growled louder and louder, waving his arms in slow motion, menacing the masses below him like something trapped and cornered. The Little Glooms danced across the bench on which the giant puppet stood, waving their sheeted arms to music that sounded like an ancient gramophone. The crowd applauded.

The Fire Dancer appeared, small at the foot of the terraced steps. The crowd yelled encouragement. All in red, costumed and masked, little David swooped and danced, higher and higher up the steps, wielding his torch, threatening Goliath, while the giant bent his head, growling at the tiny creature at his feet. The crowd shouted, "*Burn* him! *Burn* him!"

Gin shivered. It was atavistic. She always felt sorry for the giant, a little frightened by the crowd. "There he is!" she cried.

"Where?" Juan shouted.

"Over there! Head him off!"

"Head through the crowd!" the lieutenant shouted to his sergeant.

Pursuers converging on him from all sides, the man in the red devil suit burst out of the crowd and onto the middle terrace, holding the painting before him in both hands. Now there were *two* Fire Dancers. The crowd cheered. There'd never been two Fire Dancers before.

The real Fire Dancer touched the torch to the hem of Zozobra's clothes, and flames burst to life inside the puppet. Gin stopped in awe at the foot of the terraces. Flames leapt up the puppet's leg while he howled in pain and the crowd set up a rhythmic, "Burn him! Burn him! Burn him! Burn him!"

The Fire Dancer hesitated with his torch. A tomfool clown in red long johns and mask ran toward him across the step. Where the hell had he come from? Goddamn drunk. Chrice, the boob was heading straight for Old Man Gloom.

Zozobra blazed up in the night. Flames climbed his legs, his trunk, and he groaned and writhed, enveloped by smoke and fire.

Tito had his pistol out but he couldn't head the fellow off. Too many people behind Zozobra, watching from the hills and rooftops across Murales. The masked devil holding the painting ran straight for the burning giant, not seeing where he was going, looking over his shoulder at his pursuers out of the little slit eyes of the mask. The crowd roared.

The Fire Dancer cursed under his breath. Here came Tito Gonzales. What was ol' Tito doing? (Out in the crowd Tito's wife, holding one of the babies, the others clinging to her skirts, wondered, too. "Daddy-daddy-daddy," Junior yelled, his voice lost in the uproar.) Ten years ago Tito and the Fire Dancer had been high school football stars together. Now, Tito running along the bench and the Fire Dancer leaping higher on the steps, they converged on the red devil, heading him off. Tito knew how to throw a tackle when he had to. He had to now or the devil would be fried to a crisp.

Zozobra cried out in the agony of his death throes. The crowd yelled and cheered this new and original spectacle at the feet of Old Man Gloom. The Fire Dancer blocked the running man's way in front, and Juan blocked it from below. At last, the red devil looked up at Zozobra. He threw up an arm against the heat as the lieutenant launched himself into a flying tackle and landed with his arms around the red devil's feet. Out of the red devil's hands flew the painting toward the flames. Gin screamed. Juan, who had once played basketball, leapt up and snatched the painting out of the conflagration. He looked at it. "What is thees trash?" It looked like an amateur's rendering of yellow desert, green cactus, garish yellow sky.

"Hello, Ginny," the fallen devil said in a small, embarrassed voice.

Tito burst out, "You know this guy?"

"Chees!" Juan said, recognizing the voice, and with a touch of diffidence reached out and offered the devil a hand.

The crowd went wild. Out in the sea of people, Linda Gonzales held onto the babies, who wanted to run to their daddy. She smiled and accepted congratulations from the people around her for the show Tito had put on, but all she could think was, Why doesn't he tell me these things?

Zozobra subsided in his fiery death throes. The sea of faces turned up like night-blooming flowers to follow a ball of flame soaring into the night. The crowd went aaaaaaaahh as the first of the fireworks burst, showering a silver spray over the hills north of Santa Fe.

Gin said, "I knew it had to be you."

The devil pulled off his headpiece. Quillan Davies said, "I believe my next line is—I can explain everything."

29

Toby Trowber was in her room at the Sheraton, packing to go home. She thought she had it all straight now. She and Sheila had been talking of nothing else.

Only one thing Mrs. Trowber hadn't cleared. She'd hoped it would somehow come up in conversation, for asking about it would give away her eavesdropping. The habit had never gotten her in trouble so far, though whenever Bobby had lost her to the conversation at the next table he'd warned her that one day it would land her in an embarrassing situation. She hoped this wasn't it. Still, her curiosity was getting the best of her.

"But," she said, "if it wasn't the paintings, what were you selling for one million dollars now and sixty over the long haul? You know, that they wanted to give you cash for 'on the pier'?" Whatever that meant.

The crime writer flung herself down like a Raggedy Ann on one of the beds and sat there smoking. Mrs. Trowber had just yesterday given up the nasty habit. Bobby had tried to persuade her for years. She sometimes worried that she might be an addictive personality. She opened a window as a hint.

"Oh, that," Sheila said, puffing away. "Well, as you know, Victor's business was import-export."

Mrs. Trowber nodded, folding a blouse into her suitcase. She glanced around the room. Now where had she put . . . ?

"And the pod needs money badly just now," Sheila said from within her smoke cloud. "The pineapple plantation next to us is selling off the parcel on our border. No telling what could go in there, maybe a development. They want a fortune for the land, but who's got a fortune?"

"That must be very distressing," Mrs. Trowber said.

"*Tell* me."

Mrs. Trowber folded her hair dryer in the slip she'd worn yesterday and laid it on the bed beside her suitcase. It could fill a hole somewhere. "But what on earth sells for sixty million dollars?"

Sheila chuckled. "Cigarettes."

"Cigarettes!" It wasn't going to be easy to quit with these constant reminders.

Apparently it reminded the crime writer, too. She sighed and crushed out the cigarette half-smoked.

"Sixty million dollars for *cigarettes*?" Mrs. Trowber said.

Sheila nodded in her halo of smoke. "The Arabs want American cigarettes. They can buy them abroad, apparently, with American labels, but those are made with foreign tobacco, and according to the Arabs foreign tobacco doesn't taste as nice as American tobacco. For one thing, Victor said the foreign growers use more and stronger insecticides. So, the Arabs want cigarettes grown and rolled in the U.S. of A. But they have a hard time getting them."

Sheila absently took her pack from the bedside table, knocked one out, and lit up. It sure smelled good. Mrs. Trowber thought maybe she'd wait and quit once she got home to San Francisco. Then she admonished herself: You're *weak*, Toby Trowber.

She fished a sandal out from under the bed. "I see," she said, though actually she didn't.

"You have to get around the cigarette companies," Sheila said. "They all have contracts abroad with companies that make them there and put the American company's label on them. *That* ought to be illegal, seems to me. But I guess the foreign companies are some kind of subsidiaries to the American firms, so it's all according to Hoyle. But Victor found a way to buy them here, ship them to his warehouses in Honolulu, and sell them from there to the Arabs. It's all legal, I guess."

Toby Trowber wondered how many cigarettes that would be, sixty million dollars' worth? She pictured them stacked in lovely cartons to the heavens. She'd never be able to quit this way.

"Selling in large amounts, Victor said we could make a

fortune. It went through some German company, I understand. But now I guess it'll all fall through.''

''Did you like Victor?'' Mrs. Trowber asked from the bathroom, putting her toilet articles into her cosmetics bag—bath bubbles, cologne, mousse, blush . . .

It took Sheila a moment to answer. ''I wouldn't say I *liked* him. He interested me. Now I realize it was probably because I sensed something. You know, my work.''

''Yes, I see,'' Mrs. Trowber said. ''But I wonder if this was his first, you know, *offense*.''

In the bathroom mirror, she saw Sheila thinking about that. ''I guess we'll never know,'' she said. ''But he seemed to dote on Ellen. I can't imagine him harming her.''

Toby Trowber knew she would be curious about that murder for the rest of her life. She and Sheila had been awake all night, worrying it to death. Had he been jealous of Raoul Query? Had he learned of her intention to change her will and been enraged? They'd found that his business was nearing bankruptcy. Maybe he'd needed Ellen's money to work the cigarette scam and killed her to keep her from changing her will, though she'd changed it already. Toby thought very few people would kill just for money. Sheila laughed at her naïveté.

And why had he been cottoning up to Alice?

Sheila said, ''To keep her quiet. She'd just come into the museum corridor, looking for the 'Ladies,' when she heard Raoul fall, and Victor immediately rushed her out of the building and down to the plaza. He told her he hadn't been able to contain himself, that he'd seen red at something Raoul had said and he'd let him have it. She thought with his fist. He never mentioned the statue, nobody had mentioned the statue. He claimed Raoul had said that night in the Gallery of Western Art that, after all, Ellen was dying anyway so her 'swimming accident' was all for the best.''

''What'll the pod do for the money now?'' Mrs. Trowber asked, closing her suitcase and leaning her weight on it.

Sheila shrugged. ''Nothing,'' she said. ''We'll have to let that land go and hope for the best. Hanna will be pleased. She thought selling cigarettes to third world countries was like selling lethal weapons.'' Sheila sighed. ''It'll be good to get home.''

Mrs. Trowber leaned harder on her suitcase and brought the zippers all the way around, forcing them a little at the corners. What would it be like, living in Hawaii? She had a little money, though surely not enough. She gave herself a shake and put that out of her mind. She had to think of Pooley. She'd heard that in Hawaii they put animals in quarantine for months on end. Pooley would never survive that. Besides, San Francisco was her home.

There was a knock at the door and Hanna Enright came in. ''Oh, good, you haven't left yet, Toby. I wanted to say good-bye.'' She had on a navy blue dress with a wide lacy collar that Mrs. Trowber thought very becoming. It all but hid her hump.

''How is he?'' Sheila asked.

''Gaining strength every day. By Wednesday we'll be able to take him home. I'll be glad to miss flying back with Eric and Alice. Alice is in one of her primal snits.''

''What now?''

''She was questioned by the police and—you know Alice—she felt accused.''

''She sees now that Victor was using her,'' Sheila said. She was filing her nails. ''That's a blow to her ego.''

The crime writer got up and walked barefoot over the carpet to fall into one of the easy chairs by the window, the better to see what she was doing. ''I'm ready to get back to my computer,'' she said.

Hanna Enright propped herself on the edge of the dresser, watching Mrs. Trowber collect her things.

''What did Raoul tell you about that night on the beach?'' Sheila asked.

''Nothing much,'' Hanna said.

''Come on, you were never a good liar. What really happened?''

Hanna crossed to the window and stood looking out over the flat roofs of Santa Fe to the blue volcanic hills in the distance. ''He actually said very little. I had to put it together myself. He just said he'd already told us.''

''I never believed what he told us,'' Sheila said, laying the fingers of one hand lightly on the palm of the other, seeing if the nails were even.

Hanna found the view charming—the low piñons, the earth-colored adobe houses nestled in the hills. "What he told us was true, as far as it went."

"That wasn't very far."

Mrs. Trowber knew she had to hurry if she was to catch the airport shuttle, but she wanted to hear this. She went in the bathroom to renew her makeup and comb her hair, but she left the door open.

Hanna said, "The reason he didn't look for her when he came back to the beach . . . Well, he thought she'd left because she didn't want to see him."

"Had they quarreled?"

"No. She'd told him she was leaving Victor."

Toby Trowber saw Hanna's nod in the bathroom mirror.

"Don't tell me she wanted to go back to Raoul," Sheila Wadsworth said.

"That's what I gathered, but when I suggested it, he clammed up. I always thought Ellen married Victor because Raoul had that affair—you know, she'd been so hurt."

"Wowee," the crime writer said, getting up and ranging around the room in her loose-jointed way. "She was leaving Victor because she was still in love with Raoul!"

"That would explain the change in her will," Hanna said.

"Raoul didn't know about that?"

"Not till after the inquest. I gather what happened next— he was too much a gentleman to say—either he told her that was not possible, or perhaps she saw it in his eyes."

Mrs. Trowber detected a faraway note in Hanna Enright's voice, like she was recounting a fairy tale.

"He didn't want her back?"

"He always loved Ellen but was a little afraid of her," Hanna said in that dreamy voice. "I mean, when they were together he had, you know, a breakdown. Ellen was too much for him."

"Is this what he said, or is it your invention?" Sheila asked drily.

Hanna Enright ignored her. "He ran from the marriage

once and I guess he thought history would repeat itself if they got back together.''

"Well, I say," said Toby from the bathroom. "And I gather they seemed like the ideal pair." She sighed. "Nobody knows what goes on in a marriage." She put on her lipstick and pressed her lips together to get it even.

Hanna said, "That must have been a painful moment. That's why he hurried off to get her sweater. That's when he heard the helicopter."

"Victor's?" Sheila threw herself back down on her bed and dragged a pillow behind her.

"Must have been. Alice said he'd phoned from Oahu maybe two hours earlier and learned that Ellen had called and asked Raoul to drive down to Hana. He called about the time Raoul left to drive that awful highway. Victor could have easily made it from Oahu in the time it takes to make that tortuous drive."

"Why didn't Raoul tell us all this?"

Hanna shrugged. "Some mistaken sense of honor. It might even have been to protect Victor's feelings."

"Is this the truth, or is it your version of what might have happened?" Sheila asked.

Mrs. Trowber emerged from the bathroom and phoned down for someone to pick up her bags. "Do you suppose," she said, "that when they found her he thought—Raoul, I mean—that he'd *caused* her suicide? You know, because he'd rejected her?"

Sheila shrugged. "Maybe he thought because of her illness."

Hanna said, "She claimed the kahuna had cured her."

Sheila raised her eyebrows.

"Oh, you don't believe in anything," Hanna said sharply.

Sheila looked up, surprised. Hanna turned back to the window.

Mrs. Trowber thought: Now what's that all about? Pods must be like families, full of strange little animosities she would never now unravel. The bellhop knocked at the door. Sheila rose and gave her a hug. Hanna came over and hugged her, too.

"Come visit us sometime, Toby," Hanna said.

"I will." Mrs. Trowber felt sentimental about the poddies now that they were parting, but her heart was making the break. What with flying west, chasing the sun, she'd be with Pooley well before dark.

30

Would the museum prosecute? Gin wasn't so sure, and she was glad that wasn't her decision. Tito threw up his hands at the idea. Prosecute who? Whose paintings were they anyway? And who was the thief, the late Charley Burrell or Quillan Davies? "It'd be opening a can of worms! You'd be getting into British law."

Perdita assured them the paintings had been legally Charley's, and he'd replaced them with copies to avoid just such a fuss. And if Quillan Davies thought they were his, why had he gone to such lengths to *steal* them?

Lloyd Noldes was for putting Davies away, but Perdita chuckled when she heard the story. She wanted to meet the ninth Earl of Tor. She said to Gin, "It's like something Charley would have done. Tell me about him, child."

But Gin thought Quillan Davies had better tell her about himself.

"The Right Honorable Quillan Davies, the Earl of Tor," Jack announced, a look of satisfaction on his luminous face. He bowed and murmured, "M'lord."

The interim director stood smiling self-consciously under the portrait of Charley above the double doors, so like Quillan Davies ten years hence. Then Gin was struck by another resemblance: Van Dyck's rich pirate without the beard. No wonder Charley had looked familiar. It was the family resemblance.

Quillan looked a little the worse for wear after a night in

jail with his cousin Will Nevil, the commander. Lieutenant Gonzales and Sergeant Peck stood uncomfortably behind him in the hall.

"Come, sit down, sit down," Perdita said, motioning them in. She had on a fawn cashmere pullover today, and brown tweed slacks, a single strand of pearls at her throat. Her nails had been freshly done. Did a manicurist come regularly to the house?

Quillan Davies stroked his cheek with timid fingers. His jailhouse shave was less than perfect. He crossed the room with that shy little smile she had found so charming and took Perdita's hand and kissed it. You could see that pleased her.

"Yes," she said, "you're like him." Laughing like a girl.

"Awfully good of you," he murmured. "So glad we meet at last."

Gin stood watching with her back to the fire. What was it she was feeling? Sibling rivalry? She'd never had a sibling. But she felt proprietary about Perdita's drawing room, where the two of them had enjoyed their private tête-à-têtes. The place seemed invaded.

Quillan Davies explained to Perdita how it all started. "You see, I'd taken a first in art history—largely because I grew up fascinated by the treasures at Mousehole."

He glanced around at his audience. There were Tina and Pablo, too, in the window seat under the view of the mountains.

"But then as I got on in my studies I waxed suspicious about three of the pictures, the so-called Rembrandt, the Turner, the Van Dyck. I brought a knowledgeable fellow down from Oxford to, well, vet them—informally, you know. And he quite agreed that they weren't what they were—as you Americans say—cracked up to be. At once I suspected Charley. The paintings had been authenticated just after the war—World War One, I mean—so I knew the real thing was at Mousehole then."

Perdita was smiling, nodding.

"Charley was home for a while in the thirties," Davies said, "tying up some estate business, and everyone else tactfully away at Cowes for the races. That was the only time the substitution could have taken place. Clever of him. I never knew Charley, you see. I was born in the middle of the Second War. But he always fascinated me. He was a mystery, you know, and you can guess what hold that had on the mind of a lad.''

Lloyd Noldes shifted in his seat as if he'd be damned if he'd listen to this nonsense. Tito Gonzales stood uncomfortably with his hands clasped in front of him. Sergeant Peck stood at something like Parade Rest just inside the door. Pablo seemed to be drawing a strand of Tina's hair behind her ear. Tina, busy taking in the house, absently brushed his hand away.

''So you see, when several years ago I read about the Waldheimer Museum opening in Santa Fe, and the gift paintings in the collection, I vowed I'd get the originals back where I felt they belonged—at Mousehole Castle.''

Smiling, Perdita nodded. She seemed charmed by the man. As I was, Gin reminded herself.

''Well, to make a long tale short—no offense, old man,'' he said to Nemo, who flopped that furry member once against the floor and grinned back at him—''I hatched a scheme to exchange the fakes at Mousehole for the originals in Santa Fe. I took great interest in everything having to do with the Waldheimer. That wasn't difficult. I'm a museum director myself in London. I learned that the director of the Waldheimer was an Anglophile and spent a great deal of time in Britain. When I found out from *Museum Notes* that he would attend a particular auction in New York, it was a simple matter for me to be at the bidding, too. I had him pointed out to me and saw to it that he was invited to a certain cocktail party. And the rest is history.''

''Not quite,'' Lloyd Noldes said.

The lieutenant cleared his throat. ''This naval guy supposed to be your cousin?''

''Will? Yes. Will Nevil. You really mustn't hold him, you know. Will's an intrepid seaman, decorated for bravery under fire in the Falklands. But with the two of us—as boys growing up, you know—well, I was always the leader. Get the chap on land, it's still that way. I drew him in, you see, convinced him we were simply righting a wrong, retrieving stolen goods in a manner of speaking. Guess I'd convinced myself of it, too.''

''You needed him for what?'' the lieutenant growled.

''Oh, my dear fellow, to bring the Mousehole paintings into the U.S. My cousin's ship was due in Pearl Harbor sometime this year, and it would be easy for him to take a few paintings aboard to decorate his cabin.''

''A Rembrandt?'' Pablo chuckled. ''On a navy vessel?''

''Well, old chap, they weren't the real thing, you know,'' Quillan Davies said, ''and sailor fellows hardly look at what's hanging on the walls.''

''Just like the ignorant Americans, who wouldn't know a Rembrandt from a Grandma Moses?'' Lloyd Noldes said sarcastically.

To hide her smile, Gin put both hands on the mantel and hung her head between them, looking at the fire.

Perdita offered Charley's nephew the box of chocolates. He took one and passed them to the chairman, who eyed them distastefully. Jack came in with his tray of lethal coffee.

''You see, old chap, I knew I could make the switch once I'd got myself installed as interim director, but I still hadn't a clue how I'd get the copies to Santa Fe from Hawaii and the originals back aboard the *York*. Then Cousin Will called and told me he was having a devil of a time with some deuced piece of machinery on his frigate. He'd laid over at Pearl a bit early, you see. The Yanks were willing to help, but they had to get the piece machined on the mainland and shipped out. So there was Will, with time on his hands.''

''Did he really know Ellen Weldon?'' Gin asked.

''Heavens, yes. This was a piece of luck. He met her in Singapore sometime last year and formed a terrible crush. She was traveling with her husband, chap in the import business. That's Will's thing, you see—crushes on married women. It's safe, you know. But he finds it painful. I'll always believe he took to the sea out of chronic, inoperable shyness.

''Not to put too fine a point on it, with time to spare he flew over to Maui and looked her up. Learned, of course, the sad news of her death, so the poor fellow called me in the throes of grief and it all clicked into place. Her friends were leaving on a tour to Santa Fe. So I told him he must join them. He'd given his chaps shore leave. He had the time, and there you are. He brought the copies over in his luggage. He would take the originals out the same way. I'd found these wonderful chests in Chemayo and bought some for the museum gift shop. Cousin Will would pack the originals back to Hawaii. It's after all a state and no customs officials to get past. Then aboard the good ship *York* and finally home to merry old England and no one the wiser."

Certainly not, Gin thought bitterly, an assistant director who, in a course called American Museum Practices, had ineptly stuffed a weasel.

"But I'm puzzled," Perdita said to Gin. "You say the X rays disclosed that the copies were *signed*? That part fascinates me."

"What do you mean? What X rays?" Quillan Davies looked at Gin with raised eyebrows. Gin explained about the signatures in white lead paint underneath the oil. "One was signed 'Pablo' and another 'Gonzales' and one with only the initials 'M. L.' "

Perdita's beringed fingers roamed over the candy nougats, settling on none. "I see," she said. "Well, we can guess who *they* would be, can't we?"

But Quillan Davies obviously could not.

"Wherever Charley went," Perdita said, "even here in Santa Fe, he always had friends among the artists. He had a lot of artist friends in Paris after the Great War. There were the two Juans—Miró and Gris." She shrugged. "Charley knew them both. But it was Juan Gris whose real name was Gonzales."

The lieutenant wondered if they were related.

"He only told me he'd gotten some of his artist friends to paint copies of the paintings to leave on the walls at Mousehole Castle so the originals would never be missed." The benefactor sank back in her chair. "You must all be able to guess who 'the inimitable Pablo' was."

Pablo Esperanza had folded his arms in an attempt to keep his hands off Tina. Now he unfolded them and rose slowly from the window seat. "Do you mean . . . ?" he said. "Can you possibly mean, dear lady . . . ?" He walked into the room a little bent, as if too excited to straighten to his full height.

Gin turned from the fire and stared at the benefactor. Perdita shrugged, smug and catlike, looking around at her guests. "Whenever Charley did something naughty he always told me the least said the better. All he would say about this matter was that he'd had friends over from Paris for a house party—Charley loved a party. Liven up the old place you know, while the family was away avoiding him during that thirties' visit. And it was these friends who copied the paintings for him—as a lark, you know."

Pablo struck his palm with his other fist. "It was always clear these copyists were not hacks, but *Picasso*?"

"M. L.?" Gin said urgently. "Who was M. L.?"

Perdita was enjoying herself. "We can only guess," she said, and smiling popped a chocolate.

Gin dropped to her knees in front of the patron. "Marie Laurencin?"

Perdita's laugh was almost a giggle. "Well, it's not for me to say. I suppose you can vet forgeries, too, can't you?"

"Good Lord." Quillan Davies lowered himself to a footstool and pulled it closer to Perdita.

Pablo slapped him on the back very much in the American-style. "If thees is true, those copies of yours are worth a fortune, though perhaps not so much as the originals. And of course thees"—Pablo searched for a word—"*fable*, for is it not fabulous?—will make them famous. There'll be bidders from all over the world, if you've a mind to sell them."

Jack passed the tray with the Irish whiskey and whipped cream. Perdita poured coffee for everybody. She said, "But Ginevra, how very clever of you to have caught on to the plot."

"Not really," Gin said. "It just took a little sorting."

"But however did you manage?"

Gin's face went hot, but not from the fire. She felt all eyes upon her, especially Quillan Davies's.

Perdita laced a cup with the whiskey, topped it with whipped cream, and handed it to her. "Come now, don't be shy."

Gin sipped this little drop of courage. "Well, the janitorial service comes to the museum late Tuesday afternoons. And after I looked closely at the painting Wednesday morning''— she decided not to mention the pencil mark or the Pink Pearl eraser—''I went into the director's office to telephone . . .''

"In my office?" Quillan Davies said, raising his eyebrows and smiling.

"And there were crumbs of pipe tobacco on your desk," she said.

"Is all this leading somewhere?" the chairman asked grimly.

Tina said, "Give her time. It's complicated."

Gin said, "Not very." She made herself meet Quillan Davies's eyes. "You were supposed to have left Tuesday morning for Dallas. You made it a point of telling everybody. So if you left Santa Fe Tuesday morning and the janitorial service came in Tuesday afternoon, what were those crumbs of pipe tobacco doing on your desk?"

He smiled guiltily. "Perhaps the service was careless?"

"With Regina Philipson around?" She smiled back grimly. "And I found your office door unlocked that morning. If I leave the museum after you, I always check it before I lock my own. I'd have sworn I'd locked it the night before. I thought it was odd, but I put it down to my own carelessness. I hadn't put it together yet—I mean, that someone had been there after I left."

"Locks were all intact. Had to be somebody with a key to the museum," Tito mumbled.

"What first made you suspect me, Ginny?"

Gin glanced up at the emblem on the chimney. "That," she said.

"The coat of arms?" Perdita said.

Gin nodded. "It matched a seal on one of the letters that came in your mail, Quillan. At first I didn't put them together. I just thought it looked familiar."

"You went through my letters?" he murmured, that same teasing smile playing around his lips.

"I sorted the mail," she said firmly.

"Ah, yes," he said. "But why, when I called from Dallas, did you tell me to go on to New York according to plan?"

"Because I knew you were coming back here. You had

to. To unlock the museum and get at the paintings to give to your cohort, whoever that was. I said it to throw you off, make you believe I was as ignorant as you'd counted on . . .''

"Dear Ginny—"

". . . and buy a little time to figure out which pod member was your accomplice."

"But what made you think it was a member of the group from Hawaii?"

"It was while the pod was here that the pictures were stolen." She'd known the night they'd been taken . . . because of the pencil mark she wasn't mentioning. If it hadn't been for the vanishing pencil mark, would the switch have ever been noticed? "I was convinced the paintings would leave Santa Fe with that group."

"What gave Will away?" The teasing smile was tinged with a thoughtful frown.

"His cuff links."

"His *cuff links*!"

She nodded toward the coat of arms on the chimney face. "The same coat of arms on his cuff links. Red and gold— *sable per chevron or*. It meant you were relatives, and both of you kin to Charley Burrell."

"Ahhh." Quillan Davies lifted his chin in the familiar gesture of understanding. They were all looking at the coat of arms on the chimney.

"The pod was leaving town tomorrow morning. Last night in all the hubbub of Zozobra would be the time to strike."

Quillan Davies smiled. "You are very clever, Ginny."

"Hence the red devil suits—for disguise and to blend into the festivities," she said.

"But how did you know the paintings were in the museum basement?"

"I wasn't sure until I looked. But what made more sense? They wouldn't fit in a safe-deposit box. Your apartment's very small." She looked quickly into the fire. "But mainly it was because last week—we were getting that folding screen from the basement . . ." And she recounted how she'd found the dirty rags covered with acrylics on the floor, and there was also the torn scrap of aged paper she'd thought had come from the back of the Frederic Remington painting Tina had been cleaning, with part of his name on it. "Only I realized later that the REM could have been the first letters of Rembrandt, too." She turned to her friend. "Forgive me, Tina. I accused you of using the museum basement for your own work."

"I wouldn't think of it," Tina said guiltily.

"And then there was the Dürer," Gin said.

"What about it?" Lloyd Noldes asked. He'd been told the Dürer at the museum was authentic.

"Thieves often smuggle valuable paintings out of the country by painting over them with acrylics," Gin said. "But the Dürer is a drawing on paper. You can't paint acrylics over paper and hope to ever get it off. Suddenly it just all fit together. The untouched Dürer drawing, the acrylics on the rags in the basement, the torn paper with REM on it . . . I knew where to look for the stolen paintings. And when I looked, there they were in the racks with the gift paintings, covered over with amateur daubs."

Quillan Davies smiled deprecatingly and shrugged. "You're right, my dear. I am not greatly talented."

"It really only fell into place, all of it," Gin said, "when I saw the commander's cuff links and remembered the chest he'd bought in the gift shop. It was big enough to hold the paintings. So if he was leaving tomorrow morning, that meant he'd have to pick up the paintings tonight." She was repeating herself. She stopped talking and gave her attention to the Irish coffee.

Quillan Davies turned to her there in front of the fire. That little smile resurfaced. "Can you ever forgive me, dear girl? You see, I've come to like you enormously."

She looked back coldly. "You hired me for my ignorance. I was to have been no threat to your elaborate plot."

"But you were," he murmured. "Oh, my dear, you were."

To avoid his eyes, she looked at her watch. Enough. It was over. She had to get out of here. She could come back another time and have Perdita to herself. Just now she wanted to get to the hospital, where Raoul Query waited. He had identified the kahuna's card for the lieutenant, put together now with Scotch tape and covered in plastic: Exhibit A for a trial that would never happen. They'd found numerous prints on it—Raoul's perhaps, maybe those of the boy who'd found the last scrap in the parking lot, maybe Ellen's or someone at the kahuna's house who had jotted down the message from the doctor's office on Oahu, and one thumb print of Victor Weldon's. Raoul Query had told them about discovering it in the breast pocket of the blazer that was not his, and what he remembered of the encounter in the Gallery of Western Art. Gin had confessed to him she'd met Victor Weldon in the parking lot the night of his second attempt at murder and never guessed he was leaving the hospital instead of arriving. To make up for it, she had promised him a pizza for lunch. She thought he more than deserved it.